ADVANCE READING COPY

Waiting for Grace
a novel of redemption

Caroline E. Zani

Pub Date: February 4, 2020

ISBN: 978-1-948018-71-5
272 Pages, 5.25 x 8
$15.95, Trade Paperback

CATEGORIES:
FIC039000/Visionary & Metaphysical
FIC027090/Time Travel
FIC009050/Paranormal
FIC025000/Psychological
FIC045000/Family Life

DISTRIBUTED BY:
INGRAM, FOLLETT, COUTTS, MBS, YBP,
COMPLETE BOOK, BERTRAMS, GARDNERS
Or wholesale@wyattmackenzie.com

Wyatt-MacKenzie Publishing
DEADWOOD, OREGON

PUBLISHER CONTACT:
Nancy Cleary
nancy@wyattmackenzie.com

Waiting for Grace

· *a novel of redemption* ·

Waiting for Grace

• a novel of redemption •

Caroline E. Zani

Wyatt-MacKenzie Publishing
DEADWOOD, OREGON

Waiting for Grace

Caroline E. Zani

ISBN: 978-1-948018-71-5

Library of Congress Control Number: *to come*

Some permissions pending.

Wyatt-MacKenzie Publishing
DEADWOOD, OREGON

Wyatt-MacKenzie Publishing, Inc.
www.WyattMacKenzie.com
Contact us: info@wyattmackenzie.com

DEDICATION

For all of those who wait for grace.
What's meant for you will not pass you by.
Be still and know.
And for all who are full of grace and
share it selflessly, the world needs you now more than ever.

1995

"So she was still under anesthesia? And you just checked her vitals and left. Where did you go after that? You said she is claiming to remember the event, 'scuse me, alleged event."

"Listen, I can't have this—out there. I mean, these women, they blow things out of proportion and because they know you have money, they'll try anything, you know?"

"I'm just not getting the feeling you're telling me everything, Doctor—I'm sorry, I didn't get your name—would you mind telling me, again, what you remember of that day?"

"I told you, I did her breast augmentation, then her lipo and sent her to recovery. Normal day, normal procedures, nothing out of the ordinary. When I went in to check on her, she was beginning to come up out of it and—"

"Hold on, you said that she was under anesthesia still. This is where I need you to be really specific. I can't help you unless you are 100 percent honest and tell me everything that happened. I mean everything."

"Look, Cranston. This is a stupid woman and she's trying to frame me. I will not be ruined by a bitch who cares more about her breast size than her kids, career, and husband, all of whom will suffer if this becomes a thing."

"So has she pressed charges? Police involvement? Have you gotten anything in the mail?"

"No! I told you, I just wanted a consultation. I don't know if she is going forward with anything. She just called screaming and threatening me. I just need her to shut up. And I need you to be sure she does."

"Where are the cameras in your suite?"

"What? I mean, they're in the OR and lobby."

"Not in the recovery room? Why not?"

"We don't need them there, there's always someone with the patient in recovery."

"Was there a nurse there that day—in recovery?"

"Yes."

"Where was she when you went to check on the patient who's making these accusations?"

"I don't know. Lunch?"

"Are you the person who typically checks patients in recovery?"

"No. I was just worried, so I—"

"Wait, you said everything was normal and it was an ordinary day. Why were you concerned?"

"Hey, I need a lawyer on *my* side. What is going on here?"

"Well, let's back up. I'm going to need some info here ... what's your name again? Do you want to make an appointment to come in?"

"To be honest, I'm not comfortable giving you my name. You'll have to earn my trust."

"I'm sorry. I don't think I can represent you in this matter, but I can give you the names of a few people who might be able to."

"What? Why? Your ads say you win 97 percent of all your cases!"

"Yes, that is true. We pride ourselves on that and our clients feel safe in our hands."

"But you won't take *my* case?"

"No. I'm sorry, Doctor."

"Why the hell not?"

"We only take cases we can win."

1

2019

When Eli finally sat down on the bale of hay that had been beckoning from across the small barn for hours, it seemed all the bones in his tired body settled deeper, his muscles relaxed harder than ever before, if that even makes sense. Home does that to a person and oftentimes they don't realize what they were missing until they feel it.

It was Smudge who called with a shrill whinny as if to say, "Hey you're sitting on my dinner and you're still on the clock." And when Eli finally mustered the last of his energy and brought a flake of hay and a bucket of grain to the stall, the "littles" were frantic. He knew he would need to cut the door down a bit sometime this week so they could see over it and watch his every move. Ink reached up and nipped him high on the back of his thigh in his impatience. Eli swatted at him and reminded them both that he visited the animal rescue with plans to get a dog, not two ponies. He shook his head as their crazy manes meshed together while they ate from the same bucket and stomped their tiny hooves, still impatient with their constant hunger.

Eli latched the stall door and double-checked it even though he knew they couldn't get their noses over the top of the door, never mind slide the latch; with everything he had gone through and lost in the past several years, he wasn't taking any chances.

"Goodnight, you crazy kids. Be good and don't break anything, please. We just got here and I don't need the neighbors

knowing how much trouble you guys are. I'm sure they will figure it out soon enough."

As he tossed the grain scoop back into the bin in the feed
room and checked the faucet for the third time, he caught a
glimpse of himself in the dirty, dusty mirror over the sink. His
grey eyes and once dark hair seemed to be getting closer and
closer in color, but for the first time he really didn't care. The
eyes looking back at him were confident if not a bit sad. They
were bold with a hint of longing and without a question, tired.
He reached up and wiped the mirror once with his sweatshirt
sleeve and caught movement behind him. He spun around, not
sure what he would see. His heart caught up with his vision and
though it thumped dramatically, he wasn't afraid. He was curious. What else lives in this barn? Raccoons? Cats? Opossum?
He shrugged and realized he wouldn't figure it out tonight.

Closing the feed room door behind him and glancing at the
Littles once more, he sighed a breath of accomplishment. The
ponies were settled in and fed which meant they were happy.
Good enough, he thought. At least *they* are and that means
something.

He switched the light off and stood for a moment in the
dark, listening to the rhythmic sound of the ponies chewing
their hay and lightly shifting their weight from side to side, the
pine shavings making a comforting sound as they moved it
around. It was a sound that reminded him of something but he
didn't know what. He was too tired to wonder at the moment,
which meant he was actually exhausted because wondering was
something that Dr. Eli Cranston did for a living. He wondered
and he wandered, and he helped people know their truth. And
that was something that no one other than he could understand
was the only thing keeping him alive.

The barn door slid on a track that needed greasing but the
creaking sound was oddly comforting. Years of use meant there
was life here. People feeding animals that didn't serve a purpose
as food always bewildered Eli until Ink and Smudge entered his
life. He never had a pet growing up and he was quite simply too
self-absorbed to have one as an adult until everything changed.

"Isn't that the way, though," he said to the night air. "Everything is as it is until suddenly it just isn't." He got his feet moving then, a trick he learned in his graduate work. Keep the body moving so the mind doesn't go where you don't want it to. *Keep moving.* That was the theme of Eli's life now. Keep moving.

He reached the back door of the old white cottage he had signed papers on earlier that day. He turned back toward the barn for a moment and noticed how the sounds of the water beyond the trees could be heard here in the stillness. The bay quietly filling and emptying leaving the sand studded with clams. It was true that he felt more settled near water, always had. He never stopped to wonder why before his life took a left turn in the middle of perfection and dumped him head first into a foreign land akin to a desert one might drown in. But now he was a different person and living a very different life; a life he was living purposely and one that held mysteries he planned to solve. Until he could unpack and set up his office, though, he was just Eli. And that fact alone, terrified him.

The light at the start of day was different here. He had read about it but wasn't sure what was meant by "different." He thought it might be so subtle as to needing to be told about it then with concentrated effort he might see a difference, sort of like the optical illusions printed in the Sunday comics. It wasn't that way at all to Eli's surprise and delight. He now lived, also much to his surprise, close to the spot where the sun first rises on the East Coast. And the light, it was different. But as beautiful as it was in the morning, he knew nothing could compare to the evening light just before sunset. He thought perhaps there should be an Instagram filter named for it. Acadia.

The colors outside his bedroom window were muted and soft; the corals bleeding into the pinks and yellows were actually quite ethereal in nature. When he had visited six months prior, on his first ever visit to New England, he hadn't noticed much. At that time, he was on a mission to purchase a small home, or so he told himself. And yes, while he did find his little white cottage with the dark green shutters, a place to call home, the one he had dreamt of, he simply didn't allow time for exploring the area. He had stayed at the Saltair Inn and was surrounded by the beauty of the open view onto Mt. Desert Narrows and the stillness of the bay. He was there for a day and a half and flew back home to tie up things there, to be done with it all.

This morning, though, as he was waking up in this new place, and over the last several weeks, it really did begin to feel like a home. He had a routine again and could find socks and clean underwear with ease. There were just two boxes that still hadn't been opened or touched really since he dragged them in, exhausted as he was after the house went on record. He knew what was in the boxes and he remembered vividly how difficult it was to pack those items. He wasn't so sure what it would be like to take them out and see them here, thousands of miles away from where they began.

Keep moving, he thought, *get up.* Eli swung his legs out of bed and sat up, feeling the muscles in his back reminding him he could use a new mattress since this one seemed to have been here probably half as long as the cottage itself had been here. He took a deep breath and began his day the way he had for the past nine years. "I'm grateful to be alive today, to have my health and a roof over my head. I'm grateful for the opportunity to help others and I'm grateful for In—" And as though they could read his thoughts from out in the barn, Ink and Smudge were alerting him that the sun was, in fact, up and that they needed to be fed at least ten minutes ago. Eli took another breath and wondered why he hadn't just gotten the dog he set out to get. He laughed and pulled on a pair of jeans and his old UCLA sweatshirt and headed out to feed the Littles.

The air was decidedly a bit cooler than it had been when he moved in. End of September felt different here than it did back home. There was a definite change in seasons, which he had read so much about, beginning to make itself known. He was excited to experience it and whatever it brought even if that made him naive or even downright ignorant to think that way. Southern California didn't have snow and though there was beautiful foliage to be appreciated there, he knew this new place had some stories to tell him about autumn in New England. Winter, well, he would just have to experience it to know if all the rumors were true. For now, he needed to get Clem out here to finish the renovations because he knew that once winter came, it would be too late.

On his way back from the barn he heard a rustling in the underbrush that bordered his property in the back of the barn. He stopped and waited but he didn't hear it again. He realized that he was oddly comforted by the fact that he wasn't alone here. There was plenty of wildlife that had shown itself in the short time he had been here: foxes, deer, skunks, turkeys. He closed his eyes for a quick moment, the way one does when there is a realization of something they suddenly realize needs realizing. Birds and raccoons and rabbits made him feel less alone. Eli. Eli F. Cranston was making peace with nature and animals were his friends. *Huh*, he thought. *Interesting. I must be getting old.*

Back in the house Eli started a pot of coffee and made himself some scrambled eggs and wheat toast. "Chickens. How about chickens." He said it as a thought rather than a question as he had come to practice. He was manifesting just about everything he was experiencing and though he understood how it all worked, he never got over the sheer excitement of seeing that what he set his intentions for actually showed up either by his direct action or just the allowing of it. He often wondered how he had lived his life so carelessly for the first forty-one years, so oblivious to anyone but himself. Do it if it felt good, do it if you can, and do it even if there are consequences. Do it until you're not able to any longer for whatever reason.

"Huh." His head nodded back and forth a bit when he said it, like his whole body agreed. "What a waste of time. Not all ... but most. And nine years later how am I even in the same body? I'm not that person, not at all. If only I had ..." He stopped himself and said, "Keep moving."

His coffee was ready and it smelled delicious. He couldn't

wait to try this one. Rebecca from the farmer's market said it tasted like Bar Harbor and wouldn't give him any further details, but he didn't need any. He enjoyed her smile and her natural beauty, without a stitch of makeup, but a mouthful of gleaming teeth that seemed to have an arrangement with her blue eyes. When her teeth peeked out, her eyes lit up and the little wrinkles at the corners seemed to act as exclamation marks. "I'm genuine and I'm okay with life as it is, however it is!" He only imagined that was what her eyes exclaimed. He knew not everyone understood how he had an inclination toward the philosophical. To many, crow's feet or chicken eggs or the color range of the picket fence's many paint layers were simply those things and nothing more.

I used to be a surface dweller. Sometimes I wish I still could be.

He sat down at his small kitchen table with the lace tablecloth that must have seen many visitors over the decades. Charlie McCabe outlived his wife by nine years, and it was obvious that he hadn't changed much about the place in her absence. Eli thought that was sad and stoic but beautiful at the same time. It did cross his mind that perhaps Charlie didn't care to buy a new tablecloth or replace the pink floral hand towels, but he liked to think that Charlie just wanted everything to stay, the same as it was when Louise was alive. When he met Charlie at the assisted living residence, he noticed how he looked Eli in the eye the entire time except when he mentioned Louise. Charlie's watery blue eyes drifted off over Eli's shoulder and he breathed a heavy sigh, his eyes moving back and forth as if to clear the cobwebs of time away so he could see Louise again. That's what love does, it searches always and it never gives up.

The first sip of coffee was almost too warm, so Eli added a dash more cream. The next sip was confusing, so he tried adding a bit more sugar. The third sip shouted, "Blueberries!" He smiled and realized why Rebecca had said it tasted like Bar Harbor, where blueberries were featured on and in everything it seemed, from T-shirts to maple syrup to ball caps and even the color of many houses. He decided he liked it. The coffee, the cottage, the farmer's market, his new life. He liked it a lot.

The knock at the door surprised him and came just before his first bite of scrambled eggs. It was Clem and he didn't wait for the door to be answered, just knocked and walked in. "Hey-uh, fella. How we doing this mahnin?" He pushed his Red Sox cap back off his reddened forehead and looked around a bit. He sniffed at the coffee rather comically until Eli offered him a cup. Before he could get up and start toward the cupboard, Clem was there, helping himself. He knew more about this house than Eli ever would and didn't think Eli would mind, he was new here after all. He might own the place, but what did that matter?

"Today I'm gonna tear out that back room fah ya. Gut it down to the studs. You still want that door put in, do ya?" I gotta go down the town hall afta and pull a permit. They get ya, ya know. In the old days, ya just did what ya want to yer own place, ya know. Not today. They gotta know whatcha doin' and they'll tax ya just fah breathin!" He snorted a laugh and when he did, Eli could see he was missing at least one tooth in the front. He liked Clem. He was a genuine guy and a hard worker who didn't charge a dime more than he told you he would. An honest guy, a guy Eli wouldn't have ever chosen to deal with in his life before coming here. He would have judged him and made fun of his accent and the plaid shirt he wore six days out of seven. But now ... Eli needed the Clems of the world to balance him, to keep him real and grateful and to learn ways he wasn't exposed to back home.

"Well, I guess I don't mind the permits and the taxes, Clem. I love it here and let me tell you, it is a whole lot more affordable than where I came from. Just let me know if you need money for materials before I head out."

"Ay-uh, you goin' down-ah Camden today, huh?" I haven't been down that way in ye-ahs. Dated a little girl named Stella down that way in the late 60s. She wanted to marry me, did she evah. Ha! I wasn't settlin' down fa nothin'. No siree. She was a looker, too. Red hair and freckles and legs up to her chin. But I wasn't gettin' tied down yet, no sir."

Eli took his last bite of his now cold eggs and washed it

down with the blueberry coffee, something he still couldn't get over and said, "Well, there's some office furniture I saw online someone is selling and I need a few things plus I want to find some new places to explore. I'm on vacation until that office is finished."

"Yep, Gotcha. I'll get to work on it right now, fella. And if ya got some cash on ya, I'll hit the lumbah yard and get those boys to deliver it. Let those young kids haul that shit. I'm no young buck any-moah, ya know?"

2

The late morning sun on the bright blue hydrangeas peeking out from behind the white fences along Bay Road seemed surreal in a way. They bobbed their heavy heads in the breeze, almost keeping time with Eli's footfalls. The tourist season was winding down and there weren't many kids on the streets, in strollers, or running on the sidewalks carrying ice cream cones. Eli was relieved. He waited until now to come back down here. The sights of families and old couples enjoying their summer vacations proved to be a little more than Eli could bear when he first came to town. Everything was so foreign, in many ways he felt he could be in a different country altogether. He never imagined himself living anywhere but Los Angeles. He was born there, as were his parents. He loved his fast-paced life full of guilty pleasures and the privilege that came with his title. Never could he imagine the incidents that would change his entire world nor the changes that followed.

He opened the wrought iron gate in front of the yellow house and walked up the cobblestone walkway to the cobalt blue door and paused before knocking. *Well, here goes.*

He listened for footsteps but instead heard a dog barking and the whirring of a vacuum cleaner. He waited a moment and the vacuum stopped but the barking continued, then broke into a howl. "Oh Pep, die klappe halten!"

The door swung wide open the way one opens it when they know who is on the other side. "Elias. Dr. Cranston. You made it."

Eli stood up a little straighter and nodded, "Hi. I did, I made it. I'm here."

The old man in the doorway stepped back, "Come in, come in. I was just cleaning up a bit. Elise and I had guests last night but it's just you and I today. It is so good to see you."

As he stepped over the threshold, Eli felt oddly familiar with the house. He knew he had never been there, nor had he ever been to the state of Maine before his trip six months before. He stepped gingerly around the little black dog that was now whining at his owner's feet. "That's Peppercorn. We call him Pep." Eli bent down and lightly touched the top of Pep's head. He noticed the warmth of his fur and the softness of his energy. "Hey, Buddy." This was all it took for Pep to attach himself to Eli for the next several hours.

"Dr. Gunther, I am very appreciative of the invitation to meet with you. I never in my wildest dreams would have imagined visiting your home. Thank you, I ... am quite honored." He didn't want to gush about his books and sound like a fan boy, but inside he felt like one.

The old gentleman didn't seem to hear Eli as he led the way down the hall of the old Victorian with a soft green parlor on left and a winding mahogany staircase on the right. Eli stepped into the kitchen, which seemed to rapidly bring him into the 21st century: white cabinetry, stainless steel appliances and a huge granite island that seated six, stunning copper lanterns hanging above. The enormous window over the sink looking out onto the bay was breathtaking and Eli couldn't help but stare. "Wow, what a view."

Dr. Gunther said, "Don't think there is a day that goes by I don't say the same. Elise and I have thought about selling but we just don't want to leave here, and I don't think the new owners would appreciate us staying!"

Eli relaxed; Dr. Gunther wasn't what he expected. He seemed like a down-to-earth guy with a normal life and a dog named Peppercorn. He stepped closer to the enormous window and took in the panoramic view of the water, the lawn leading down to it, the blood red roses along the edge.

"Come, Eli. Let's go to my office. It's more comfortable in there. Can I offer you a drink? Some lemonade or some coffee? He turned to peer up at Eli, who at 6'2" enjoyed a good vantage point most of the time. Dr. Gunther was a much smaller frame and carried himself with vigor to make up for it. "No thank you. Maybe a little later."

Dr. Gunther led the way through the formal dining room and past the family room, Peppercorn second in line and Eli bringing up the rear. The French doors to the office looked original to the house and as they swung open Eli felt like he was going to step back into the 1800s. The view did not disappoint. The dark bookshelves that lined three of the walls had a rich patina and the craftsmanship was something to behold. "Reminds me of my law school days," Eli said.

"Oh, I suppose so, young man. I suppose so. Have a seat, won't you?" Eli gazed out the back of the office through two more French doors that led to a stone patio covered by a white pergola, covered in climbing roses as red as red could be. Beyond the patio was the bay dotted with sailboats and off in the distance, a cruise ship, the only hint that they were not in 1860s Bar Harbor.

Eli sat in one of the worn leather chairs while Peppercorn waited for an invitation to sit in Eli's lap; when it didn't come, he curled up at his feet and almost immediately began to snore softly. Dr. Gunther sat opposite Eli and pulled out a humidor. "Now, I don't smoke these very often, but it seems that today might be a good day to do so. What do you think?"

Smiling, Eli said, "I think today is a great day for a cigar." He chose the third one from the right as Dr. Gunther held the beautiful box open for him.

As Otto Gunther snipped the top off the cigar and began lighting it, Eli looked around at all the leather-bound books that lined the shelves. He always wondered if people read all the books on their shelves or if they were more for reference, or perhaps decoration. He doubted that Dr. Gunther had this collection for decoration, though. He was still stunned to be sitting in his home with him.

"Elias, you know when I read about your work and your experiences, I just couldn't believe you hadn't been doing the work your entire career," he started, the leather creaking under him as he leaned forward. He handed the lit cigar to Eli.

"That is to say, it can take a lifetime to develop what you have in a few short years." And then to learn that this is, in fact, your second career just really intrigued me. I don't ever remember feeling that anyone has had any new insights in this field for such a long time. It's truly refreshing and I have to say, quite daring, on your part. I do believe youth has a tapferkeit, a bravado that has long been scared out of anyone over the age of forty—in any field." He sat back and looked out the window to the water. "But ... alles was Sie brauchen ist hoffnung."

Eli watched him, staring at his profile and wondering what this man's life was really like, how long he'd been in this country, his accent still so strong but his English perfect. His nose had a slight concave hump and his glasses sat exactly on the precipice seemingly undecided about which direction they wanted to travel. The scar on his cheek was not a slight one but he knew the story behind that. He had read about his run-in with the SS officer who beat him for calling to a girl he thought was his sister.

Eli handed the cigar back to Dr. Gunther. "I sometimes think I was given a second chance at life, Doctor. I mean, not the life I was looking for by any means, but a second chance at making a life I can be proud of. The life I have now is not one I would give up for anything. But I had to lose everything to get it. You must know what I mean."

Otto Gunther looked at the younger man sitting in his office and thought back to the start of his adulthood in Germany just after the war. He remembered thinking that a man Eli's current age was so old. And then he thought what it would be like to be fifty-two once again.

"Yes, Elias. I do know exactly what you mean. And it is only people who have been through their verletzung, their wounding, sufficiently who can say such things. I trust you understand that about your clients as well. The ones who have been beaten

so badly by life that they are open to anything, all their precon-
ceived notions and cares gone, just like that. They quite literally
have nothing left to lose."

Nodding, Eli took the cigar back, feeling quite at home here
and comfortable with this man he'd only read about in inter-
views and in other therapists' research.

"I know that to be true, Doctor. It wasn't until I turned
forty-one that I knew real pain. I couldn't understand how the
absence of someone could hurt so much and the unabating urgency to make it stop was just absolutely brutal. I wouldn't wish
that on anyone. Not any one."

Otto turned to look directly at Eli and said, "One man's pain
cannot be compared to another's. What is unbearable for one,
is just a bruise to another."

Eli sat stunned for a moment. "Well, if that's so and I'm not
saying it isn't, what is the difference?"

"The difference, Dr. Cranston, is hope."

3

1991

"Happy Anniversary, Babe!" Antigone jumped into Eli's arms when he walked through the door carrying a bouquet of roses.

"Happy Anniversary, Tig!" I can't believe it's been a year, can you?"

"No, it seems like just yesterday we were out on the beach saying I do. It was definitely the best day of my life. Until now anyway." She looked at him in anticipation, wanting him to ask her what she meant but she recognized that look on his face.

"Babe, please. Just this one night—for Christ's sake, it's our anniversary! Just tell your father you can't work tonight. Please?" She knew it was useless, but she wanted her husband to stand up to his father, to stand up for them as a couple.

"Tig, you know I want to be with you, especially tonight but … but I can't. I have to get back to the office in like forty-five minutes. He let me …."

Antigone turned away. "You mean he *let* you come home to give me flowers and that's supposed to be enough?" She walked into the kitchen and turned off the oven, defeated.

"I made us a nice dinner, Babe. C'mon. What's he going to do anyway, fire you? He can't. Just tell him…" her voice trailed off as Eli answered his phone,

"Yea, I'm heading back now, Jay. Tell Dad I'm on the road."

He put the roses on the kitchen table of their condo and kissed the top of Antigone's head. "I promise to make it up to you, Honey. I do. It's just this case … time is running short and we have to get it right. We have a deposition and ..." he stopped when he heard Antigone gulp for air. He hated when she cried. "Tig, I'm sorry. I have to go. Don't wait up. I'll see you in the morning. Love you."

Antigone threw the roasted prosciutto-wrapped asparagus in the trash and walked to the refrigerator. She reached for the handle, paused, then flung the door open so it hit the corner of the counter. She hoped it dented the door, and as it turned out, she got her wish. She reached in and took the bowl of lobster tails on ice and brought it over to the table. She slowly poured the ice water and four raw lobster tails out on top of the roses and shut off the lights.

She climbed the stairs to the second floor and got ready for bed. She didn't care that it was only 7:00 pm. Antigone had gotten up early that morning and gone to yoga, then to the spa to get her hair and nails done for this special night. On her way home, she had stopped at the market to get fresh lobster tails and champagne. And on a whim, she popped into the pharmacy. Her cycle was always like clockwork so for her period to be six days late was unlikely to be a fluke. So later, when the blue line appeared on the pregnancy test, she wasn't completely shocked but she was indeed completely thrilled. She had the perfect evening planned for her husband. A romantic dinner followed by a walk to the Bistro Le Rouge a block from home for dessert, and back to the condo for the news that their lives were about to change.

But that's not what happened. Not at all. Eli was under his father's control and until Eli was made partner at the firm, this would continue. Antigone knew it and she had received fair warning all along. Her mother, Eli's mother, and even his brother, Jay, all told her what her life would be like married to Richard Cranston's younger son. It would be controlled by the needs of the firm and her father-in-law's insatiable appetite for wealth and for winning.

It all seemed a fair price to pay for being the wife of the man she fell in love with. She could have married Julian, the premed major she dated in college before she met Eli and whom her parents loved. If she was honest with herself, she would refer to him as the boy she was dating when she met Eli but she didn't want to feel badly about that anymore. It just wasn't meant to be. She was meant to be Mrs. Elias Cranston, the wife of a defense attorney in one of the biggest firms in the state of California. And she was.

4

The chilly air was a bit sobering when Eli stepped out of his office and onto the stone patio at the back of the house. Feeling like he was nearly ready to open for business, he instantly pulled away from the feeling of accomplishment with thoughts of all the work that still needed to be done in the rest of the house. He thought about going back to grab a jacket but decided against it. He'd just hurry. "C'mon boys!"

The ponies could be heard before they could be seen barreling around the corner of the cottage and raced to him, knowing what time it was. The leaves on the ground crunched beneath their small hooves as they came to a halt and immediately began searching Eli's hands for carrots or peppermints but there were none. "C'mon you two, it's time for dinner. Get up to the barn. They stuck with him, still sniffing and waiting. He shook his head and pictured tossing a ball to a chocolate lab and getting him to run in any direction as simply as that. He jogged up to the barn behind the house and slid the door open, eight little hooves clamoring into the barn with him. When he first moved here, he offered them each a stall of their own in the small barn but from day one they insisted on sharing just the one stall, the other standing empty with perfectly spread pine shavings and a brand new water bucket hanging on the wall, untouched. "Goats. I'll get goats," Eli said.

The ponies came from a hoarding situation down in Saco and each were in rough shape when removed from the owner's a year before Eli had even heard of Bar Harbor. They were rehabbed and loved by the foster, who named them Ink and Smudge for their markings. Black and white and sassy is how they were described. Eli saw their pictures on the website and was immediately captivated by their faces and gentle eyes. He remembered thinking, "What's happening to me?"

"Okay you two, your blankets should arrive by the end of the week, you can stop growing that coat anytime now. I had no idea that ponies even had blankets. That's really a thing?"

A week before he had started to think they had gotten shorter somehow, but knew that such a thing was impossible. He realized that their coats had thickened so much they didn't even look like ponies anymore. He wasn't sure what they looked like, but it was not ponies. Rebecca asked him if he planned to blanket them for the winter when he showed her pictures on his phone the previous weekend. Her eyes were smiling at his, saying, "If only you would ask me on a date, you'd realize what you're missing." He shrugged off his interpretation of her friendliness. He knew he wasn't ready and started to doubt he would ever truly be ready.

On his way back down the hill to his office, he felt pulled to the side of the house and just as he rounded the corner he caught a glimpse of someone in a purple-hooded sweatshirt leaving his gravel driveway. He stopped himself from shouting "Hey!" when he realized it looked like a child or a small adult, likely female. He shrugged and walked around the perennial bed that would need attention in the spring. Peering over at the small front porch he had only sat on a few times while Clem was changing locks for him when he first moved in, he noticed a white piece of paper sticking out between the storm door and the dark green one behind it. He enjoyed the crunching of the leaves beneath his feet. Reaching up, he could see the paper wasn't the size or shape of an oil bill receipt.

> Hi—I noticed you have horses and I was wondering if you needed any help with them. I know a lot about horses! You don't have to pay me. Here's my number.

Eli held the note and smiled at the obvious "tween" girl penmanship and the smiley face next to the phone number. *No name but definitely thoughtful.* He held the note for a moment longer and looked back out to the road. He couldn't see anyone there and even if he had he wasn't feeling like engaging anyone with so much still to get done back in the house. Eli wrinkled the note and stopped himself. *Breathe. Feel it. It's okay to feel it. Sit with it for a moment. You're okay.* He straightened up and pulled his shoulders back, clearing his throat. He smoothed the paper out best he could and neatly folded it. He wiped a tear off his cheek and tucked the paper into his back pocket as he pushed the front door open and walked back into his new everyday life.

5

"Tig!" Eli shouted from the top of the staircase in their new home. "Tig, come look!"

Antigone lumbered slowly through the living room and peered up the curved staircase at Eli who was covered in paint and still had the roller in his hand. She started up the steps and grabbed the railing to help haul herself up each one. *Any day now,* she thought. *I hope it's tonight.*

"Need help?" Eli walked down to meet her. He took her free arm and helped her up the rest of the staircase. "I wanted to surprise you, come on."

They walked down the hall past the guest bedroom and bathroom and stopped at the next door. "Okay, Tig, close your eyes."

Antigone closed her eyes and put out her hand for help walking. Eli led her through the nursery door and said, "Okay, open 'em!"

She stood for a moment in disbelief. "Pale grey with a hint of sage green." She turned to look wide-eyed at her husband. "Oh my God, Babe. You nailed it. I can't believe you were even listening."

Eli looked away and pulled back the corner of his mouth as he always did when he knew someone disapproved. "No, I mean, it's perfect! I love it—you were listening and I'm obsessed with it! Thank-you."

"You're welcome. I know I'm not around much and I know you want me here. I will be when the baby comes, just not sure how much ...."

"Stop," Antigone covered his mouth comically, "let's just enjoy this time together. I feel like this baby will be here soon—hopefully in like five minutes."

They laughed and turned to the unassembled crib in the corner. "That's next," Eli said and put his phone up to his ear at the same time.

"Yea, Dad. Yea, of course. I emailed that to them last night. I cc:d you and Jay and Alan on it and ..." Eli walked away as he usually did when it was a business call. Antigone was left standing in the room that was painted the color she loved and with the next project waiting to be started.

She walked to the window and felt the warm breeze against her face, blowing her long blonde beach waves back from her ears and neck. She watched the men below laying the second half of the pavers around the complex's pool and noticed how they worked so efficiently and as a team. Side by side, they handed each other tools and pavers and water bottles, as they worked rhythmically to get a big job done.

"Tig! Antigone!" She could hear him and started to move, smiling as she remembered when they first met. He looked at the napkin she wrote her name on. "Anti-gone? That's your *name*?!" She rolled her eyes, having heard this her entire life. "An-tig-oh-nee," she told him slowly. That was when he started calling her Tig.

Eli was downstairs now and she knew what was next so she didn't bother replying.

"Tig! I have to run. I'll be back—I won't be long. Tig?"

She walked to the open balcony in the loft above the living room and looked down at her husband, who from this vantage point seemed so small. Like an ant, scurrying to grab his keys and shoes and being controlled by a colony she wished didn't exist.

"Tig!" He looked up and realized his wife was standing within earshot.

They looked into each other's eyes from a distance and realized that no words were needed. This was their life, their routine. Small bits of joy strewn among the stress and disappointment, both of them unhappy about the obligations they could not tear each other from.

"I'll see you soon, Tig. Tell the baby to wait—definitely can't be tonight."

Antigone stood listening to the familiar departure. Kitchen door to garage, *Don't leave.* She closed her eyes, three steps down into the garage, *Why do you always leave?* She took a breath, engine firing up, *Here it comes,* garage door rumbling open *and* the shift into reverse.

She put her hands on her belly. *Bye, Babe.*

6

"Smell it. Don't be silly, just smell it." Rebecca held up the jar to Eli's nose. Feigning anxiety, Eli pulled his head back as far from the jar as he could. "I'm terrified."

Rebecca's laugh was a surprise to them both and caught Eli off guard. They both devolved then into fits of giggles and neither cared what the other might think. "Okay, so terrified might be a strong word but I have this thing about jars of stuff. I'm not entirely sure why, but when someone says, 'Here, smell this,' I instantly become suspicious. *Please* don't judge me."

Rebecca had turned the lid back onto the mason jar and began to lower it onto the long table where all her items sat on the autumn-themed tablecloth in the golden sunlight of mid-morning in October. The light danced on the crown of her light strawberry hair as she caught Eli looking at her in a way that made her heart quicken.

"Treadway's Tonic. I will drink Treadway's Tonic." Eli was committing to this act although he hoped it would be sometime in the future. He could never stomach things well that he wasn't used to, and he didn't want to embarrass Rebecca or himself. He looked at her in short snippets as he was suddenly self-conscious and was beginning to realize it, which made him more so.

"Okay, well it's here when you're ready." Rebecca placed her hands on her hips and looked from side to side along her table which was covered with apple pies, jars of honey, custom blended coffee, peach preserves, blackberry jam, blueberry pie filling, rosehip, cranberry and citrus tea, golden milk, and Treadway's Tonic. He reached into the basket on the chair next to her table and touched the soft mittens and scarves that suggested the cold was on its way. "In this jar is the best immunity booster for the winter and made with love by yours truly." Her attempt at a half-hearted Treadway's Tonic pitch was endearing because he knew her table was a popular one. She would sell almost everything she unloaded from her van this morning. She didn't need him to purchase anything. She simply wanted to be a friend. *If only you'd trust your gut, Eli, I'd help crack your cold heart open.* Her eyes taunted him, or so he imagined, but this time they were a little sad in the way that the coneflowers seem at summer's end. At once vibrant and healing and full of color, and the next day frostbitten and drained. They must go the way of the seasons and shrink back to the ground, hunkering there until spring; gone, but not forgotten.

Eli knew that he was playing a game for which he didn't know the rules, and he did not intend to actually roll the dice. He was just sitting on the board looking at all the possibilities and directions and feeling like the best outcome would be to have someone call, "Bedtime, kids. You can play another day."

Rebecca turned her attention to the customer who was inquiring if she made her own pie crust. He must have liked the answer, Eli figured, because he bought two pies, leaving just three left on the table. He put his hands in his jacket pocket and turned, feeling uncomfortable now and looked toward the next vendor's table. He picked up a small pumpkin bread and smelled it, then turned back to see Rebecca pulling out more items from beneath her table. Her apron, clean and white, was obviously not the one she used while baking. He watched her slender arms as she neatly lined up five more pies: three apple and two blueberry. He quickly released the pumpkin bread and walked back to Rebecca's table. "Wait a minute. You waited until I left to bring out the best pie ever? Okay, I see how it is."

She huffed and rolled her eyes as she checked her phone. When she looked up, Eli had both blueberry pies and a jar of Treadway's Tonic in the crook of his arm. He placed a fifty-dollar bill on her table and as Rebecca took out the roll of cash from her sweatshirt to make change, Eli walked away and over his shoulder said, "I'd like to start an account, please."

Rebecca stood with the bills in her hand, wisps of hair that had escaped the grasp of her ponytail moving gently in the breeze, and shook her head slightly. And though Eli couldn't see her eyes at that moment, they shouted, "You are something, Mister!"

Back in his truck Eli put the pies safely on the passenger seat next to him and sat for a moment, the sun warming his face and making his truck feel like a good place for a nap. He turned the radio on and then quickly turned it off, deciding this might be a moment to take a few breaths and just be. Inhale for four, hold two, exhale six, hold two, repeat.

"Get in the cah! You useless bitch! Get. In. The. Friggincah!"

Eli's eyes opened as his head spun toward the sound of the yelling. The man in the dark green Corolla was waving his hands wildly at the woman in the parking lot. "I said get in the cah! You stupid whore!"

Eli's eyes widened to see if anyone else was seeing what he was. He got out of his truck and took a step in the direction of the Corolla but the woman had stumbled into the passenger's seat. The door slammed shut as the car tore away. Eli looked around. A couple of people laughed. "Barlow Family keepin' it classy," said one.

And then the scene was as it had been just before the yelling. Families walking around with wares they just picked up, everyone in sweatshirts, children happily scuffling through brightly colored leaves with a recently purchased honey stick or candy apple. Mums exploding with color—burgundy, purple, pink, gold, orange—against the bland hay bales stacked two or three high at the corners of the large tent exclaimed, "It isn't winter yet!"

The smell of mulled cider and freshly made fried dough hung in the cool air; a seagull cry overhead, and the sound of a boat signaling its approach to the harbor cemented the feeling.

This was autumn in New England. It was a time of harvest and gathering after the tourists mostly went home; a short, exuberant lull before the long winter ahead.

7

"What do you mean, Ivermectin? Is that medication?" Eli cradled the phone the best he could on his shoulder as he tossed hay to the fat and happy ponies. "Oh, the dewormer you gave me. Umm, to be honest I don't know how to do it but if you explain it I can figure it out, I'm sure." Eli waited through the pause. "I mean, I can find it on YouTube, I'm sure. Right? It can't be that hard." He hung up the phone with the vet. He was realizing there is a lot more to horse care than there is with dogs or cats, though he hadn't owned either.

He turned back to the Littles and shook his head. "I'll be back."

The cool air felt good in his lungs. He decided to take a walk instead of heading back into the house. Sunday was a day he had carved out of his schedule for the last nine years. It didn't sit well with him at first, felt odd, wrong in some way. A waste. But now he looked forward to it and cherished it. *My time,* he thought.

He paused at the end of his driveway, then turned left, wearing his navy fleece vest over a red and white checked button-down shirt and Red Sox cap, jeans, and his first pair of L.L. Bean hiking boots. No one from back home would have recognized him and the very thought made him happy and settled. This was home now, and he couldn't imagine ever going anywhere else.

He walked down Ogden Point Road and breathed in the pines and the sea salt. The road beneath his feet was feeling more solid and familiar than it had when he first moved in. Up ahead he saw a truck that looked like Clem's. He wondered if Clem took any time off during the year or if he could afford to. One thing Eli quickly realized when he moved here was the juxtaposition of the multimillion-dollar properties that dotted the coast and the small dwellings tucked farther back behind the trees. It wasn't really that different back home. The crime rate and homelessness in Los Angeles was the stark reality in a town also full of the ultra-wealthy and entitled. Sometimes it seemed to Eli that his life there was just a hazy dream, memories poking at him like broken glass through the comfortable, more recent blanket of memories.

Eli bent to pick up some pinecones on the shoulder of the road and wished he'd thought to grab a bucket to put them in. He loved the feel of the cones in his hands, so light but so important, carrying the seed of such mighty trees inside. *Nothing short of a miracle.* He stuffed three cones in each jacket pocket and pulled a pine bough down to his face and breathed in the scent he had grown to love. Closing his eyes then he felt enveloped by the energy of the forest. He stepped inside, not wanting to be seen by the approaching vehicles for no other reason except that he wasn't looking to interact with anyone. He found a well-worn trail and decided he'd walk just a little way to see where it might lead, but knew it wouldn't be wise to go too far and risk getting lost. He came to a corner in the trail with a large rock covered in dried pine needles. He swiped it clean and sat for a moment, leaning back with his face open to the bit of sky above. He closed his eyes and drew a deep breath, held it and let it go slowly through pursed lips. He heard the forest inhale with him. Out of the corners of his closed eyes hot tears escaped. Eli wept for all the changes he didn't choose and for the ones he did. The forest swaying above and around him, whispered, "All is not lost. I, too, was once an empty field."

Back out on the road Eli heard the clip-clop of hooves and turned back to see how far down the road they were. He didn't think the carriage roads were close enough that these would be the giant drafts that pull tourists in the park. He could make out the swish of a tail on the dark horse down the road, heading away from where he was going. The tail swished opposite the ponytail of its rider.

Back to nine Ogden Point Road and up the short driveway, the gravel crunching under his feet, Eli admired how the house was beginning to shape up. Just as he was approaching the small picket fence gate that leads to the back of the property and keeps the ponies in, he heard a motor. He turned to see Clem pulling in with a delivery. "Hey Clem. Working on Sunday, huh?"

Clem's window was always rolled down. It never occurred to Eli that it might be broken. He just figured it was because Clem smoked which became a bit of an issue while he was working on the interior renovations for Eli. Now that he's moved on to the outside, Eli no longer worried about it, although he did wonder what shape Clem's lungs might be in.

Clem leaned back in the truck seat and swung his legs out the opened door and sort of slid out. He straightened up slowly and said, "I ain't gettin' any youngah I guess." He walked around the back of the truck and Eli's eyes followed him.

"Oh! My sign!" Eli walked over and enthusiastically reached out to touch it. "That came out perfect, Clem, good job, man."

He ran his fingers over the dark green oval sign with carved lettering in bright white paint.

Dr. Elias F. Cranston
PSYCHOTHERAPY
GRIEF COUNSELING
HYPNOSIS / FLP

It was sitting next to the post and hooks it would hang from soon enough.

Clem reached out and ran his weathered and scarred hand over the surface. "Came out pretty good, fella. Sorry it took so damn long. Been busier than a one-ahhm pay-pah hangah."

Eli laughed. "I've never heard that one, Clem."

Clem's eyes had a habit of disappearing into his round face

when he laughed. "Ha! Well, I got a million of em—stick around an' ya might hear a few mo-ah. I won't keep ya, just want-ah ta drop it off for ya so ya didn't think I took yah money and ran."

He laughed again, followed by a cough and then another.

"I knew you were good for it, Clem. I didn't have any doubts. Hey, listen I bought an extra pie at the market yesterday, you interested?"

Clem's face brightened up, "What kinda pie and which mahket??"

"Blueberry—I got it fresh yesterday at the farmer's market but it's still delicious today." Eli intended to fetch it for him but Clem reached into his truck and turned the key. The truck chortled as it shut off and it was clear Eli had company.

Through the gate they walked up onto the small porch and as Eli reached for the door handle, Clem said, "Ya got a bunch a bulbs in the ground here. Mrs. McCabe, she loved 'em. Tulips, daffodils and a bunch of some kind I don't know the name of. Charlie planted some for her every year after she got sick. He kept plantin' after she passed, too. He was nevah the same though. Crocus! That's it. Look there. See that spot undah yer dryer vent? He planted a handful of purple ones there. They start poking through before anything else from the heat. Charlie had a way of keeping Louise smiling. Not easy up here in the woods in March."

They walked into the entryway and wiped their feet on the rug there. "You need a dog, fella. Don'tcha think? He'd be right here in the dooryard." Eli turned, a little surprised at the sudden question. Clem had been working on the cottage at least four, sometimes five days a week since late August. He had never mentioned a dog to Eli.

"Well, that was my intention when I moved here but I ended up with Ink and Smudge and they are a handful as it is."

"Ha! Little bastards. Rats with a mane if you ask me. Hosses just eat and shit and I don't know one person who isn't broke on their arse because of 'em."

Eli wasn't sure that was true, but he did have to agree that the Littles seemed to only eat and shit. It was beginning to pile up behind the barn and he was wondering what he'd do with it in the spring.

"Hey, do you know what Ivermectin is? Horse dewormer in a tube."

"Ah-yah, sure. Used it on cows when I worked at the dairy. What about it?" Clem took off his worn and less-than-clean Marines ball cap and hung it on the coat hook on the wall, the same knotty pine that had been there since the 1940s when Clem's father helped the McCabes turn the cottage into a year-round residence.

"Well, I have to give it to the ponies but I've never done it. It doesn't look hard, but they are feisty and I've been bitten more times than I can count. Their teeth shouldn't hurt that bad for animals that don't chew meat. Seriously, it hurts."

Clem giggled as Eli gingerly placed generous slices of the dark purple dessert on the dainty yellow dishes from the cabinet. He watched as the filling oozed like violet lava over the tiny roses in the center or Mrs. McCabe's finest plates. "Coffee?" Eli resigned to the idea his afternoon wasn't his alone but once he did, he felt happy to see Clem relaxed and not working.

"Oh sure, thanks, fella. I didn't expect ta stay ya know but I sure appreciate it. Evah since the Missus has been gone, it gets a little lonely ya know?"

Eli knew Clem was single but didn't know much beyond that. "Sorry to hear that, Clem. When did she pass?"

Clem laughed and wheezed and revealed his missing tooth again. "She didn't pass! She left my sorry arse three years ago. Haha. She couldn't put with my drinkin' no more and I guess I can't blame her. Funny thing is, as soon as she left, I quit! See, she drove me-ta drink. All women will do that, ya know."

Eli was amused but could feel that Clem was feeling hurt as he spoke of his wife.

The coffee finished brewing and filled the kitchen with the scent of pumpkin spice, something new to Eli. Rebecca said it tasted like joy. He poured them each a cup and turned to the refrigerator for the cream. Out the window Eli could make out the shape of a cat on the stone wall. As he focused his eyes, he saw its tail wrapped neatly around its feet. He had seen him or her a few times but not recently. It was a grey tabby and as such blended well into the stones. Eli didn't know if it was a stray but didn't think it wise to start feeding it. He asked Clem if he knew whom it belonged to. "Humf. You're a charactah, fella. Cats are everywhere. It's pob'ly feral. Leave it alone and if it's got a home, it'll get back there."

Eli and Clem enjoyed the rest of their pie with talk of the impending winter. Rock salt, shovels, sand, flashlight and reflective boundary markers, and firewood for the stove. That was Clem's list and advised Eli to copy it.

"What do I need the reflective boundary markers for?"

Clem stopped for a moment and squinted his eyes at Eli. "C'mon, you think you're gonna shovel that driveway? Haha. You ain't seen a Maine winter, fella."

"Yeah, I figured it might be tough. You know anyone who plows?"

Clem said, "I don't know nobody who don't 'round here."

"Oh cool, man. So you'll ask around for me?" Eli was puzzled as to why Clem kept squinting at him. Suddenly it dawned on him, "Oh, you mean you'll plow for me?"

Clem took his last half sip of coffee and stood up. "Atta boy. There's hope for you, yet."

8

Antigone had grown into her role as mother as well as anyone. She loved baby Grace with all her heart and energy. An easy baby makes it easy to want another and since this one was almost two, Antigone was feeling like it was time for another. Maybe a boy would make Eli happy. Sometimes she wondered if he even knew what it was to be happy. He seemed to be when they met at UCLA. She was visiting friends there and they wound up at a fraternity, already drunk. Meeting Eli didn't happen until the next morning when they woke up not knowing where they were. Eli was in the hallway sleeping on the floor. She tried to step over him but tripped and fell on top of him. They started dating the following weekend and they both knew right away they wanted to spend their lives together.

"Ha. Together," she said to the wall. She finished folding Grace's laundry and put it into her dresser drawers, admiring the size of the clothing, so small and yet more than double the size of the clothes she wore when she was a newborn.

Her phone buzzed in her back pocket. Eli.

Antigone took a deep breath and answered. "Hi Babe, are you on your way? My parents will be here in a half hour. We can make the 9:10 movie and grab something to eat beforehand if ... what? What do you mean? You said you were leaving when you called a half hour ago. Where are you now? Okay, I'll be ready when you get here."

Pulling out of the driveway onto the street always seemed like an accomplishment to Antigone. It was never a sure thing until they were both in the car and had actually pulled out of the driveway. She couldn't count how many times Eli's father or Jay would call and force him back to the office. She wanted to throw his phone into the Pacific and force him to leave the firm so they could have a life together.

"What did you do today, Tig?" She looked at her husband and knew that she needed to say more than, "Took care of Gracie." She paused and then said, "Well, after Gracie went down for her nap, I looked up a few houses we could look at this weekend and Mom came over after lunch so that I could run some errands and ..." She looked at Eli and realized she really didn't have anything more to say than, "Took care of Gracie." It was an important job but Eli felt his job was more important and it showed in his refusal to help with housework, taking calls out in his car in the garage, and leaving the house to get work done.

"I was thinking, Eli. Maybe it's time we start thinking about making Gracie a big sister soon. She's almost two and a half and ..." Eli pulled his hand away from hers and turned the radio down. "What do you mean? You want to have another baby?" Antigone hoped that she was hearing excitement and not fright in her husband's voice.

9

The frost on the corners of the bedroom window caught the sunlight and twinkled like a thousand lights. Eli stretched one leg out beneath the down comforter to see if the house was warm. *Nope.* He pulled on the socks he had left on the floor before letting his feet touch the wooden boards. He walked into the living room and saw through the glass door of the wood stove that the fire was out but there were still some red embers. He tossed a couple of pinecones in and few pieces of kindling on top of them and shut the door. He pulled on his boots over the long johns he slept in. Starting the coffee was an incentive for getting his barn chores done quickly. Knowing you have hot coffee waiting for you while your cold fingers wrestle with buckles, buckets, and baling twine helps a little bit.

Coming in from the barn, Eli could see the kindling had caught and was beginning to burn. He opened the door again and the fire roared as the oxygen blew life into it. He tossed two stove lengths in and shut the door again before the smoke could set off his fire alarm. He hadn't anticipated the learning curve that is a woodstove in the house. He warmed his hands over the top of the stove and breathed in the scent of the fire and hot coffee. "I'm grateful for this day, for my house, my friends, Ink, Smudge and—" He stopped and turned toward the kitchen. "White paneling. I'm going to paint the paneling white." He shrugged his shoulders and wondered when he'd have time for that. Monday he would begin seeing clients in his new office, finally. He felt like it had been years since he saw his last patient but in truth it had only been since mid-August. So much had changed since then. He nodded in agreement with his thought and peered out the window to the stone wall. Again, no cat. He hadn't seen him or her for a few days and wondered if perhaps whoever it belonged to, began keeping it indoors as the weather rapidly cooled off.

He walked over to the cupboard and took out a pink mug that had become his favorite, not because of the color but because it was given to Louise McCabe by Charlie for Valentine's Day according to Clem.

Eli scraped the last of the peach preserves from the small jar and spread it on his toast. He was disappointed at the thin layer. He took a bite while his eggs sat in the pan, fluffy, and pale yellow like the plate they would sit on in a moment. He wasn't a great cook, but he had recently perfected breakfast. He loved timing the eggs and toast and coffee so it was all ready and still hot at the same time. Home fries. I will learn how to make perfect home fries."

The coffee done, he poured the cream into his coffee and watched it slowly turn his black coffee to light caramel, the *exact* color of baby Gracie's hair when she was very small before it darkened to Eli's color. *Keep moving.*

"No."

Eli sat at the kitchen table and took a breath to steady himself. "Stay with it, sit with it." He took another breath and could smell Gracie's hair and feel her little body on his lap. "Gracie."

The tears that fell onto the scrambled eggs went into Eli's mouth and were destined to be recycled. He didn't stop the fresh tears that came; he had long ago learned to let them flow. Tears are healing and necessary, he told his clients. They are part of the magic and mess of being human so the sooner you embrace it—all of it, the quicker you will begin to heal.

The sun was getting brighter outside his window and it promised to be a beautiful fall Saturday, the last day of the Bar Harbor Farmer's Market.

When Eli's truck came to a stop in the parking lot, he realized he was a little early and contemplated taking a drive down to Hulls Cove for a bit to watch the boats out on Frenchman's Bay. He sat forward to start the Chevy but glanced to his left and saw Rebecca's van pull in. He brightened then and decided he would wait for her to park and then offer to help her set up. He had missed the last couple of weekends trying to get caught up on paperwork for the state and the county and the town in order to open his practice; raking leaves, holding the ponies for the vet, and everything else that needed to be done. If he was honest with himself, he would recognize that he was avoiding Rebecca because he hadn't been ready to ask her on a date. But now, he felt ready and if nothing else, he wanted more peach preserves.

He put his hand on the door handle and stopped, drawing in his breath. Rebecca was unloading her van, handing her table and chairs to a man who reached up and kissed her with each item she handed him. He could see her smile and recognized the look on her face. It was the same look Antigone had beamed when they were dating: bright, fresh, excited.

Eli turned the key and hoped his diesel engine didn't draw attention. He didn't wait around to notice if it did. As he was pulling out of the parking lot, in came the green Corolla he remembered from a few weeks ago. Same guy, same woman, and this time with a girl in the backseat who looked to be about Gracie's age at her last dance recital.

This is not a day I am prepared to watch unfold if this morning is any indicator of how it might go.

Eli headed back toward Ogden Point Road and the safety of his newly anointed world. He had been so busy readying his office to open for business and eager to be a part of his patients' healing that he had forgotten his wounds still needed tending. He realized then that it would be a long while before he could call them scars.

10

It wasn't until Gracie was almost four that Eli and Antigone began to hit their stride together. The trial that Cranston and Cranston PC won, the one Eli promised would set them up for life, was finally over. It was indeed a battle to the end and there were many ugly skirmishes along the way. She didn't always understand what Eli was talking about when he described preparing for a trial, or motions made, sidebars, objections and the appeals process. She just knew that all of it kept her husband too busy to be a part of her and Grace's life.

"Eli? Eli can you help Gracie get her dance stuff together so that I can shower real quick?" Antigone got out of bed and knew she would have to get Gracie ready after her shower from the sound of the snoring coming from the other side of the bed.

Grace was still sleeping, too, so she would be easy to dress when she first awoke. Antigone had hoped they would have another baby close the time Grace turned three, but it hadn't happened yet. She was beginning to worry a little but felt there was a lot of stress between them and with Eli gone most evenings, she admitted that it made sense why she hadn't gotten pregnant.

To her surprise, after her shower she found that Eli was up and had Grace ready for dance class, cereal and orange juice included.

"Morning, what are you doing up so early, Babe?" Antigone was always surprised and appreciative when Eli did anything at all family related. And this small gesture wasn't lost on her.

"Well, I thought we could check something out after Grace's' class if you want," Eli responded.

"Sure, what did you have in mind?" Antigone had planned to get a manicure and take Grace to lunch but she knew this was not an opportunity that came up often.

"Well, Tig. It's a surprise but I think you and Grace will love it. Trust me."

And with that he kissed them both good-bye as they headed out to the car.

"Text me when you are out of class, and I'll meet you two."

Antigone opened her mouth, closed it and then opened it again, appearing to attempt to communicate like a cartoon fish. She put her sunglasses on, mostly to avert Eli's gaze and give herself a second to control what almost came out of her mouth. *Why don't you just come with us* would have ruined the smooth start to the lovely morning. She looked back up and smiled, "K, Babe. I will."

The summers in Los Angeles can be brutally hot and today was no different. Grace and Antigone stepped out of the dance studio into the humid wall of heat and instantly slowed down, as if suddenly they were walking in the ocean, the weight of the water holding them back.

"Mommy, can we get smoothies?"

Antigone held Grace's hand and tugged her along. "Not now, Honey. Daddy wants to surprise us with something. I wonder what it is."

Gracie yawned, picked up and hugged her less-than-clean stuffed bunny; the one Eli's mother gave her when she was born. On not just a few occasions, Antigone had spent hours searching for this very bunny: in the car, in the condo, out on the lawn. This bunny was the key to bedtime, naptime, TV time, and when it went missing, nothing was okay in Grace's world.

Antigone looked at her daughter in the rearview mirror just as her phone buzzed.

"Eli, where are you, we're in the car, waiting. What? Where? Oh, okay. I guess, yeah just text me the address. Okay. Bye, Babe."

The text came in and she pulled away from the curb not knowing exactly where this address was, but she thought it sounded familiar.

"Holmby Hills," read the sign. *What is this about, she wondered. I don't remember there being anything to do up here.* She glanced back at Gracie, sound asleep. Her GPS insisted she had arrived at her destination, but she couldn't see how. The driveway on her left was gated and it appeared to be a residence. Just as she started to pull away she heard a motor and turned to see the gate slowly swinging open. She cut her wheel hard and slowly turned into the drive that immediately began climbing upwards. Not sure what was happening, she called Eli. "Babe, am I supposed to be in a driveway? Where *are* you? What do you mean you see me— all I see is trees? Okay, okay, just stay on the phone until I see *you.*"

As her Lexus slowly came off the curve in the driveway Antigone could see the house ahead, sitting at an angle on the huge expanse of lawn, and she pulled up around the circular drive. She wasn't sure where Eli was, but he sounded excited.

Antigone put the SUV in park and waited until she saw Eli step out of the house onto the stone entrance in front of her. He had his sunglasses on top of his head and squinted into the sun to smile at his wife, her beautiful blonde hair tied up in a hurry this morning as she rushed to get ready before Grace's dance class.

"Babe, what is even happening right now? Who lives here?" She felt her heart quicken at the thought that something was wrong. Eli has said nothing.

"Give me Gracie." Antigone hesitated for a moment and then handed Eli the sleepy four-year-old in her pink leotard and tights and turned to look at the man who had appeared on the front steps.

"Dad," Antigone looked at her father-in-law and felt even more confused.

"Welcome home, you two." Richard Cranston, the odd combination of loving father and militant president of the family law firm stood aside and pushed the front door open.

"Wait. What is this, Eli? What does he mean?" Antigone felt drawn up the front steps but wanted to take Grace back into her arms at the same time, her little bunny in a sense.

"It's ours, Tig. This is our new house!" He put one hand on her lower back as she stepped through the front door and into the foyer which immediately drew her eyes upward. The soaring ceilings and chandelier above her were dizzying and the coolness of the stone floors made her feel like she was back in Europe on her honeymoon six years before.

She turned back toward Eli. "Is this real life? I don't understand, how can this be happening?"

"That's a question for Dad, actually." Eli turned to his father and as he always had, Richard stood tall. Eli always saw his father through a superhero lens and it often made him feel inadequate, as though nothing he would ever do in life could compare to his father.

"Antigone, Sweetheart. Come here." He held his arms out to his only daughter-in-law and though she was still stunned and unsure of what this surreal moment meant, she stepped into Richard's embrace.

"On the first of next month, Eli will become the third Cranston partner at Cranston, Cranston and, well, Cranston!"

Antigone stepped back and looked into Richard's eyes and then to Eli.

"Babe! That's amazing! Partner?! You have wanted this since the day I met you. Oh my God this is unreal!"

Richard gently took Grace from Eli's grasp so Antigone could have her turn.

"Shall I give you a tour, Mrs. Cranston?" Eli offered her his arm.

Slipping her arm through his and walking beside Eli down the hallway toward the next chapter of their existence together was, in a way, a contract she hadn't yet read thoroughly.

11

"Welcome, come in. Please. I'm Dr. Cranston." Eli stepped back and held the door open to the woman dressed in a long scarlet winter coat and black gloves. She walked past Eli and he could smell her perfume. It wasn't overwhelming but he knew it wasn't high end. Eli once believed one could tell a lot about a person by the clothing they wore and grade of their perfume but he is no longer the same Eli and though he was happy about that fact, he also often wondered how many people he excluded, even hurt, by his old beliefs. *Keep moving.*

The woman looked around and visibly relaxed. "I wasn't so sure I was at the right address. This looks so different in here than it does when you pull in."

Eli took her coat and hung it on the coat rack in the corner. "Yes, I've only been here since August, so the office was the first renovation to be done. Springtime, the outside will hopefully catch up. Please, have a seat and make yourself comfortable."

The woman, dressed in dress slacks and a heavy sweater, Eli guessed, was always cold. It wasn't yet Thanksgiving and though the temperatures were definitely dropping by the day, he welcomed the change. Perhaps she knew something he did not.

"So, I have here that your insurance will cover six sessions, but I will take care of this if we need to go beyond that. You don't have a co-pay and—" Eli looked up from the folder open on his lap to see that Jacqueline already had tears falling from her chin onto the collar of her cardigan. "I'm sorry," she said and waved her hand in front of her face, embarrassed.

"Don't be," Eli bent forward with a box of tissues and instead of taking one, she took the box from him and said, "Thank you."

Eli took a deep breath, hoping she would mirror him, which she did. He looked slightly to her right so that she wouldn't feel as though she was being observed.

"Can you tell me a little about why you're here, Jacqueline?"

"Jackie," she said and seemed to immediately gain control over the wayward tears.

"Well, I'm a wife, a mother, and a nurse in the emergency department at MDI Hospital here in town. I'm fifty-two years old and I just feel like there's something more. I don't know, it's hard to explain. It's like I have what most people would say is the perfect life, but—"

"Why would they say that, Jackie?" Eli felt she was comfortable enough for him to start subtly taking notes.

"Well, I have been married for twenty-nine years, I have two amazing kids."

"Ages?" Eli nodded to keep her going.

"Alexandria is twenty-seven and Gigi is twenty-four." She straightened up in the Navy blue and cream-striped Crate and Barrel occasional chair opposite Eli's identical one.

"They're so different from each other personality-wise, but they are everything good and I put my life into them. Joe did, too, my husband. He is a good father, he really is."

Eli waited. He often felt therapist was the easiest job once you knew what you were doing. You facilitate, you wait, and you let your client untangle the raw wool in their head. You let them wash it, card it, and spin it and roll it up into a neat ball and hopefully, if they don't quit, eventually toss it into the basket by the rocker in the room that is their life.

"What sort of husband is Joe?" Eli didn't look up, as though he hadn't asked the question at all. He waited.

"Umm, well he's ... he's just there. I mean, he's always there. He handles things, fixes things, he's a hard worker. He ... is ... just ... there." Jacqueline lifted the tissue to her nose and blotted twice. She lowered the tissue to her lap and folded it neatly, patting it against her thigh apologetically.

"So you need more from him. You need something from him he isn't providing?"

Jackie inhaled deeply and looked beyond Eli at the picture on the wall behind his secondhand desk that looked as if it was original to the house, well worn and sturdy. The painting came from a yard sale Eli stopped at one morning on the way back from the farmer's market in late September. The woman on the dock looking out onto the water reminded him of Rebecca if he was honest with himself. If he wasn't being honest, he'd say it's a good focal point for clients to look at and relax as they tore at the issues that were holding them back and keeping them from living their true authentic lives.

"I can't imagine that he could give me what I need. I mean, can anyone really give you what you need?"

Eli made his best Robert DeNiro smirk and nodded with his brows at attention, but said nothing. Truth be told, Eli was hard pressed to answer. He wasn't sure he could give an honest answer, though he knew he'd love nothing more than to say, "Yes, absolutely!"

"So how about this. Let's talk about why you're here. What made you want to enter therapy?"

Jacqueline looked past Eli again but this time she was looking out the window. A single tear slid down her face.

"I'm not sure I can put it into words, Dr. Cranston. I just know that there is something else for me. It's not here in Bar Harbor. I'm not from here and as much as I have grown to love it and the people I have come to know, it's not where I belong.

Eli waited, not wanting to ask the obvious. He shifted his weight in the chair and took a breath.

"Or, rather not *where* I belong, but how I belong. I think I belong, I think I belong alone."

12

The forecast called for an early dusting of snow, which excited Eli in a way he wasn't sure was entirely naive. He took Clem's advice and stocked up on firewood, salt, sand, and reflective driveway markers. He felt like he was ready and his office proved to be more than comfortable. "Bring on the snow," he told Clem the day before.

He was looking forward to doing Skype sessions with clients while snowed in. He wondered if he was romanticizing the notion of winter in Maine. He was well aware of the effects that long, dark winters and isolation have on people. And maybe just because he hadn't conquered one yet, he was eager to have the experience.

Many of his former clients were waiting for him to come online and pick up where they had left off with him. If he took all of them on, he wouldn't have much room in his schedule for new local clients; until he made his presence known here, he'd rely on the clients he left behind in California. It wasn't about the paycheck. He had more than enough in savings to last him a very long time. There were moments Eli thought that cutting ties with all of it, every last cent, could bring some healing to himself and others. But he knew the reality of money, the energy of it. It can be a drug for some, a lifeline for others, and it can destroy the greatest of dreams. Currency needed to be learned and it needed to be respected, much like the oceans he had lived near his entire life. It didn't matter which currency or which ocean, they were all powerful and with the ability to swallow up everything you thought you had.

The vestiges of his old life were thankfully few. Two cardboard boxes still in the corner of his bedroom begged, *When? How?* He moved away from the thoughts each time they presented themselves.

He was enjoying the routine he had settled into and woke without his alarm each morning mostly because he hadn't yet gotten blinds for his windows. The sheer pale blue ones left behind were no match for the early sunshine. Eli liked it and he knew that the natural circadian rhythms of his body followed the sun if he allowed it.

"Chilly." He wrapped his bathrobe around himself while his feet found his slippers. He paused and stretched out his back muscles. "I'm grateful for this chilly morning, for my home, my clients, for my ... experiences that led me here." He took a deep breath. That was a tough one. That one hurt to say but he knew he needed to heal; he deserved to heal.

"Oil the hinge on the stove. I'll do that this afternoon." He glanced over at the firewood and added, "And bring in more wood."

While he primarily heated with wood, he kept oil in the tank and took the edge off the cold with a couple of hours here and there with the furnace. He preferred the wood stove though, the way it worked—so simple and the way it smelled was comforting.

He started the last of his special Rebecca-blended maple cinnamon coffee. He frowned as he looked into the empty bag. Into the recycle bin he tossed it and slipped on jeans, boots, and his Patriots winter hat.

The cold air showed him the breath leaving his mouth and he suddenly was more awake than his coffee would make him when he got back inside. He had been keeping the barn door closed since blanketing the Littles. It slid reluctantly open, squeaking louder than before. He grimaced at the sound, "Add that to the list of things that need greasing."

He was greeted with the shrill whinnies of Ink and Smudge as they stuck their fuzzy faces over the top of the pint-sized stall door. "Starving. You guys seem to always be starving but you eat all day long. I don't get it." Hay, grain, and fresh water was pretty much their routine and then out to tear up the acre of land that was fenced in behind the house. He never had them out front and didn't think it was necessary to destroy the entire place. Those tiny hooves were like tines on a tiller.

He straightened their puffy red blankets and checked their water bucket, then opened their door and latched it to the outside wall of their stall so they could come and go during the day.

He looked at the clock on the wall. 6:45 a.m. "The whole day to myself."

He loved his Sundays now. He turned to leave but thought he ought to toss a couple of bales down from the loft since he had the time and there were just a few flakes left in the feed room, about a day's worth. He climbed the stairs to the loft and flicked the light switch at the top. He froze when he heard rustling. Nothing. He took a tentative step and heard scurrying again. *Rat? Racoon? It's big, whatever it is.* He held his breath as he carefully made his way toward the 20 or so bales neatly stacked along the back wall. He got to the hay and heard the first meow. He jumped back and focused his eyes on the scene in front of him: five tiny kittens, eyes closed and huddled together on top of a hay bale. He looked around to see where the mother was, his heart pounding a little faster. "What are you doing in here?" Eli had played with his friends' dogs and cats as a child, but his family didn't have any. His mother was allergic to everything so it was never even a question. It just wasn't a possibility. He wasn't sure if he should touch them but knew they must be getting cold. Suddenly he felt something rub up against his leg. He startled and stepped back, prompting the cat there to hiss.

"Sorry. Sorry!" Eli stepped back further not sure what to do or if she would attack him. "I didn't touch them. They're okay."

The cat jumped up on onto the bale, laid over the top of the kittens as they blindly followed her scent and her heat to find what they were looking for. He noticed they all latched on but one. It was so tiny and couldn't find the right spot to nurse. Eli felt it was best to let the cat do her job and let nature do what it does best. He turned to leave, then remembered he needed hay. He walked to the far left of the loft so as not to upset anyone. He opened the door in the loft floor and dropped two bales into the feed room. Clang, clang, bang. He missed his target—the wooden trough next to the bench—and knocked off the metal bucket that he used to scoop grain when he forgot to replace the actual grain scoop. The ponies jumped and kicked at the wall of their stall. "Sorry, boys!"

He walked back toward the stairs and peered over to see the same little runt still struggling, his little mouth open but his body lacking the strength to latch on. Something in Eli set itself in motion and he found himself reaching down slowly to guide the baby to his mother and held it there until he could see it suckling. The mother blinked slowly and purred her approval. "Barn cats. I have barn cats." Eli made a mental note to get cans of tuna and a water bowl for the mother. Eli was excited. His family was growing.

He had wondered where she had gone and why and now suddenly here she was, with babies.

"Barlow. Why does that sound familiar?" Eli picked up a second apple cider donut and held the box with the last one out to Clem who put his hand up, "No thanks, fella. I'm watching my girlish fig-ya."

"Barlow, I feel like I've heard that name recently, but I don't remember where."

Eli got up to get the coffee pot and thought about Clem's idea for an invention: a table with a built-in coffee maker.

"If ya been in town moah than a month, ya gonna he-ah about the Bahlows. Stan is a drunk and his wife—can't remembah her name, young thing—she's just as bad but she got into that hard shit a few years ago. Can you believe anyone would wanna stick a needle in their own ahm? I don't get it. I just cahn't imagine doin' that knowing ya ain't got no chance of evah gettin' off it. Evah. He beats the piss outta the poor girl, too. In public even. He goes out lookin' faw'er and by God when he finds her, everyone knows about it. She use ta be wicked cunnin' when she was the bahtendah at the Chaht House but that crap makes er look like the livin' dead from down cell-ah. Drives a piece a crap Toyota, not even registered is my guess but the cops, they don't mess with Bahlow none. Nobody knows why either. Just the way it is."

Eli suddenly remembered the car at the farmer's market and the man screaming at the woman to get in. That's where he'd heard someone say Barlow family.

"Well, Clem, every town in every state has a drug issue, don't think it's just here."

Eli had many clients who had addictions and they came in every shape, size, color, profession, and socioeconomic slice of the pie chart.

Clem nodded. "He wasn't always like that. Grew up here, good kid. Joined the service, came home and married a girl from Bath. He moved down that way. She goes to school and gets a job as an x-ray tech and he's working construction. Then she gets pregnant and goes to the doc-tah. Don't ya know, the poor thing finds out she got a tum-ah. She decides to try to have the baby, ya know and not have the chemo and all that shit. So she does it, God love 'er. The baby was wicked early though and it didn't make it. Can ya imagine that, fella? So then she goes shot'ly aftah that. And Stan, he was messed up as all get out. Stahted drinkin', got in trouble. He comes back he-ah and has been an angry son of a bitch evah since. Not saying I faut him or nothin' but the way he treats the new wife, she was so young. People talk ya know. Says he kidnapped her but I don't believe it."

"Wow, that's a sad thing, Clem. For everyone, you know? Oh yeah, by the way, I'm heading to Camden again Tuesday, do you have any projects lined up?"

"Nope." Clem's face brightened and Eli realized he was probably hoping for an invitation to take a ride.

"I was thinking you could start taking out that wall upstairs and maybe see if it's possible to get that plumbing working up there. I was thinking that might be the next big project."

Clem's face fell and Eli could feel the sting of disappointment radiate off him.

There was something about the guy that Eli felt grateful for, something he couldn't describe.

"What are you doing for Thanksgiving, by the way?" Eli got up and put the coffee cups in the sink and ran some water in them. He could hear Clem getting up and pulling his Carhartt jacket over his arms.

"Ah nothin'. Prob'ly head over ta Rosalie's down the road apiece." He had his hand on the doorknob and decided he'd wait a moment, put his gloves on first.

"Oh, cool. Who's Rosalie?" Eli hadn't heard Clem mention any women in his life.

"Rosalie's Pizza—little place down on Cottage. They're open on Turkey Day."

Eli's heart sank a little at the thought of Clem eating pizza alone on Thanksgiving.

"Maybe I could join ya? Or maybe there's a place that serves Thanksgiving dinner?"

"Well-ah, there's Gayln's but ah, I haven't been there since, well, since my old lady left."

"Oh, okay. I gotcha, man. No problem. Maybe I'll catch you at Rosalie's then if you don't mind?"

Clem was out the door and just before it shut, Eli heard the old man say, "See ya Tuesday mahnin'."

The note read:

> Hi again—I'm not sure if you got my last note so I
> came by again. If you need help with your horses
> during the winter, I have a lot of experience with
> horses and ponies and other animals, too.
> Let me know.

It was followed by another smiley face and phone number, this time with area code.

Eli took the note, folded it up and grabbed his grocery bags off the bench on the porch and entered the house. He put the note on the kitchen table and the bags on the counter top. After switching on the oven, he sorted his groceries on the yellow

Formica. As he glanced out the window at the sun setting low behind the trees, he noticed the Ivermectin dewormer still sitting on the windowsill above the sink. "Dammit, I have to get this done, somehow."

He slid the frozen lasagna into the oven and turned toward the kitchen table. His eyes fell on the folded paper there. *Hmm.*

He shrugged, pulled out his cell phone and dialed 207—he stopped. *Text is easier.* **"Hi there. My name is Eli. You left a note on my door. Thx for the offer. I could use help with deworming if you know how."**

Send.

Eli grabbed the can of tuna, opened it with the old electric opener on the kitchen counter, wondering just how many hundreds of cans it had opened over the decades. He took one of the yellow plates from the cupboard and the water bowl he'd picked up at Hannaford's and headed for the barn, hoping he would find the littlest kitten still alive. It was moving that morning when Eli went in after feeding the horses. He had brought some leftover chicken and a plastic pint takeout container to fill with water for the mother. He didn't want to bother them but looked to see that they were all alive.

There was a peaceful feeling in the loft he hadn't expected. As cold as the air was outside, in the loft it wasn't that bad. The meow was a welcomed surprise and it gave Eli a tingling in his chest. He smiled. "Hello, everyone."

He carefully removed the sharp top of the tuna can and before he could dump it onto the plate, the mother cat was at his feet, yowling louder than Eli was comfortable with. He bent down and placed the can on the floor and before he could let the can go, she was eating ravenously and purring like a motor. Eli watched her for a moment before stepping around her to check the kittens. One, two, three, four, five. All five were squirming. Eli marveled at their little bellies as they rose with each breath. He wanted to pick one up but knew he shouldn't. Instead, he took off his coat, then his UCLA sweatshirt and rolled it up and stood in his t-shirt, shaking his head at how smitten he suddenly was. He made a little nest on the hay bale next to where the kittens awaited their mother's return.

When he turned around, the mother cat was licking her paw and Eli could see the tuna was gone. "I'll bring you some more tomorrow, how's that?" She brushed up against Eli's leg with her back arched as he put his coat back on, then hopping up to sniff at his sweatshirt. Eli flicked off the light switch and climbed down the stairs to see who was being murdered.

"You two are so dramatic. Hold your horses." He wondered what you were supposed to tell horses when they needed to slow their roll. He shook his head and tossed the hay over their little heads so they would be distracted and wouldn't trample his feet when he poured the grain into their shared bucket.

Back in the kitchen, Eli grabbed his phone and decided to unwind by the stove until the Pats game started. His phone buzzed in his hand: **Hi Eli—I could come give the horses the de-wormer tomorrow. That's easy. LOL**

He smiled at the phone and texted back: **Great! Thx! I have to leave early for work. I can leave it out on the porch for you unless you want to wait until I get home.**

He could see someone was typing a response already so he just waited.

I get home from school at 3. I'll come then.

Eli responded: **I won't be home til around 6pm but I can leave it on the porch!**

Ok.

13

Antigone flew home, her pink blouse wrinkled at the back and only half tucked in. She looked in the rearview mirror. No makeup. She reached in her purse and pulled out a tube of lip gloss. As she swung into the driveway, she hit the brakes. She still wasn't used to this stupid gate even after three years. The wand fell from her hand and smeared three dots of hot pink, sticky gloss onto her white skirt. "Shit! What the actual...."

She took a deep breath and at the top of the drive, she pulled into the garage. Eli's car wasn't there. She sat confused for a moment and then grabbed her purse. Her phone was buzzing. Eli.

Hi? Where are you, I thought—oh, okay, but what about? Oh, okay whatever, we can go another time. K, bye.

Relief washed over her from head to toe. "Well that sucked more than most things."

Since starting this job, Antigone was always rushing. To the school, to the office, home, the market. It was more difficult than she had thought it would be but it was the best thing for her. The job was changing her and she could feel it, which she thought was quite amazing in and of itself.

She dialed the sitter, "Hey, Arianna—we aren't going to need you tonight. Eli can't get time off as usual. I'll pay you anyway. No, really, I'm sending it Venmo now. Please keep next Friday night open, okay?"

She hung up and rested her head on the headrest behind her. She focused on her breath as her chest rose and fell. Her phone buzzed again.

I love you.

She tossed the phone in her purse and got out of her new Escalade. It felt good to make her own money and though she had heard it was hard to get into real estate in this neighborhood, she had done it. She was proud of herself for having the confidence to do it, and being successful was just the icing on the cake. With Grace in second grade and no more babies, she had plenty of time to focus on herself.

The refrigerator was usually stocked with fruit and yogurt, milk and orange juice for Grace, the odd beer and sometimes a takeout container, but even these were scarce. There was enough to make something for she and Grace and she'd stop at the market on the way back from yoga in the morning.

She glanced at the clock: 5:30. She had an hour before her mother-in-law would drop Grace off from dance class. She stepped out of her heels and bent to pick them up. Her phone buzzed again:

No response?

She went upstairs to scrub the lip gloss out of her skirt. Before she had a chance to grab the stain remover, she heard, then felt the familiar notification that meant a prospective client was interested in viewing a property. She sat at the edge of the bed and opened the listing they were interested in. Her eyes widened when she saw the address. Beverly Hills. She quickly responded to the prospective buyers that she could set up a time to view the property and asked if they were working with someone on financing.

A text dropped down from the top of her screen.

I miss you.

She swiped it away and sent her message. This would be a huge deal if she was able to sell this property.

The gloss came out as far as she could see but she set the washer to hot anyway and tossed in her skirt, blouse, and the towels that were in the hamper. Walking into her closet, she let herself sink into Eli's dress shirts. She always loved the way they smelled. Not like him, exactly, but because they were his, the smell reminded her of him. She recalled the first time he let her wear one of his shirts. She loved how long it was on her, falling to just above her knees and thought she could simply add a belt and no one would know it wasn't a shirtdress. That seemed like a lifetime ago. How did things change between them so quickly? How did they change between anyone?

Just as she reached the bottom step of the staircase, the front door was opening. "Gracie, Macie!" She was always thrilled to see her daughter after a long day at work.

"Mom, guess what?! I'm going to be Elsa in the recital! I couldn't believe it!"

Antigone hugged her close and greeted Eli's Mom. "Would you like to stay for dinner? I haven't cooked yet but I was just about to."

Eli's mother was a quiet woman; kind, but kept to herself as much as she was allowed to as the wife of a high-powered attorney who had several black tie events and dinners to attend all throughout the year.

"No, thank you. I have dinner waiting at home. Bye, Gracie. Grammy will see you next week."

The woman in front of Antigone looked at her. She didn't say anything, but in a way, spoke volumes. Antigone wondered, Is it my hair? My lack of makeup, the fact that I'm in sweats after work?

After the front door closed, Antigone went to the kitchen to cook some pasta and vegetables. Then she would need to decide how she should answer those texts.

14

"Eli. You are just in time." Otto Gunther wasn't someone who slept in and he had been ready for this visit since 5:00 a.m.

"Morning, Dr. Gunther. I'm a bit early, sorry. I expected a little traffic but there wasn't any. Eli stepped over the threshold and was welcomed with the smell of freshly baked banana bread.

"I'd like you to meet Elise before she goes out today. She is going down to Rockland with her friend Susanne to visit a senior center to help with Thanksgiving preparations. Come!"

Eli felt a different energy from Otto on his second visit. He followed the man he knew so much about professionally, but was eager to hear about the experiences that had shaped his young life, though Eli knew it was a deeply painful experience.

Before Eli entered the kitchen, the woman Otto married in Cologne with a borrowed suit when he was nineteen turned and with her arms open, walked toward Eli. He bent low to hug her and could smell the combination of shampoo and perfume, both high-end, he was certain. Antigone often smelled exactly like this combination.

"Eli, this is my wife, Elise. Elise, meet Dr. Elias Cranston."

"Pleased to meet you, Elise. I've heard so much about you." He looked into her deep green eyes and saw there many years of wisdom and a warmth that spoke of someone who has made peace with life and all it brings forth.

"I will be getting out of your way, boys. I made banana bread and there's whipped butter in the fridge. Otto, take it out so it'll soften a bit and spread easier. Now the coffee is set to start at 8:30 but I'll start it now. Otto, if you get a chance, would you pick up the pickling salt today for the brine? It's the one thing I forgot for the big day."

"Yes, my dear." Otto bowed as she whisked past him.

Eli smiled and Elise called over her shoulder, "Don't be fresh, Otto."

She appeared once more and kissed her husband of 61 years. "I'll be home tonight."

Otto reached out and buttoned her coat for her.

He walked her to the door while Eli took in the view of the water, so blue and a bit choppy today, white caps rolling in. He couldn't see any boats today and he realized that preparing for winter was not something you did last minute around here. It was something on everyone's mind starting in late August.

Gracie never saw snow. I always meant to bring her up north or to Colorado to teach her to ski.

Otto was next to him then, cutting into the warm loaf of bread filled with raisins and walnuts. "That woman has saved my life, Eli. Many times over. I have only a few good memories of life without her. Come now, let's sit in the parlor. I want to hear the bell if it rings. The turkey is going to be delivered and I don't want to miss it. They won't come back."

He laughed at the memory of last year when he was working on his latest book, *Love, Not Time, Heals Wounds,* and he hadn't heard the doorbell. Elise arrived home later that evening from the hospital and asked where the turkey was. Otto had no answer.

"I won't make that mistake twice in a lifetime!"

Eli sat on the wingback chair facing the sofa and took a bite of the banana bread.

"This is a very comfortable house, Dr. Gunther. You've made it a home with Elise. It's very obvious."

Otto sipped his coffee loudly and brushed crumbs from his mustached face with his napkin.

"Hmm, yes. We like it here. It is a far cry from where we came from and we still have to remind ourselves it all happened in diesem leben, in this lifetime. It has become a home and a sanctuary from the world's madness. You know, you can choose to engage in the verrücktheit or you can choose to make a life that will feed you. You see, the madness is still there. I think, and sadly so I must admit, it will always be there. But only you can decide if you want fuel it. It reminds me of when I was very young, before the war. My father ..." Otto looked now out the window at the morning sunshine. *How bright it is,* he thought. *But it's so cold nonetheless.* He continued, "My father was a schneider, a tailor." We had the finest clothing, my family. And there was so much talk about taxes and who owned what and who owed money and who had a right to what. I think in some ways, people have always been this way. So concerned with what others had and did they deserve it."

Eli sipped his coffee and let the warmth of it relax him further. He enjoyed listening to the wisdom Otto was sharing.

But my father, you see, he knew that if he could help someone else, he was, in a way helping himself, too. My vater, he was a thinker. He knew that when you gave someone something they truly needed, you were helping them in one sense, sure, but you were also helping them to understand that they were worthy of being helped, you see? And that perhaps, at a later time, that person would then help another or even perhaps yourself."

Eli nodded and hoped he would continue.

"He was so busy in his shop and making sure Mutter and Hannah and I had what we needed. But he had ears, too. People talked to him as he took measurements and made notes. I think he knew what was coming. That is to say, no one *really* knew what was to come but I do think it was a collective feeling that our lives were not ours to live the way we had been living. But my vater, he gave the mantels, you know, coats, to men who had no way to pay him and das kleid for girls if their parents were working but didn't have enough money to keep their growing children in clothes that fit properly. My vater, he looked the other way when there was strife and he focused on what he could do."

Otto shifted in his chair and finished his banana bread.

Eli put his coffee mug on the colorful lighthouse coaster sitting on the table between he and Otto.

"Dr. Gunther, how old were you when ... when you had to leave your home?"

Otto was cleaning his glasses with the navy sweater vest he was wearing and nodding as Eli spoke.

He held his glasses to the stream of light that came through the parlor window and through his lenses he could see the farm truck, with his turkey inside, three driveways down. He placed his glasses back on his nose and gently shifted them into the well-worn valley on the near side of the hump in his nose. "I was seven years old, Hannah was five. We were just finishing our dinner with our mother when we heard them. The shouting in the street was frightening. We didn't know what was going on but Mutter ran from the kitchen to look out the parlor window and when she returned, she pulled us close to her. "Sich verstecken," she whispered loudly to us. "Go hide." So I took Hannah's hand and we went up the stairs to our parent's bedroom. We hid in the small closet as we had been instructed to do if ever there was an intruder or emergency. I remember feeling my mother's fur coat. It was so comforting to pretend she was standing there wearing the pelz and that I could touch her hand if I wanted.

But then there was louder shouting and the glass was breaking everywhere. Kristallnacht, the night of broken glass it would be known as for years to come. You could hear the screaming of the people in the shops and houses. The women were crying for their husbands. The men were forced to come out of their businesses and homes. They were arrested immediately. My mother was crying downstairs. We could hear her, and Hannah covered her ears and pressed herself against me. I tried to be brave for little schwester. I heard my father's voice. I know I did but I didn't know it would be the last time. Calling to Mutter from the street. "Sich verstecken!"

Eli hadn't realized he had been holding his breath until he let himself exhale. He felt instantly relieved by the loosening in his chest.

The doorbell seemed too loud as it rang twice. Otto jumped out of his chair almost comically and hurried to the front door calling, "Coming!" He opened and greeted the young men delivering the turkey. "Good morning to you. I saw you coming over from the Iverson's and I wondered if there was time to go for a run around the block, but I thought I'd better wait here."

Eli heard the men, no more than twenty-one by Eli's estimation, laugh.

"Well, you can go jog now, Dr. Gunther. The turkey has safely arrived, Sir."

Otto reached into his trouser pockets and handed the men the money for the turkey and then reached into another pocket for his wallet. Eli could see he handed each man a tip.

"Thank you, Dr. Gunther," they said in unison and offered to take the turkey into the kitchen.

"No, no. Be on your way and finish your deliveries."

Eli jumped up to take the turkey from Otto. "Here, let me get that. You open the refrigerator."

Back in the kitchen, Eli felt far removed from the story he was engrossed in just before the poultry intrusion.

"Eli. I want to talk more about your work today and the things you have been doing with it. After our last visit I have so many more questions for you. I feel like as much as I have learned in my lifetime, there is much more to unfold. I know that I will only see a kleines bisschen, a small bit, because I cannot live forever, but I feel like you are someone who understands that going backwards isn't always the key to understanding. It's not always the key to healing, though it does have its part."

Eli was disappointed that he wouldn't hear more today about Otto's early days but certainly it wouldn't be polite to ask him to continue.

"Yes, of course. I'd love to share what I know and what I do. I am just so intrigued by your background and work. I'm not used to being asked about mine."

"Well, you know, you don't always have to be asked. You can let the world hear what you know. The caveat being that the world might not be ready to accept the truth of it. But you have to hold onto wahrheit, your truth, no matter what. It was given to you and you alone. To do so is to let God work through you. It is nothing less than God's grace."

15

Eli picked up his laptop and Barnes and Noble bag and stepped out of his truck. He was home twenty minutes earlier than he had anticipated. Entering the house, he could feel the warmth of the stove. Clem told him that morning he'd light the fire around midday so it should be warm when Eli got home.

He quickly changed into jeans and t-shirt then bundled up in his down jacket and boots to head out to the barn. He opened another can of tuna for the cat and grabbed a flashlight, as it was definitely not staying light out as late as it had been just a week before.

He slid the barn door open and flicked the lights on. He stood for a moment and wasn't sure it was the same barn he had left this morning at 5:30 a.m. The floors were swept, the lead ropes all hung up, cobwebs completely MIA. "What ...?"

He realized the ponies were not screaming at him and demanding to know where dinner was. He could hear them chewing their hay rhythmically and contentedly. He was confused. He looked over the stall door and again, wasn't sure what he was seeing. The stall had a thick layer of clean shavings, the hay was hanging in a net on the wall and there was what looked like a brick in the grain bucket.

"Boys?" Smudge's neck swung around and Eli could see his eyes. That was the first clue that something monumental had happened while he was gone. He tapped on Ink's hindquarters and he slowly turned to look at Eli. Yup. Eyes.

He checked the bucket on the wall and it was full of clean

water. Closing the door and latching it, he remembered the texts from the night before. *Oh yea, someone was coming to deworm the horses.* He realized then that he had no idea who this person was or their name.

Suddenly Eli remembered the kittens. He climbed the stairs to the loft and turned the light on. There was mother cat nestled in his college sweatshirt with kittens nuzzling her and each other. She saw Eli and let out a plaintive meow as if to say, "You're late and I've been stuck here with these kids all day."

"Hey everyone. It's dinner time." Before he could place the can on the floor, the cat was at his feet, meowing. He put the can down and pet her as she purred and ate. He went to the kittens and stroked the tiny bodies, feeling their heat and their tiny hearts beating. "Hi guys and girls. I'm home."

After the cat finished her meal, she purred and rubbed against Eli. He bent down and scratched her ear. He didn't stop to think about what he was doing as he instinctively scooped her up into his arms. "Definitely not feral," he said as the cat rubbed her face against Eli's and purred so loudly he could feel it in his chest. "Hey there. I bet someone is missing you somewhere. Maybe I should try to find out who."

He placed her back onto the bale that had become a nursery. He didn't like the idea that the cats might someday be gone.

Back down in the feed room, Eli checked to be sure the hose was drained and wasn't frozen. Otherwise, he'd have to haul water up from the house in the morning. "A dog. I was going to get a dog." He laughed as he reached for the light. On the small whiteboard above the light switch was a note. "I dewormed the horses and I pulled their manes a little. At least they can see now. LOL. I can come tomorrow and finish cleaning."

Finish? The place was spotless. He shrugged his shoulders and thought it wouldn't hurt to let this kid work through the winter so he could focus on the house and work.

He remembered Otto's sentiment about doing things for others so that they knew they were worthy. He had a feeling there was more to that story and he wanted to hear it. He wouldn't see Dr. Gunther again until after the holidays, so he needed to put it out of his mind for now. Eli wanted nothing more than dinner, a beer, and bed.

16

"Hello Kate! How have you been?" Eli sat forward a little to be sure he was in the center of his monitor screen.

"Dr. C! I've missed you! How is everything over there on the right coast?"

Eli smiled, "It's very different but I am enjoying it quite a bit. So listen, I contacted your insurance and they are telling me there's a lapse in coverage. Are you aware of that?"

Kate's young face betrayed her lengthy rap sheet and problems with addiction. "Yea, I guess it's being worked out. I'm on SSDI now so I guess I'm covered but ...."

"Oh, okay, I'll contact the state then. Don't worry about it. So, let's catch up on what's going on now with you."

"Well, I've been clean for the most part, just one relapse since you left. I saw Max at a party and he was using and it all just went south from there. I didn't even use with him, I went over to Lola's after and picked up there."

"Okay, well how long ago was that, Kate?"

"The week after you left."

Eli could sense that Kate wanted him to take responsibility for her relapse.

"Kate, do you recall how many relapses you've had since entering therapy?"

She fidgeted with the vape she had on a lanyard around her neck. "No, I don't remember."

Eli sifted through the notes he had on the desk next to his monitor. "Four times, Kate. I have it here, four times."

"Oh, wow, okay. I hadn't realized that." Kate sucked on the vape cartridge and let it fall back to the dreamcatcher tattoo between her breasts.

The session ended fifty-five minutes after it started and Eli instructed Kate to check in within a few days and that their next session was going to be the following Thursday. He had fit her in today because the following day was Thanksgiving and her voicemail had sounded desperate.

Eli rubbed his eyes but the screen was still blurry. "Might be time for cheaters." He texted himself a message to remind himself to pick some up. He pushed himself away from the desk on his wheeled chair. The end of his first full day of sessions was more exhausting than he had anticipated. He enjoyed the Skype platform, though; felt it provided people a way to feel comfortable at home during their most difficult discussions.

Eli looked at the corner of his office. The boxes. He had moved them from his bedroom so as not to have them taunting him the moment he awoke each morning and haunt him each night when he went to bed. But here they were, taunting him. He walked out into the hall toward the kitchen and wondered where he might store them so they would not be a constant reminder that Eli still had things to look at, to take care of, to move through.

Entering the kitchen, though, he felt safe enough and put it out of his mind. He turned the oven on and pulled a frozen pizza from the freezer. Movement outside the window caught his eye and he saw a dark ponytail bouncing back and forth as the frame of a small girl pushed the wheelbarrow around toward the side of the barn. He waited to see her return, but she didn't right away. Eli went into the living room and opened the woodstove. He felt the heat rush out at him as he put in two logs and swung the door closed. He double-checked the handle and turned on the TV.

He slid into his boots and reached for his coat to go talk with the girl and thank her for the cleaning she obviously did in the barn. He heard an engine screaming up the road and he froze to see if her could catch a glimpse of the vehicle. It stopped before reaching his driveway and he could hear the drivetrain shift into reverse, then squealing tires again. He waited, and as it got closer he then could see it was an older dark green car, four doors. He wondered if it was the Barlow vehicle.

He walked back to the kitchen and slid his pepperoni, mushroom, and pepper pizza into the oven, pulled it out and reached for the spices in the cupboard above the stove. Italian seasoning and a pinch or three of red pepper flakes. "See, I'm cooking."

He set the timer for fourteen minutes and realized he had to make his visit quick.

As he stepped out of the back door in the kitchen he saw that the barn door was closed. She was gone.

His phone buzzed. He took it out of his pocket.

Ponies are fed. I brought cat food for the momma cat, too. They are all set.

Eli was stunned. "I have a farmhand. I need to pay her."

He texted back: **You really are a huge help. I'd like to pay you. Please don't come tomorrow. Enjoy your Thanksgiving. I'll be home Friday if you come then, I'll see you. What's your name? LOL.** And he added a smiley emoji.

Eli ate his pizza and a Blue Moon in his recliner in front of the TV and watched the sunlight fade. He picked up his phone and dialed Clem.

"Hey Clem, it's Eli. What time should I meet you at Rosalie's tomorrow? Oh? Really? That's cool! Yea, do we need a reservation? Oh, okay, great. Meet me here and we'll head over. I can't wait. Have a good night."

He looked at his phone assuming the buzz was a reply to the text he sent to the stable help.

Eli, Your father and I miss you very much. We hope you enjoy Thanksgiving in your new home. Please call us. We'd love to hear how everything is going. Love, Mom

He smiled at the screen and the way his mother signed her text message as if he would have no idea who was sending the message.

"Maybe," he put the phone down.

"Maybe."

17

"Hi ya fella, Happy Turkey Day." Clem reached up to the handle at the top of the doorframe of Eli's truck and hauled himself in, grunting as the weight of his body came to settle in the seat.

"Hey, same to you, Clem. Nice to have a day off, huh?"

"Maybe fah you, but I was workin' this mahnin' over the Flat Tire Fahm. Nah, that's not the name of it. I don't know, people come up with all sawts a names these days. Used to be yah fahm was called Smith or Fontaine or Devereaux. Anyway, it's down the road apiece ovah by the Sals'bry cove. She got a leak in her roof and I climbed up there. She's gonna need a new roof soonah than latah but I patched it good 'nough fah now. I'll go over again ba-foah the snow and seal it up. Get her through the wintah anyways."

"What's on the farm? Besides a leaky roof?" Eli was in a good mood and was curious to know more about Clem and the town and its people. He'd been here three months and realized he had only met a small handful of people.

"Ah, let's see, she's got gahdens, apple trees, peach trees, blue'bry bushes, ras'bry. And ah, those llamas there, goats, bee-hives, sheep, a hoss. Not like yours, but a real hoss. A beauty and you know I don't like hosses much. This one should be in movies and he whinnies to me when evah I'm there. I bring 'em a pepp'mint from my truck."

Eli smiled. The horse is cool because it likes Clem. Ink and Smudge are rats with manes because they turn their hindquarters on Clem. *We are all little children looking for love and acceptance.*

"So what's on the menu for tonight? I didn't have a chance to look it up."

Clem looked out the window, his elbow on the bottom of the frame. "Oh they got everythin' there. Bugs, ah-coss, and scallops the size of yah fist. 'Coss tonight there's turkey and pah-day-ahs, and all the fixin's. They make their own cran'bry s-ahs, too. Not too sweet, ya know?"

Eli looked over, "Bugs?"

Clem's whole body laughed, eyes squinting in the dimming light. "Lobstah!"

Eli laughed, "Oh geez, man I didn't know what you were talking about."

"They got the finest kinda chow-dah, ya gotta staht with that."

Main Street Bar Harbor was decorated for autumn festivities with straw bales and pumpkins, cornstalks and the odd scarecrow. This morning's turkey trot was over and within a day or two all the decorations would be whisked away to make room for the Christmas decorations. It was most definitely the quintessential New England storybook town. But as anyone can tell you, every town has had its struggles, its families with genealogy reaching back to the Wabanaki, Penobscot, Micmac. The hurt never really leaves when the blood in one's veins still feels the bitter sting of injustice. And there are families from away. If you haven't had family in town for a hundred years, you were "from away." When these families clash, the pulse of the entire town quickens and prepares for fight or flight.

They parked on West Street and walked over to Main where Gayln's simple white and light blue appearance sat humbly between Geddy's hot pink exterior and the darker Blueberry Patch. There was a chill in the air that made Eli feel alive and he welcomed it. He noticed Clem was wearing a button-down shirt that wasn't his usual blue plaid. It was tucked into a pair of trousers cinched with a belt, his belly hanging over. Without his usual Marines cap, he looked more his age and it made Eli a little sad for him. Eli hoped he wouldn't find himself alone at that age.

Stepping through the door, the atmosphere almost yelled, "Surprise!" the difference so great from the outside. Surrounded by warm, dark wood and local street sign decor, the smell of stuffing and apples wrapped Eli in a blanket of familiarity. *Gracie at my parents' house enjoying the whole family. Jay, Gracie, Dad, Mom, Tig and her parents. Keep moving.*

The hostess greeted them, "Welcome to Gayln's. How many?"

She brought them around the far side of the bar and seated them at a table set for two. Handing them each a menu and wishing them a Happy Thanksgiving, she asked what they wanted to drink.

Eli shrugged his shoulders at Clem to see what he'd order. Clem said, "I'ma have Coke, please, De-ah."

"Make that two and water, please," Eli said.

"Yah pacin' yaself, fella?" Clem's eyes pulled their disappearing trick again and Eli could see now with his jacket off that Clem had an undershirt on also, his button-down ironed to perfection with two opened buttons at the top.

"Ha. You're a character, Clem." It was clear that Clem was happy to be out with his new friend and enjoying the spirit of the season.

"Wha'cha gonna have, fella?" Clem was looking over the menu but had an idea of what he was going to order.

"Not sure, everything looks really good. Any suggestions for a newbie?"

"Well, like I said, ya gotta have the chow-dah, even it's just a scrid. If yah aimin' ta have seafood, I'd get a honkin' bug if I was you."

"I'm not even sure what you said, but I might just take your advice. We'll see."

Their Cokes arrived and the young waitress said she'd give them another minute to look over their menus. Clem reached over and took the top of the paper wrapper off Eli's straw, an old habit he had when Annie sat across from him. He wondered just how many straws he had unwrapped for her since 1975 when she finally decided she'd let him take her out on a date. *Couple thousand, prob'ly. Ya nevah know which one is the last straw. Hah.*

"Well I think I'ma get the whole shebang. The turkey supp-ah. Why not?" Clem put his menu aside and twisted in his seat to look around as the tables were filling up fast. "Last night this place is open til spring, ya know." He looked at Eli who was still deciding what to order. He wished they had a tapas option. It all sounded so delicious. That's when he realized the frozen piz-zas had to stop. He needed to get out and eat real food.

"Okay, I think I'm ready."

The waitress came back, pen and paper in hand. She looked at Clem.

"I'm going with the turkey dinnah and a cup a chowd-dah, De-ah."

Eli took a deep breath and said, "Well I'm going to have to try the chowder too, a cup. And I'm going to have the lobster."

"Which one, sir?" She looked at him as if he hadn't finished a sentence or perhaps had two heads.

"Oh um, I'm not, ahh, I'm not sure." Eli flipped the menu over and realized there was an entire page he hadn't seen.

"Well the twin boiled is popular but you could try the baked stuffed or the Lazy Man's or the medley which comes with shrimp, haddock and a hawf dozen oysters on the hawf shell."

Eli looked panicked. He had only had lobster at sushi restaurants and it wasn't even his favorite. He felt like a heel for not knowing what he was doing and almost gave up and or-dered the turkey dinner. The waitress kindly reassured him, "Most people get the twin boiled with slaw and baked pah-tay-da." Eli smiled at the slight accent and wondered if it deepened with age.

"Perfect. I'll have that. Thank you."

Clem pulled out a pen from his jacket pocket and circled an ad on the paper placemat in front of him. "Two fahty-nine fah oil. Hah, that's a good price. I membah when it was fifty-nine cents. Thought that was a killah then. Gahd help us."

Eli noticed someone approaching then but didn't look up. A woman's hand rested on Clem's shoulder and he craned his neck around to see who it was.

"Becca, de-ah, long time no see. He reached up and hugged her as she bent down to meet him. He clapped her on the back three times. When she straightened up, Eli saw it was Rebecca. He drew in a sharp breath and waited.

She turned to him and said, "Hi. How are you?" Her eyes were the way he remembered them, blue, but now lined with dark liner and a dusty brown shadow. Her hair was not in the ponytail he was familiar with; instead, it flowed past her shoulders and curled in long, loose tendrils around her face. She wore a deep plum dress, accentuating her narrow waist and slender arms, and tall black boots.

"Hi, Rebecca. Good to see you!" He wasn't sure if he was supposed to hug her or put his hand out but her body language wasn't inviting either so he just sat and smiled up at her.

"This is the gal I told ya 'bout, fella. She owns the fahm." He turned to Rebecca and asked, "What's it called again? Full Tank, ah somethin'? I only know it as the Boudreau Fahm from way back."

Rebecca revealed her beautiful smile and laughed, "Full Circle Farm, Clem."

Eli hadn't thought about where Rebecca lived or that she had an actual farm. He felt a bit foolish now, for many reasons.

"Is it open year 'round?" Eli hoped he wasn't unknowingly asking a stupid question on the heels of his crustacean faux pas.

"Farms never close," she laughed, "but as far as taking my things to markets, that's over 'til late spring. I sell my things year round and take orders for sweaters, mittens, socks, and ...."

A man's hand slipped around Rebecca's waist from behind and she turned to include the man in the conversation. "Hey, Brendan, this is ...."

The man remained behind her and said, "Food's ready. C'mon."

She stopped, embarrassed, and hesitated before turning back to the table.

"Well, it was nice seeing you again." She smiled, this time without teeth, at Eli.

Her eyes said, "See, you missed out and now I am, too."

Clem and Eli wished her a happy Thanksgiving and she turned to leave. Impulsively and feeling like he deserved, somehow, to finish his chance at messing up, he said, "Hey, Rebecca. How can I get more peach jam or do I have to wait 'til Spring?"

She smiled and said, "Preserves? Have Clem pick some up for ya next time he comes over."

Dinner arrived and Eli felt overwhelmed with the amount of food on their table.

"Now that's wicked good food, fella. Not like that stuff yah was prob'ly eatin' out west there. This will make up fah it."

Eli picked up his Coke glass, "Cheers, Clem."

He was too embarrassed to admit that he didn't realize twin lobster meant two lobsters. "Hey Clem, there's plenty of lobster here, help yourself."

Clem had a mouthful of stuffing already and shook his head. "I'm gonna have all I can do to get this down. It's the finest kinda stuffing. Annie always wanted the recipe. Try it."

Eli scooped a bit onto his fork and tasted it. "Yea, you're right, that's amazing. What's that flavor? It's earthy.

Clem shrugged, "Secret ingredient, I guess!?"

Picking up the lobster cracker reminded Eli of times when he had to fake it 'till he made it: driving a manual transmission, swinging a golf club, using a condom.

He was relieved when the shell gave way to the claw meat beneath it, perfectly pink and fragrant. He pulled it out gently and dipped it into the melted butter in the small tin on his platter. He tapped it on the plate so as not to drip the butter on his shirt and put it in his mouth. To his surprise, all of his taste buds stood at attention. *This is why Maine is called Crustacean Nation.*

Clem was watching his expression and laughed. "Better than sex, huh, fella?"

Eli laughed, "I'm pleading the fifth on that one."

"Hey-ah, that's what the bib is fo-ah, fella. Put that on and don't pay no mind ta that there butt-ah. You're in Maine now. You might not always need the bib, but fah staht-ahs, everyone uses one. Dig in!"

When the check came, Clem reached for his wallet, another habit he had of always picking up the bill.

Eli already had his credit card out and handed it to the waitress. "Don't take his money, please."

"Oh hay-ah, fella, you din't have ta do that, ya know."

"Clem, you have been a lifesaver with the house renovation and making my sign. And I'll remind you that you said you'd plow." He cleared his throat loudly.

"Shit, that's what we do 'round here. We help each oth-ah."

"Good, then we're even."

"Well, I'll thank you very much, Eli. Sure makes me happy ta know ya."

Stepping back out onto the street, the cool air wakened them from their food comas and reminded them it was late November on the coast. They closed their jackets around them and walked toward West Street.

Pulling away from the curb, Eli said, "You know you never have room for dessert at the restaurant but once you're home, you wish you had something sweet."

"Yah, you'd think rest'runts would figure that out—but they stuff ya to the gills. Hey-ah we could run by Rosalie's and get som-ah their balkava. Best around."

Eli pulled onto Cottage Street and saw the sign for the pizzeria. He pulled in behind a plumber's van and put it in park. Clem said, "I'll just run and get it. Gimme two minutes."

Eli turned the radio on and thought about Rebecca and her anti-social boyfriend.

The van pulled away and Eli could see the green Corolla in the next space up, empty. *That's the only reason it's quiet.*

He looked through the window at the people inside: Clem at the counter, shifting his weight back and forth, hands in his trousers as the waitress placed the gooey confection in a plastic container. Eli looked to the left and saw people in a booth; a balding man in a Carhartt coat and faded jeans, and a woman, possibly his daughter, in a black parka, tights, and the boots Eli couldn't understand were so popular. Eli shrugged his shoulders. "Uggs must mean ugly in another language."

When Clem left the building the bells above the door jingled. He opened the door to the truck and said, "Okay, let's blow this popsicle stand. Baklava and them I'm going home to get some shut-eye." Clem hoisted himself up into the truck again.

"Hey, Clem, is that the Barlow Family?" Eli pointed to the people in the shop.

"Ay-uh, staht drivin't ba-foah Stan picks a fight, will ya?"

18

Eli didn't hear the side gate open outside his bedroom window. After Clem left the night before, he had taken out a bottle of Jameson and relaxed by the woodstove, looking at the boxes next to the TV. *Not tonight. It's Thanksgiving.* Eli was never a big drinker but there were a few occasions during college that he hit the bottle pretty hard. His job demanded a lot from him at the firm and the one time he showed up in court hungover he swore he would never let that happen again.

So the three shots he drank while watching a documentary on Netflix that night just ensured he would sleep well.

His most vivid dreams always came just before waking. *Little Gracie playing hide-and-go-seek, shrieking, "Daddy! Daddy!" But Eli was looking in all the wrong places. She didn't know why he couldn't hear her." Daddy!" He kept peeking behind doors and trees and buildings. Each time he looked, he was expecting to see her. But she wasn't in the spots he looked. "Daddy, don't give up hope!"*

The second time the gate clicked closed, Eli heard it. He sat up but by the time he looked out the window, there was nothing to see.

Out in the kitchen, Eli took stock of the sad few groceries he had in the cupboards. Rice, half a box of penne, a packet of instant oatmeal and a bag of sugar. The refrigerator wasn't much better: a stick of butter, two bottles of Blue Moon, one egg, and a piece of baklava from the night before. "Going to the store today, I guess."

He put on a pot of coffee and sat at the kitchen table rubbing his face. His phone buzzed.

Horses are fed. They need their hooves trimmed. Do you have a farrier?

Eli sighed. That was one thing he knew nothing about. *How did they let me take these horses home? I know virtually nothing about them.*

He texted back: **No, I don't but I'm guessing you do!**

She texted back a smiley, then: **I'll call the one I know if you want.**

He laughed and shook his head as he responded: **Thank you. I'm going to leave some $ for you in the feed room since we keep missing each other!**

"Oatmeal it is then." He got up and stretched the muscles in his back and wondered if he should catch up on paperwork today since he wasn't seeing clients or Skyping with any. *Maybe,* he thought.

He pulled into the Hannaford's Market on Cottage Street and sat for a moment, listening to the end of an NPR segment. He looked up at the sky which was darkening as the clouds rolled in off the harbor and promised rain or maybe even snow. Eli never minded rain, as there was very little back home. He admitted he liked the excuse to hang out at home, whether or not he spent it on paperwork. There was a comfortable, safe feeling in his cottage that he attributed to the McCabes. Simple furnishings, delicate, colored plates, and little pictures and plaques around the house wishing Irish blessings and messages of faith for anyone who entered.

One, two, five, eight raindrops spattered Eli's windshield and he realized he had sat too long. He pulled his hood up over his head and opened his door.

In the coffee aisle, Eli looked for something different ... French vanilla, hazelnut, Christmas Sugar Cookie. *Already?* He shrugged and tossed it into his basket. He wished he had one of Rebecca's blends. He hadn't realized what he'd miss once it was gone. Rounding the corner toward the frozen foods section he slowed down and watched as the woman in front of the freezer stood, swaying slowly back and forth. He wondered if she needed help. Before he could approach to ask, a man walking passed her remarked, "What the f—-? Get a life, junkie." Eli was taken aback. He looked at the man as he passed where Eli was standing. "How ya doin?"

Eli didn't answer. He looked back to the woman who was now slowly shuffling her way to the register with a box of frozen waffles, unsteady in her leggings and worn out Uggs, her parka engulfing her slight frame.

Cereal, coffee, steak, an onion, mushrooms, cheddar cheese, potato chips, beer, tuna, eggs, English muffins, potatoes. *That's good. No, wait.* He turned back to get some half-n-half and on his way back, grabbed some honey ham, rolls, cheese, and three frozen pizzas. *Habits take time to change,* he reminded himself.

Eli carried his overflowing basket, the pizzas under his arm, to the self-check-out. He waited for the machine to spit out his change in coins then carried his three bags toward the door when he caught sight of the woman again. Nodding back and forth, she was counting change as if in slow motion. The girl at the register, clearly uncomfortable, nervously checked her cell phone, dropped it into her apron, then took it out again. Eli wanted to step in to help but thought he might make things worse, so he kept walking.

He sat in his truck for a moment to see if the woman was going to try to drive or if she was walking. *Then what, give her a ride?* He wasn't sure of the answer but didn't feel he should just ignore the situation. He turned his radio on and turned to a music station. *The Diary of Jane ... Oldie but goodie,* he thought. Out of his side view mirror he saw a Bar Harbor police cruiser pull up and when he turned to watch it approach the fire lane in front of the store, he heard a siren approaching from the street behind him. He turned to see an ambulance enter the lot. He thought about waiting, but knew that she was in good hands—or at least better than his, since he doubted he could do anything for her. He watched the expressions of the shoppers as they left the store: concern, hesitance, apathy, he wasn't sure what else. He saw one woman shake her head and make a quick sign of the cross. Eli felt better then, knowing that not everyone sees an addict as a junkie or worthless. That couldn't be farther from the truth.

Back on Ogden Point Road, Eli put his groceries away, looking forward to his steak and baked potato dinner much later that evening. He had a to-do list a quarter mile long, as Clem would say, and he intended to get it all done. Paperwork, sadly or not, didn't make the final cut.

He made himself a three-egg and cheese omelet and more coffee, the ticking of the old wooden clock above the doorway to the living room the only sound. The clock's face had a Celtic cross on it and the hands were tipped with four-leaf clovers. He had mentioned to Clem right at the start of the renovations that everything pretty much needed to go. But looking around now, he realized he had become accustomed to the knotty pine, although he decided he'd like it painted off-white, much to Clem's chagrin. "Those knots are a bitch to cov-ah and they like to bleed through but whatev-ah ya want, fella. I'll get some Kilz."

The clock, the little sign that read, "You Are My Sunshine," and the Hummel figurines on the cornice above the sink all had a certain charm. He hadn't seen any of it at the auction. He stood on the front lawn with four other bidders as the auctioneer read the rules, one of which was no entrance. Never having bid on anything in his life and it being a sealed envelope auction, Eli figured he probably bid too high but he really loved the location and wanted it no matter the condition inside.

He wondered if he'd see Clem tomorrow since it had become a regular occurrence now. Sometime around 8:30 a.m. each day, Clem had pulled in, beeped once, and come to the door with donuts. He hoped he would see Clem tomorrow as well.

After laundry and sweeping, Eli took a shower and let the warm water wash away the feeling that he could have/should have asked the woman at the store if he could do anything for her. He knew it wasn't his job or really his business for that matter, but he was a firm believer that when people say, "Well that's society today," what people are really saying is, "We are blaming something outside of ourselves, when in reality **we** are society.

He toweled off, dressed, and decided he wanted to check on the kittens even though he knew they had been fed.

He climbed the loft to hear them squeaking for the first time. His heart beat faster as he approached. The mother was gone and they were calling for her. "I'm sure she'll be back. Don't cry." He looked around and called to her, "Momma, where's Momma? C'mon, your babies need you."

He felt silly not giving her a name. He thought about what to call her but only baby girl names came to mind. Grace, Ellie, Emma, Madison were all names he and Antigone had discussed. He had never named an animal before. He looked around to see if he could get an idea and saw: hay, rafters, dust, and an empty tuna can. Bumblebee. He said it out loud, "Bumblebee." He called to her now, feeling odd. Who was he to name a cat that probably had a name already and would she even like the name he chose? "Bumblebee! Where are you?" He felt like she would return, but in the meantime welcomed the opportunity to sit with the kittens. They squeaked their little squeaks and to his surprise one of them began to squint and open his tiny eyes. "Oh my gosh, look at you." Eli held it close and examined its little mouth, nose, and now the bits of blue he could see in its almost open eyes.

He looked up when he heard the soft whisper of the mother cat's feet on the steps. "Bumblebee!" Eli was stunned to see a mouse hanging from her mouth. She softly walked up to Eli's feet and dropped her catch at his boot. "Gross."

She purred and rubbed against his leg as if to say, "It's okay if you don't understand. I'm still proud of my kill and I'm trusting you with my babies as I do it."

"Your babies are growing, Bumblebee. They are starting to open their eyes. You're a good momma."

Eli tossed a bale down to the feed room and noticed the slop sink was scrubbed clean.

Back downstairs, he looked into the stall to see that the brick was still inside the grain bucket. He wasn't sure why someone would need a weight in a bucket like that. As he reached down, he could see it was pinker than a normal brick and it had smooth edges. He touched it. "Why is it slimy? What is this?" He brought it out into the light of the open barn. He sniffed it. "Apples?"

He tossed it back in the bucket. "I'll have to ask about that." Checking out the feed room he saw that the floor was swept, the baling twine wrapped into a big ball and stuffed into a grain bag. The window adjacent to the sink was clean and even the top of the grain bin had been dusted clean.

Just before leaving the feed room he saw the note on the board: "I brought them a mineral lick—good for their electrolytes."

Wow, who knew? He reached into his pocket and pulled out a twenty and a ten and placed them on the grain bin. He looked around and grabbed the rock he used to prop open the grain room door sometimes. He placed it on top of the bills and headed out. The horses were grazing at the far end of the property, rhythmically, methodically looking for any grass worth eating. Rustling through the leaves, their hooves now on semi-frozen ground.

Eli decided he'd try to get more leaves raked and off the front lawn. His muscles thanked him for the opportunity to work. He looked around and realized they should be careful what they wish for.

After a half hour, he peeled off his fleece and started thinking about his new client coming Monday, a woman from Boston. Looking up at the new sign to the right of the driveway he felt a sense of accomplishment, and a pride that never played a role in the courtroom dramas he starred in, defending people he had no doubt were guilty as sin. It was a job, a game, a way of life. His father had taught him this from an early age.

"Someone has to defend them and they will pay a lot of money to that person. It may as well be me."

When the leaves were bagged and raked, Eli bent down to pick up the dozen pine cones he purposely avoided bagging. Both hands full, he walked to the porch and placed them in front of the black bench with the bright white letter C painted on the backrest. "Perfect, how that worked out," he said to himself.

He lifted the seat of the bench to take out one of the small cardboard boxes he noticed was there when he moved in. He boxed the pinecones, intending to finally get some wax and make fire starters like the ones he saw in the L.L. Bean store in Portland when he bought his boots in early October. He liked the idea of making his own. He just needed to find where to buy beeswax.

Picturing Rebecca's smile, and the way she had looked when dressed for Thanksgiving dinner, brought a smile and regret to Eli. He wondered if she was happy with the guy she was with and if it would last. As Eli has learned to do, he shrugged his shoulders and thought, "If it's meant to be, it will."

He sat on the front step and admired his work. He was hoping to replace the flagstone walkway with poured concrete and bring it around to his office door at the back of the house. Once the snow came this year, he'd have to have people come through the living room, which didn't thrill him.

Eli looked at his phone. He wondered why weekend days went by so much faster than weekdays.

He took the canvas firewood sling and walked around to the right of the house where his woodshed stood, packed full of seasoned firewood. He filled the sling and just before he turned, he caught a glimpse of Ink rubbing against the fence at the back of the property. *Must feel good to have no blanket on during the day,* he thought.

Three trips out to the woodshed and his bin in the living room was full. He glanced at the cable box, 2:45. Too early to start dinner, too late to tackle picking up manure in the pasture. The sun was just starting to peek out from behind the thinned clouds and suddenly Eli decided to take a drive. For half a second he thought he ought to put the boys in the barn but shook his head. He was only going for a short drive. He grabbed his keys off the key holder on the wall by the front door which read: Please Don't Drive Faster Than Your Guardian Angel Can Fly.

He pulled out onto Route 3 and headed toward town, thinking again about the woman at the supermarket and wondering if she was okay. He put on some music and enjoyed the sparkling bits of gold on the water as he passed the harbor looking out to Frenchman's Bay. He continued onto Eden Road. The sun was fully out from behind the clouds just in time to say farewell in a little while. Not wanting to go too far out before it got dark, remembering the boys were out in the pasture, he turned down a side road and saw a sign with an arrow that pointed to another arrow and another almost like the recycle symbol. FULL CIRCLE FARM. He slammed on his breaks as if he was doing something terribly wrong. He glanced behind him and saw no one coming so he put the truck in reverse and hit the gas.

He pulled back onto Eden and glanced around to see if anyone had seen him. He challenged himself. *So you don't want anyone to see you, a stranger, accidentally driving down the road where the woman you can't stop thinking about lives, because they might tell her and she then would know you like her. Is that correct?* He answered himself out loud, "Pretty much." And just then the skies opened again and the rain came down fast and furious as if to wash the worry away and say, "Try that again, son. All of life is an experiment."

Pulling back into his driveway, he felt something was amiss but wasn't sure if it was how hard the rain was coming down, his hunger, or his near collision with the possibility he might drive by Rebecca's farm and she would, against all odds, see his truck and know it was him.

He was beginning to see how quickly the weather can turn in this neck of the woods and decided to feed the horses early and be done for the day. He ran to the side of the house, through the gate, and up to the barn with urgency fueling his uneasiness because he had left the horses out and now he couldn't see them in the pasture. "Boys?"

He entered the barn and could feel the stillness. The feeling was familiar and it was terrifying. "Boys!"

This time it wasn't a question but a command. Nothing.

He ran back out and looked again. No horses. Just as he was turning back to the barn, he noticed a section of fence lying on the ground. "What? How?" He remembered seeing Ink at that spot rubbing against the old wooden fence. "I should have put them in, dammit!"

He went into the feed room and scooped some grain into the metal bucket and turned to run. "But where am I going?" He grabbed two lead ropes and a flashlight and ran.

He had no idea where they could be or how hard it might be to catch them. He'd only ever kept them in the pasture. His heart raced as he stepped over the splintered boards and into the woods. There was a little shelter from the rain but he could feel the difference in the energy of the trees. The overgrown trail that the McCabes' boarders used to ride was all but invisible, but Eli just followed the ferns as they wove their way through the trees. Thunder in the distance added to Eli's panic and he yelled, "Ink! Smudge! Dinnertime!"

It seemed that with every step, the woods got darker and the last thing he wanted was to get lost out here.

The light from the flashlight bounced off the trees and more than once, Eli heard something scurry up ahead. His heart pounding with each careful footfall, Eli wanted to turn back. *I can't. It's my responsibility, my fault. They need me to find them, they are small and vulnerable. They need me. I'll never forgive myself.* His tears mixed with rain as he remembered the night Grace came into the world, so tiny and perfect. She whimpered and squealed much like the kittens in the loft. And then, as if someone turned up the volume, she let out a wail that had everyone laughing. *I am here. I am Grace and I will change everything about you, one way or another.*

Eli stumbled on a tree root and took two giant steps forward, *Mother, may I?* and fell to the forest floor, hurling his flashlight several feet ahead of him, his grain whooshing out like a farmer feeding young farrows.

He got to his knees, and realized he still held the now empty bucket. Suddenly he realized he was watching the light coming toward him, gently bouncing up and down. He stood, ready to run. He didn't care if it was a person or a ghost. He had reached his limit and intended to flee.

Just then, he heard the soft nicker or one of the horses. The light no longer shining in his eyes, he could see the outline of person between, what he assumed were, his boys. They were stopped a few feet from Eli who was simply speechless.

"I found them!" The voice, female and soft, came from somewhere behind the light.

"Oh, thank God." Eli breathed in the relief. "Are you ... ?"

He reached for the flashlight.

The answer came, now in darkness and confusion as it often does.

"I'm Hope."

19

"Daddy! Daddy, I'm here! I'm here!" Gracie's voice was the sweet and excited giggle it always was when she was little. Eli looked through windows and in drawers, opened gates and pushed through shrubs, climbed inside dumpsters and under vehicles.

"Daddy, Where are you?"

Gracie's voice calm and fading. "Where are you?"

For the first time in many years, Eli awoke before morning, drenched and shivering. He sat up and drew a deep breath. "Gracie."

He sat like that for several minutes, slumped forward, shoulders hanging in the light of the moon. He heard the ticking of the Celtic clock down the hall, steady and comforting. He allowed himself to slowly lie back, turn on his side and hug the cool pillow next to him. And there in the stillness of his cottage, thirty-two hundred fifty-four miles from where he started, Eli Cranston realized that, in fact, Grace wasn't the one hiding.

Time has a way of speeding up and dragging on and sometimes seemingly spinning backwards. Eli came to realize all of that was much better than when it stood still like a stubborn mule staring you down. With just a couple of weeks until Christmas, Eli tried to fit in as many clients as he could because he knew they needed him. He was tired, though. He hadn't anticipated the three-hour time difference in Maine making for some very late evenings.

"Hey Kate, before we end here, I'd like to ask you to do

some breathing with me. Let's do some box breathing together." He was afraid she would refuse. Her session was a particularly difficult one tonight and she was shutting down.

"Ready? Inhale through your nose, one, two, three, four, hold it, two, and exhale slowly, two, three, four, five, six. Good, inhale, one, two—he saw her lip begin to twitch, three, four, hold it, her eyes squeezed tighter and she burst into sobs. Her arms, fully covered in beautiful ink, filled most of the monitor screen as she covered her head, protecting herself from the shrapnel: the explosion that had become her life. Staring at Eli was the intricate detail of a snake in beautiful greens and blues, spiraling around Kate's thin arm and resting its bejeweled head on the back of her hand which was also wrapped in black ink with rosary beads.

"Kate. Listen, I am going to put you in touch with a local outreach."

She made a guttural sound he recognized as disgust. "Hey, you need it, come on, Kate. You've done this before. It's okay. We know that relapse is part of the journey. Hardly anyone has kicked it the first time. It's not easy but we can do this."

Her face slowly came back into view, eyes smeared with black mascara, face red and gaunt. "I don't want to do this anymore. It's too hard. It's just too—"

"Hey Kate, remember what you said to me when we first started working together?"

She shook her head, the corners of her mouth drawn downward.

"Well I do. You said, 'Dr. Cranston, do you think I'd be sitting here if I didn't want to get better?'"

She closed her eyes and more tears followed the tracks that were laid a long time ago.

"And I said to you, 'Kate as long as you show up, I promise we can get you better. But you have to promise you will show up.'"

She nodded and chewed on a hangnail that may or may not have been on her index finger.

"You showed up. That's good enough, Kate. That's good

enough for today. And maybe next week it'll be a little easier. Just show up, okay? Just keep showing up."

She nodded. "K."

Eli made some notes in Kate's file. Call Boulevard Outreach ASAP, ask for sponsor list. He circled ASAP and closed the folder. The time on his monitor was 9:03 p.m.

He pushed his chair back and began to stand. The dream from that morning begged to be remembered but there were just blips and gaps. "Daddy, where are you?"

He sat back down and logged back onto the computer. Boulevard Outreach, Los Angeles.

He dialed the number. "Hi, I need assistance for a client on Berkshire. Yes, she's there now, alone. Yes. Wellness check and possibly a pick up. No police unless absolutely necessary.

He logged off again and shut the light. He closed the door to his office, a tip Dr. Gunther gave him to help create a distance between work and home.

He turned on the TV and walked into the kitchen. *Ice cream? Nah, beer.*

In his recliner he flipped through the Cabela's catalog that he retrieved from the mailbox earlier. Christmas Sale! Great Deals for the Whole Family! He thumbed through each of the first seven pages, then five or six at a time. He wanted to get something for Clem for Christmas but wasn't sure what he might need or like. He tossed it back on the end table next to his chair and picked up the L.L. Bean catalog. Flannel sheets? A bathrobe? A couple of chamois shirts? He flipped and flipped. "Slippers. Those look comfortable. Maybe I'll get myself a pair, too."

He felt his phone buzz. It was Hope: **So the farrier can come out tomorrow if you want. She said it would be $50 to trim both hooves.**

He sat and thought for a moment. She? Both hooves?

Then the next text: **Both *horses'* hooves LOL.**

Eli smiled. *This kid knows her stuff.* He replied: **Sounds good! Thank you.**

Then he sent another: **Is that the going rate BTW?**

Hope texted back: **It's a bargain LOL. She owes me.**

"So my stable hand is connected. Good to know," he laughed.

He texted back: **Well thanks for calling in a favor on my behalf.**

He looked at the screen: **NBD**

He had to google her response.

20

"Mom, I just told you. I'm going to Brit's house. I'll be back later."

Antigone looked at her daughter, knowing she wasn't being honest. "Gracie, it's a school night. You know the rules."

Gracie rolled her eyes and furrowed her brow. "I'll be back before curfew, Mom."

"Okay, be sure, Gracie, because—" Antigone stopped when Grace spun around and ran down the stairs. "Your father and I don't want—"

Antigone winced in anticipation of the Grace's embellished laugh. "Yah, like Dad would even know if I didn't come home. He's never here."

"Grace Antigone Cranston! Your father and I love you more than you will ever know and work hard to give you everything you have. You should be grateful, Sweetie. Just be careful and please, be good."

Grace looked up at Antigone, upset at her mother's tone. "Sorry, Mom. I'll text you later."

Antigone went back to the master bedroom and checked her phone to see if there was a notification from the showing on Willowcrest in Beverly Glen. She had a love/hate relationship with showings of her listings. Her success early on hinged on her knowing what it takes to make a showing an experience. When she wasn't present, she obsessed with everything another agent might be doing wrong. And the wait after the showing was torture. It was during that time that she consumed most of her daily calories. Nonetheless, she trotted down to the kitchen to see what would make waiting easier.

The card Eli gave her for their anniversary was still on the island next to the roses that were just beginning to curl at the edges. She sat on the barstool while the pasta warmed in the microwave. Touching the edge of the card absently, it tipped over. "For My Beautiful Wife" sat crookedly looking up at her. She smirked and flipped it open.

"When I think about us I get filled with the same exciting love—" She stopped and placed it back, upright next to the vase.

The microwave announced her comfort carbs were ready. She grabbed the bowl and sprinkled a little sea salt on the mound of angel hair. She fished a fork and wine glass from the dishwasher, had second thoughts about the wine and headed toward the living room but remembered her phone was upstairs. She went back up, taking the stairs two at a time to burn a measly few calories before sending down dozens more.

Her phone had four notifications.

Mom, I am going to stay at Brit's and go to school from here. Her mom is cool with it. Love you!

Antigone had played her parents plenty as a teen, thinking she was outsmarting them as most teens assume. Parties, boys, joyrides. She trusted, Gracie though, for the most part. She was a smart girl and her grades were always "A"s. What more could she ask of her?

She went back to the notifications.

Feedback on the 6:00 p.m. showing at 17 Willowcrest Drive. She took a breath and clicked on the next one.

Viewing went well, party is somewhat interested. Wants to know about property line, dispute per the county. Would have liked more updated kitchen—possibly negotiate for new appliances. Felt the price was inflated but they are pre-approved for 2.3 so that's not an issue.

"Oh my God, these people." She put her fork down. *If they read the remarks on the listing sheet, they'd see the dispute has been settled. And those appliances are less than two years old.*

She clicked out of the notification and clicked on the text icon.

Tig, I'll be home in about an hour. I'm starving. Don't cook—I'll just eat the leftover pasta from last night. Love you. Kiss Gracie for me.

"Okay, now I have to cook," she sighed.

She clicked on the last text and finished her angel hair.

Eli pulled into the garage and left his briefcase and laptop in the backseat. He was exhausted and just wanted something in his stomach so he'd be able to sleep. He'd need to leave early enough to miss traffic, which meant plenty of prep time before the courthouse even opened. He grabbed the Apple bag off the passenger seat and wished he had wrapping paper or something.

"Tig, I'm home! Gracie, I have something for you!" He didn't hear anything as he placed the bag on the island, sending the cheerful anniversary card over again. "Tig?"

Antigone called from upstairs. "I'm up here, Babe. Your dinner is on the stove."

Eli walked to the foot of the staircase and yelled, "I told you I was fine with leftovers. Gracie!"

"She's sleeping over Brit's. I told her it was okay."

"On a school night, though? Tig, we've talked about this."

Eli turned back to the kitchen and lifted the lid of the skillet.

"Chicken." He replaced the lid and put the pan into the refrigerator.

He took out a bottle of beer and went to watch TV, not aware that he hadn't seen his wife or daughter in three days. Tomorrow's showdown, if won, would allow him to take some time to relax, head up to Malibu with Tig and Gracie for a few days. He reached for his phone, forgetting he was going to call his father on the drive home. It rang in his hand.

"Hi Dad, just going to call you. I just got in. Listen, I'm not complaining but I do need to get this off my chest. No, I get it. I really do. But Jay has been leaving early again and he leaves me to—no, I know. I get it, yea. Has he met someone? No, I just know how he is. I can't imagine another reason he would leave early. Yea, I'm all set for tomorrow, it's going to be wild, I can feel it." He laughed, enjoying the thrill of the game with his father, one of the best in the business. "Hey Dad, I think we have the Baker case by the way. Yea, heard that. Okay, yea get some sleep. See you tomorrow."

Eli finished his beer, set his phone alarm and fell asleep on the couch.

21

The morning sun came through Eli's window and tickled his eyelids as if to say, "Come out, come out, wherever you are!" He rolled toward the wall and settled back into sleep. His breathing rhythmic and deep.

Eli saw the boxes. They were empty and waiting for him. He tried to leave the room but he couldn't find the door. The boxes got smaller and smaller. "Wait, how will I fit everything in!?" He ran toward them as they continued to shrink until they were the size of a jewelry box. "I'll never get anything in there now." Antigone's voice was there but she wasn't. "You had your chance, Eli. You had a million chances." Eli spun around, searching. "Antigone! Where are you?"

Her voice, fading, barely registered with Eli. "I'm waiting for Grace."

He woke up and looked at the clock on his nightstand. 6:23. He swung his feet out of bed and heard the shrill scream of the horses. He didn't bother with coffee. He dressed and went out to feed the ravenous duo. He remembered the farrier would be coming around ten but had no idea if there was something he was supposed to do to prep for it.

He climbed up to feed Bumblebee and found her purring softly in her little nest. The cat food that Hope had brought over was almost gone. "I'll have to get some more. Huh, Bumblebee?"

The kittens now had their eyes open and the blue gems stared at him; their squeaks still sounded so plaintive and sad. He pet each one, wondering if he would eventually name them all.

He was becoming accustomed to his little farm life. When he spoke to his parents after Thanksgiving, he asked them if he had ever asked for a pet. He couldn't remember, but didn't think he had. His parents agreed that they didn't remember either.

Back in the house, Eli tossed some wood onto the hot coals and thought about how his future fire starters would come in handy right now. He shut the door and knew eventually it would catch. He put on some coffee and reached for a coffee mug. None. They were all in the sink. Instead of washing one, he opened up another cabinet hoping to find a clean mug tucked somewhere. "Treadway's Tonic," he said. "Hmm ... I never did try it. He picked up the jar and turned it slowly in the morning light. The shimmery golden liquid inside caught the rays coming through the window, condensing it, making the jar look as though it was lit from inside. He rolled the jar and saw: horseradish, ginger, garlic, onion, and what looked like flower petals and chopped pepper. He put it back on the shelf and closed the door.

His first Skype session wasn't until noon. He enjoyed the mornings he could start late, but it also meant that he would be working straight through until 9:00 p.m.

He went online. He put two pairs of fleece slippers in his shopping cart at L.L. Bean and cruised around their site. Ever since meeting Hope, and even before, he had only ever seen her in the purple Old Navy sweatshirt and jeans. He looked around but didn't see anything that seemed to suit a tween. The Hollister site had a much larger pool of possibility. He really didn't know what size she wore but she was so little. He felt if anything, she'd grown into a small. He knew how crazy their sizes were from when Gracie shopped there.

He put two sweatshirts into the shopping cart and stopped. He realized then that he had no idea what her parents thought of her coming to his house every day to take care of his horses. He clicked out of the Hollister tab and made a mental note to ask Hope about her parents. Back to L.L. Bean, he added a warm hat with earflaps for Clem. If nothing else, he'd be warm.

Eli opened the stove again and poked the logs around to get some oxygen under them. The flames leapt up and so he tossed a third log in. He shut the door and miscalculated where the poker stand was. It made a loud thump as it hit the boxes that sat there, probably located too close to the woodstove for the last several weeks.

He stood with a lump in his throat. "Christmas." His voice was a croak and not a very good one at that. "Well, this Christmas will be a good one." He turned on his heel and went to make some eggs.

"I really need some recipes. This is getting old. I keep saying I'm going to learn to make home fries."

He turned to the refrigerator and opened the freezer drawer. "Ha! Tater Tots!" He turned the oven on and decided he would cheat.

Just before 10:00 a navy blue pickup truck with a utility body pulled into the driveway. Eli was folding laundry and didn't hear the truck come to a stop, so the doorbell made him jump. The only person who had rung the bell was Clem and that was just the first few times he came to the house. Since then, he announced his arrival with a beep of the horn and came right in.

He swung the door open and Eli stood there, shocked. He couldn't even get a word out of his mouth.

"Hi, Eli. I didn't know it was your house I was coming to. How are you? Happy Holidays."

Eli didn't know which part of her greeting to respond to. "Yes, good, Happy Holidays. You're the ... you're the farrier?" His grey eyes shouted his excitement.

Rebecca smiled her toothy smile and said, "Yep. Farrier, farmer, beekeeper, artist. At your service."

Eli rocked back on his heels. "Wow, I'm intrigued. A woman with many talents."

She stood on the porch and looked up at Eli, his gaze meeting hers. "Umm, so the horses are out back I assume?"

"Yes, out back. Let me put some boots on and I'll meet you back there. Do you need to drive up?"

"No, not for a trim. I'll just get my stuff." She turned back to her truck in time to miss Eli's eyes dropping to see the rest of her.

He put his boots on and went into the bathroom to brush his hair and teeth. When he reached the barn, Rebecca had already taken Smudge out of the stall and he noticed she had him tied by two lead ropes, one on each side of his halter. He looked to see where the other end of each rope was anchored. The round metal eye hardware on the post between the stalls was one and the other identical one, which Eli had never noticed, was on the center post in the barn. *Huh,* he thought. *Who knew?*

He rubbed Smudge's tiny pink nose. Smudge softly bobbed his head up and down as Rebecca held his tiny hind hoof and gently trimmed the outer wall. She moved to his other side and trimmed the other hind hoof but Smudge was pulling his leg away from her over and over. She elbowed him in the flank, "Knock it off, Squirt," she laughed.

He stood quietly and let her finish. Rebecca straightened up and Eli could see her flinch as she put her hand on her lower back. "Not getting any younger," she said with an eye roll for effect.

"So what are those pants called, anyway?" Eli was trying hard not to sound foolish but when she came to the door of the house she had on blue jeans. Now she wore something over them.

"Chaps?" She looked at him as if he was joking.

"Oh yea, I guess I knew that. I mean, I think of motorcycles when I think of chaps, I guess."

"Well, cowboys wore them long before bikers."

"Huh, yea that makes a lot of sense. I just never ... let's just say I'm learning a lot here."

After Ink's feet were trimmed, Rebecca returned him to his stall. "Be good, you two."

Eli asked what he should do with the curled up hoof clippings. "Give them to your dog. They love them."

Eli raised his eyebrows, horrified, "What?"

Rebecca was rubbing her nose with her arm because she

still had her gloves on. She bent forward and laughed, her eyes crinkling at the corners. *You're just teasing me with these questions, they said.*

"Dogs eat them, just like they eat cow hooves and pig ears from the pet store,"

Eli stood, stunned. "Uh, I don't have a dog and now I'm kinda glad?"

Rebecca straightened up and suddenly had a flash of recognition appear on her face. "Wait, did Hope say you have kittens?"

"Yes, I do, I have five of them and Bumblebee. She's the Mom."

"Bumblebee? How do you know her name?"

He employed his best poker face and said, "She told me."

Rebecca shook her head. Eli smiled, "Wanna see them?"

Her blue eyes glistened in the cold air. Her ears were pink and Eli wanted to warm them for her. "Come on up, they're in the loft."

Bumblebee stretched her neck and moved her head back and forth to look around Eli. She knew there was a new visitor.

Rebecca gushed over the little family. Bumblebee closed her eyes and purred loudly as Rebecca gently scratched the side of her face.

"How old are they?" She looked back at Eli as he was admiring her warmth and wonderment.

"They are almost a month now. I can't believe how big they are."

"What are you going to do with them?" Rebecca held the tiniest one up to her face and nuzzled it. The mewing made them both laugh.

"I'm not sure yet. I mean, I'll have to talk with Bumblebee. I mean, they are hers."

"I'll take one if you have any left after Bumblebee makes her decision."

This surreal moment that Eli never thought would happen was unfolding right here in the loft with his very own kittens.

"Well, we'll have to wait and see." He shrugged comically.

They climbed back down and walked out of the barn together, Eli carrying her tools and bucket.

"So how do you know Hope?" Eli asked.

Rebecca put her tools in the back of the truck and closed it up. "Hope works at my farm, too."

Eli started to speak but stopped when he almost gave away the fact that he knew where her farm was.

"Really? That's cool. She's a hard worker. What does she do there?"

"She mostly takes care of the animals for me and I let her ride Cayenne in exchange. I mean, I pay her, too, but she really just wants to ride mostly. She's a good little rider and yes, a hard worker. She rides her bike over after school three days a week when it's not too cold. Lately I've been picking her from school since it's closer to me anyway."

"So do you know her parents at all?" Eli crossed his arms, then reached up and rubbed his chin.

"Yea, they are, ah, they're kind of a mess. So, I uh, I just do what I can for her, ya know. She's a great kid but you know, without guidance ..." She shrugged and smirked at the same time.

Eli wondered what it would be like to kiss her. "Wow, that's a shame. Poor kid. I had no idea. She just left a note on my door one day wanting to take care of the horses. I didn't know if that was a thing around here or ...."

Rebecca was bent forward again, laughing. "Sorry. I ... sorry. She waved the air in front of her face.

"Well, I don't know. I'm still getting used to things around here. Bugs, chow-dah, Clem, God bless him."

"Yes, Clem is the best. I adore that man and his stories. He has done so much work on my place over the years and charges next to nothing. Where I come from, that never happens."

Eli brightened, "So you're from away, too?!"

She nodded, "Yup, can't you tell? I drop my 'r's sometimes but not like around here and I certainly don't go adding extra 'r's where they don't belong."

"Well, where is this mysterious 'r' dropping place?" Eli felt comfortable now.

"That's a secret and if I told you, it wouldn't be a secret any-more." She hopped up into her truck and started the engine. She rolled the window down, adding, "Good seeing you, Eli."

"Yes, thank you for coming out. Oh, wait, I have to get you some money. Wait just a sec." He turned toward the house.

"You can pay me next time. Plus you still have a credit on your account."

He looked at her and wondered if she was flirting with him.

"Well, I must owe you something?"

"Next time."

Eli walked back into the house thinking of five hundred things he could have/should have said.

22

Hope finished scrubbing the water bucket, careful not to get her gloves wet. The holes weren't really a problem but getting wet was. She returned the full bucket to the hook inside the stall and kicked the shavings out from the spot directly beneath it. "You two play more than you drink," she said.

Ink nudged her hand and she rubbed his forehead. "It's almost Christmas, guys. I hope Santa brings you something. But ... you might be on the naughty list since you escaped and everything."

She sat in the corner of the stall and watched the horses' muzzles sift through the hay and pick just the pieces they wanted, which she thought was funny because they end up eating every last blade. She felt a little chill since she stopped moving but she liked the company of the well-kept horses and always took pride in a properly cleaned stall. She imagined they liked her company as much as she liked theirs. Christmas was a week away and she just wished it would hurry and get here so it could go by. The following day would be the furthest she could ever be from the next Christmas and that's how she liked it. Hope's small chest heaved as she sighed, suddenly remembering her homework: to interview your parent or grandparent about their holiday traditions. She knew she would have to just make something up and really, how would anyone know?

The slant of the sun's rays as it came through the bars in the window was a better clock than any. It meant there would only be about twenty minutes until sunset. She closed her eyes as the sun warmed her face. In the stillness and muted sounds of a barn at day's end, Hope thought that no matter what happens in life, there would always be a barn nearby for reprieve. She knew that she just needed to seek one out and make herself useful.

She hoisted herself up in the corner of the stall and walked around Smudge, hand on his hindquarters to let him know where she was. "Goodnight, boys."

Back in the feed room, she picked up her backpack and fished out the items Rebecca sent to Eli and put them on top of the grain bin, replacing the envelope Eli left her. She looked in and saw two twenties.

If Eli could have seen the smile on Hope's face, he would have been overjoyed. She could hear the soft patter of the kittens running in the loft and wished there was a bedroom up there. "That would be heaven."

The bag on her shoulder was lighter than it was when she arrived but still had the crackers and peanut butter Rebecca gave her the day before. The cheese and fruit were long gone.

She closed the gate of the picket fence under Eli's window and zipped her sweatshirt up to the top, then tucked her chin into it. Just as she reached the driveway she heard a tap on the window. She spun and searched for which window the noise was coming from. She saw Eli wave and hold his finger up. She walked around to the front and waited for the door to open.

Eli had his phone in his hand and his work clothes on. "Hi Hope. Hey, do you want a ride home? It's getting dark."

Her heart quickened. "Oh, no. Thanks. My dad is going to pick me up."

"Oh good! It's chilly out, huh?" Hope noticed Eli seemed nervous but had no idea why. "Hey, do you want to wait here for your Dad? Text him to let him know and you can wait in the living room. Fire's going."

"Oh, no thanks. He's on his way. He just texted. See you later."

Eli watched as she left the driveway and pulled the hood up over her head. He wondered if she had a coat. Or a dad.

"Good morning, Kiley. How are you? Eli stepped back so the young woman could enter his office. "Cold enough for ya?"

She let out a nervous laugh and looked around. She had never been to this office but she was no stranger to therapy. "I like your office," she said as she looked around while sliding out of her peacoat and handing it to Eli, and tossing her long dark hair behind her shoulders.

"Have a seat and get comfortable." Eli opened the folder on his lap with her intake information. "So you indicated that you've been in therapy for several years but not continuously. Is that because things had gotten better or ..." He waited for her to finish the sentence.

"My insurance changed and I couldn't afford to continue."

Eli opened his mouth to speak but Kylie beat him to it. "I'm paying out of pocket. No worries."

"Okay, no problem. I can reduce my rate a little bit if you decide to continue. My notes here say that you are interested in FLP. Just briefly, can you describe what you know about it and how you think it might help you?"

Kylie crossed her legs and then her arms. Her emotion was very visible on her face. Her long bangs hung to her eyebrows and bounced back and forth as she shook her head. "I don't know that much but from what I've read, it sounds like it might be able to help me get past some trauma."

Nodding, Eli silently urged her to continue. "I have tried talk therapy a million times, but all they want to do is replay crap over and over. I just stay sad."

Eli raised his brows but kept the rest of his expression as bland as possible. He crossed his legs, too, and leaned slightly to his right. "Have you tried other modalities, other types of therapy?"

She looked down at her fingers, which seemed to be wrestling with each other.

"Uh, yes. I did cognitive behavioral therapy, didactic therapy, and what's the other one? The one with the lights?" She looked up at Eli for an answer.

"EMDR." He was taking notes but not taking his eyes off her. Nodding again, he said, "And did any of those seem to help?"

Kylie took a deep breath and looked back at her tired fingers and shook her head.

"Okay, well tell me what you know about FLP then, and how you found me."

Kylie straightened up in the chair and said, "Well, from what I understand, FLP is like PLR except you move to a future life instead of a past one. Right?"

Eli nodded, accepting the rudimentary understanding.

"And I found you online. I can't remember how or what I was googling but it came up and then of course I saw it all over Facebook the next day, all the ads."

"Yea, pretty interesting how that happens." Eli rolled his eyes to see if she would smile and she did.

She shifted in her chair then and let herself take a deep breath.

"So Kylie, I think I mentioned in my email reply that the initial session is an intake so we won't be doing the FLP today. You understood that?"

She nodded and seemed to brighten a little. "Yes, I get it. I just want to feel better so I don't care what I have to do. I'll do it."

"Okay, good. So what's going on? What made you start googling?"

"Well, Dr. Cranston, I ..." She picked at a piece of lint on her dress slacks. "I want to be able to see what life could be like for me. I know that people tell me I should just live my life and leave the past behind but ... but they just don't know what it's like."

Eli nodded and took notes. "Yes, and I'm sure some are well-meaning when they say that."

She shook her head, brows furrowed. "No. They aren't well-meaning. They aren't!"

Eli was a little surprised at the sudden anger but given her long list of therapy attempts, he wasn't shocked. She had a lot hiding behind those bangs.

"Okay, perhaps they aren't well-meaning. Could you venture a guess as to why they might say that, then? Why they wouldn't be able to understand why you can't leave the past alone?"

"Because they don't want to admit what they did to me. They don't want to go to jail and they would if I wanted to go through all of that but I don't. I want to move forward but it's like I have bricks tied around my neck."

Eli took a deep breath and another and another until she followed suit.

"So can you tell me what they did to you that makes them afraid?"

Kylie, the professional-looking young woman in her late twenties pulled up her sleeve and showed him her arms.

Eli leaned forward and though he kept himself from gasping, he drew his breath in quickly. Kylie's arms were covered in small round scars, dozens of them. Before Eli could say anything, Kylie lifted her poncho and the thin shirt underneath. From her navel to the bottom of her bra were several long, pink scars, one resembling the letter "K."

Eli stopped for a moment, deciding how to approach his next question. He knew it could build a bridge or burn one. He waited a moment before saying anything.

She lowered her poncho and smoothed it over her thin frame, eyes on the floor.

"Hmm ... I'm sorry you had to experience that, Kylie." He waited but she wasn't budging.

"So when we are traumatized, our wounds are often invisible and others, because they can't see them, don't know they're there, or that they're still there." Eli was treading carefully still. "But you have these very visible scars and that must be quite difficult for you."

And then, as often happened in his line of work, Eli was reminded of the bravery of the human spirit.

Kylie, the forlorn, meek-mannered woman in front of him

sat up tall and looked square at Eli with eyes that seemed to suddenly come alive.

"These scars are just the diary I kept of what they did to me."

23

"Huh, what do ya know?" Eli picked up the jar of peach preserves and bag of coffee marked Rudolph's Christmas Blend. The sticker on the bag had a Full Circle Farm, Bar Harbor, Maine sticker on it. He held it up to his nose and inhaled. He couldn't place all the scents but he recognized the nutmeg, cloves, cinnamon, and ginger. He wondered what else was in there.

The forecast was calling for snow, the first real accumulation of the season. He was excited; he didn't care if it was going to be a lot of work. He wanted to feel alive and to have a purpose. Keeping the horses and the cats warm and fed had become a great joy in Eli's grey landscape. He was building an existence and though he wasn't sure what the final copy would look like, he was enjoying editing the rough draft.

Walking back to the house he swore the air smelled different, but he wasn't sure how he would describe it. *Does cold have a scent?*

He heard a motor in the driveway and as he came around the corner of the house he saw the UPS driver walking back toward the road to where his truck was parked. Eli called, "Thank you."

The man turned with a wave and hopped into his truck. Eli turned to see two packages on the front porch. His heart quickened a little. Two cardboard boxes. He bent to scoop them up and went inside to make breakfast. He tossed the boxes on the sofa he had never sat on. He realized time was running out to get wrapping paper with less than a week until Christmas. He hadn't looked forward to the holidays in over a decade. In fact, he had tried to avoid them altogether until now.

Eli checked his watch, wanting to leave plenty of time to prep for his Skype session. Eggs, tater tots, coffee. He shrugged, "Nothing wrong with routine."

His phone buzzed twice which meant it wasn't a text. He wondered who would be calling this early, and noticed the call was from area code 916. He declined the call.

Keep moving.

His truck fired up at the click of his remote start and he hoped he had remembered to turn the heat dial up when he shut it off the day before. After washing the breakfast dishes, he stopped to see if he could remember latching the stall door, somewhat traumatized from the search and rescue mission. *Yes, the boys are secure until I get back.*

Driving through town a week before Christmas was both enchanting and nostalgic: watching kids with their parents, everyone bundled up and enjoying the sights; the promise of Santa visiting, if only the children could behave just a little longer.

Eli had a memory of taking Grace shopping for Antigone on Christmas Eve. He promised her they would find Mom a great gift, be home in time for Rudolph on TV, and early bedtime so that Santa could leave her gifts.

Staring at a beautiful wreath hanging from an antique lamppost, he didn't realize he was sitting at a green light. The car behind gave a short honk: a reminder, not condemnation and as such, Eli waved an apology.

The Christmas Spirit Shop, hmm. Eli was aiming for Rite Aid but liked the brick exterior and since there was a car pulling out close by, he felt it was the place to go.

Stepping inside he inhaled the scent of pine and cranberry and looked around. He had never seen so many ornaments before. The store was busy with shoppers and the music added to the atmosphere. The song playing, "White Christmas," reminded him of his grandmother who used to play it over and over.

He looked in a few spots and finally found the wrapping paper. He picked up a roll that was shiny red matte with small gold foil wreaths. Heading back to the register he saw another bin which contained rolls of classic prints, a few of which had horses. He felt he would never find such a thing if he was actually looking for it. And yet, here it was, horses and ponies, kids in show turnout and some foxhunting. He took the two rolls to the register and happily paid the premium price.

Back in his truck, Eli looked forward to his Skype sessions today, including Kate. He realized that being in the same room with someone is obviously ideal but given the tools available, he was grateful to be able to continue working with Kate and some others who stayed on with him.

He started the engine and pulled the gearshift down to reverse. Looking over his shoulder, he was just about to pull out when his eyes caught a familiar sight. The black parka hood was up now on her head but he recognized not only the Uggs but the way they shuffled rather than walked. He put the truck back into park and realized someone was waiting for his spot. He rolled down his window and waved them around. The blare from the horn was not the friendly one from earlier.

Watching as the woman seemed to be walking in the way one with Parkinson's did, he was fairly certain what she had used. And though she was strung out, she was making her way along the street without stopping. She came to rest on a bench and seemed to be grateful to have a place to perch. People didn't seem to notice her and he wondered if she was glad or if she wanted someone to say, "Hello! Merry Christmas! Can I help you? Do you need something?"

The woman slowly pulled out a box of cigarettes and after a few attempts, she got one lit. Eli was growing anxious, watching her try over and over to get her lighter back into her pocket.

"Now what?" He glanced at his watch and saw that he had plenty of time before his first session. He watched as an older gentleman stopped to speak with her. He had bags and packages in his arms but placed them on the bench next to her as he fumbled with gloves and his coat. He handed her some money, picked up his things and moved on. Eli was relieved. He wasn't sure if he was relieved that someone was willing to help her or relieved because it meant it didn't have to be him.

Pulling back into the flow of traffic, Eli put on some music. "I'll be home for Christmas, if only in my dreams."

24

Eli set his away notification on his work email and before logging off, checked and double-checked for any client emails he might have missed. None.

Not satisfied, he checked his trash folder and scanned through all the Viagra spam and 50%-off Christmas email ads. Nothing. Next, he clicked Spam and laughed at all the "date" offers he missed from all over the world.

He sighed and rubbed his cheek, not ready to quit. He went to the top of his email and in the search box, typed Kate Cromwell. Dozens of emails loaded, all read. The most recent one was dated August 8th, a reply from Kate to Eli's email about a start date for seeing clients in his new location. He remembered she was the first to respond.

"Hi Dr. Cranston! I am stoked that you decided to email me today. I am having an amazing experience and I can't wait to share it with you. Everything is better than I could have imagined. Can't wait to tell you! My days are open and most nights too, so just send me a date and time and I'll talk to you then."

-Kate

Her email signature at the bottom read:

"The sun is gone, but I have a light." – Kurt Cobain

Eli was officially on vacation. He planned to take December 23rd to the 27th off, something he had never done. He closed his office door and decided he wouldn't go back in until the 27th and although he would check his emails, he wouldn't respond unless something was urgent.

He stepped into the kitchen and flipped open his laptop. Pandora, Christmas channel. While the oven preheated, he went to get the boxes off the sofa but when he got there, they were gone. He thought for a moment, *did I move them?* He was sure he hadn't. Then it dawned on him, "Clem."

Clem had been there weather-sealing the windows for him and scraping wallpaper on the second floor. He wanted to frame out the new doorway in the expanded space up there but it would be too much noise while Eli was working. They decided he could start the day after Christmas while Eli was in Camden.

"Hmm, if I were Clem, where would I put those two boxes?" Eli surveyed the room. He didn't see them at first but knew that when he surveyed this room in the past looking for the remote control, a misplaced folder or slippers, he avoided one corner. The corner. The corner with *the* boxes.

He walked up to the woodstove and peered to its right and sure enough, the packages that came via UPS were sitting neatly on top of the two boxes that had made the trip from California, the ones that sat in a dark storage unit for eight years. Gone but not forgotten.

"Soon."

In the kitchen, the oven timer chimed, as if to say, "Keep moving."

Tonight's answer to "not pizza" turned out to be a ready-made meal from the market: fried chicken, mashed potatoes, gravy, and green beans. He felt pulling it out of the oven would make him feel better than microwaving it.

The wrapping paper, tape, and package of bows were on the kitchen table and he was excited to see if he could remember how to fold the ends and make the gifts look presentable.

Eli's ears perked up at the sound of an engine knocking on the road, almost idling, then tearing away. "Green Corolla strikes again."

He went back into the living room and retrieved the boxes containing his Christmas offerings. He opened the L.L. Bean box and pulled out the packing slip, setting it aside. Underneath were two pairs of Wicked Good Scuffs as well as a red and black Maine Guide wool cap. He scooped up one pair of slippers for himself and tucked the other items in neatly and closed the lid. He wished he had thought to buy some tissue paper. He wondered if there was anything left from Mrs. McCabe. There were items in the eaves and basement. Not wanting to venture on a wild goose chase, he decided to wrap them as is. It was Clem; he wasn't going to care if there was no tissue paper. Eli cut the foil paper and carefully folded the edge where he cut so it would create a smooth seam and taped it closed. Then came those dastardly ends. He took a breath and remembered his grandmother teaching him how to fold it so it created a nice triangle and then pulling the triangle on each side of the end so that they came to a point which would then be brought up to complete the maneuver. Once he finished both ends, he turned it over, admiring how the wreaths were in neat diagonal rows, gleaming in gold. He chose two bows, one green and one gold, and taped them to the top.

"One down." He opened the other box next. He pulled out a pink hoodie lined with fleece, and a yellow one. He held them up and felt they would definitely fit Hope, even if they might be a little big. He reached back into the box and took out the fingerless gloves with the flap that converts them to mittens. The last item was a bag of chocolates that resembled piles of horse manure. He shook his head, not sure why he thought it was so funny but liked it anyway. "Fresh Road Apples for Your Favorite Equestrian." He folded the sweatshirts back up and placed them back into their box, nestling the road apples in the center. Eli looked at the clock on the stove and said, "Okay, whatever I can find in six minutes, thirty-eight seconds will have to do. He went down the cellar steps carefully and crouched so as not to hit his head. He turned on the additional light near the oil tank and perused the neatly arranged items: gas can, tackle box, fishing rods, a box of sockets, various tools. He moved to the right and saw a box marked "Xmas." Pulling the lid off he could see it was all ornaments. He moved it aside and opened the top of the box behind it.

"Motherlode!" Eli picked up the box and placed it on the washing machine a few feet away. He grabbed the white tissue paper with the tiny green trees and two gift tags.

"Thanks, Mrs. McCabe."

Back in the kitchen, Eli finished wrapping Hope's gifts and stacked her and Clem's boxes on the end table next to the recliner.

As he filled a water glass to have with dinner, he saw Hope pushing the barn door closed and pulling her purple hood up over her dark brown hair. He wanted to offer her a ride again but she had refused before and he didn't want to make her uncomfortable. He wasn't sure where she lived but assumed it was close by.

He moved to the living room window and watched her walk down the driveway looking at her phone, the bright light bobbing up and down as she walked out onto the road.

Eli's phone buzzed. He assumed it was Hope with her usual barn update. He stared at his phone as it rang with the 916 area code again. This time he blocked it.

25

The snow outside Eli's window was as silent as the cold air it rode down through. Piling softly on the fence, it created comical little hats on each picket, the gate becoming a rounded mound of silly characters, which stood guard below Eli's window, ready to chase away anything that wasn't beautiful and serene; but inside the house, it had no control.

Eli called out in his sleep, "Tig! Oh my God, Antigone! I found her."

He settled back into a deeper sleep and wouldn't remember much of this dream, come morning. The one about Rebecca, though, he would remember and it would put a smile on his face for weeks to come.

Eli began setting an alarm now that the mornings were darker but he hadn't needed it this morning. He went to sleep excited about the next day, Christmas Eve. His eyes opened with the realization that it was morning and then opened wider when he realized what day it was. He had, however, forgotten about the forecast.

He noticed the light was not quite the same and that there was a bit of wind whipping. He pushed the pale blue curtain aside to see that his property was blanketed in a stunning white quilt, the only color being the shadows and dapples of light. "Wow!" Eli was excited and wanted to get outside as quickly as he could. He donned his boots and jeans and pulled on his jacket over the t-shirt he had grown accustomed to wearing to bed and admittedly, around the house. It read: Bah-Habah - Where Lobst-ahs Rule and Rs Drool

He took Hope's gift off the end table and stepped out the front door, keeping to his promise not to open the office door at all on vacation. He knew it would be too tempting to organize notes, make some phone calls, draft emails, and fill out the endless insurance documentation and reminders for payment.

The crunch under his feet was music to his ears. His only snow experience was skiing with Jay in Colorado when they were in college. He loved it then and now without the influence of booze, he appreciated the experience in a whole new way. He stepped off the porch onto the first of two steps. He miscalculated where his foot should fall and he immediately slid down to the next step. "Geez!" He steadied himself and stepped out from under the overhang. The snow was deep: deep enough that he had to work to get through it. It was still falling but he didn't feel it warranted a hat since he would shower when he got back.

Feeding the horses and righting their crooked blankets, Eli wondered if he could throw the dirty garments into his washing machine. He noticed the mineral brick was slowly being licked to death as it was meant to be. He asked Smudge, "Does that hurt your tongue?"

Sour Patch Kids, he remembered, hurt Gracie's tongue but no matter how much she complained about it, she continued to eat them.

After tossing the hay and grain to the ponies, he realized the water bucket was solid as a rock. "I knew this day would come."

He put the bucket in the sink of the feed room and ran water over it, hoping it would melt at least a little of the ice. He took Hope's gift and placed it on the grain bin that had unwittingly become a place of information exchange, payment center, and all around conduit between the estate owner and the livery-girl.

He hoped she'd like the gifts and wished he could invite her in for hot chocolate and hand them to her, but it seemed she preferred to just keep her distance. He reached into his zipped jacket and pulled out a card with her Christmas bonus in it. He smiled, imagining her emerald eyes sparkling, or as they said around there, sp-ahklin'.

The sound of a truck engine caught Eli's attention, but he was on his way up into the loft to check on his feline companions. "Kittens everywhere." He watched as they scurried about and batted at each other. Bumblebee purred loudly as he poured some dry food into her bowl and realized she'd need unfrozen water, too. "Hmm."

One of the orange tabbies made its way to him. He reached down to pet it and to his surprise, it hissed and grabbed his arm with both front paws, scared itself and scampered away and as it did, performed a full somersault as one of its siblings attacked from the side. The laughter Eli heard come from his own mouth surprised him. *It's okay to be happy again.* He wondered if he should start looking for homes for the kittens soon. Then he shook his head. "No. Not yet."

Eli discovered his driveway plowed and a mountain of snow pushed off to the right between the gravel edge and the pine trees there. "Oh, that's what the space is for ... I get it." He remembered Clem telling him not to place the reflectors there but right up against the trees instead.

Turning slowly around in a full circle, Eli would have appeared to be dancing on a mountain top à la *The Sound of Music* if only his arms were lifted to the sky.

Back in the house, Eli saw there was a missed call from the 916 area code.

He put the phone down and went to shower.

26

Eli put his coffee on and replenished his firewood bin while he waited for Clem. He turned on the TV and watched scenes from Frosty the Snowman, ads for Christmas clearance sales, and flipped through his email, hoping there wasn't anything urgent. "It's been quiet," he said and was grateful. He stopped scrolling. Kylie. He tapped on the email: "Hi Dr. Cranston, I wanted to let you know I took your advice to write out what I want to resolve through FLP and honestly it could be a book. It would have to be sold as fiction though since no one would believe it. Anyway, Merry Christmas. See you next week."

He kept scrolling. Nothing else.

The engine sound alerted Eli to the impending honk as Clem pulled in, "Three, two, and ..." just then Clem sent out his "I'm here" honk and Eli smiled.

Eli went back to the kitchen and pulled out some mugs. He turned to see Clem walk in and if Eli had already poured the coffee, he'd have gotten a pretty bad burn because he jumped, almost cartoonishly, with fright. Clem *was* Santa Claus. If anyone was made to be Santa it was the man standing in Eli's kitchen with a felt sack over his shoulder.

"Ho ho ho!" He smoothed his long beard and then his belted belly.

"Holy shit, Clem!" Eli put the mugs on the counter for safekeeping and put his hand over his heart.

"Ah ha, got ya, fella! Merry Christmas!" He pulled up a chair and sat down.

"You sure did! Merry Christmas, Clem. Do you ... always ... dress up like Santa?"

Clem's eyes disappeared in his round face and now Eli realized this was that one magical trait that all the best mall-Santas seemed to possess.

"Only on Christmas, ya son of a gun! Kids love it. I drive all over, plowing if there's snow, or just drivin' and waving if there ain't. Anybody out playin' or drivin' gives a big wave. The adults know it's me now but the first ye-ah, they called the police on me."

Eli laughed along with Clem, picturing Clem getting pulled over dressed like that.

Once the coffee was on the table, Clem reached into the sack next to his chair and pulled out a pastry box and placed it on the table. "This is the best coffee cake ya evah gonna have. The Independent downtown. Good people and good cake."

"Oh cool, Clem, thanks." Eli wasn't sure it was the best time to give Clem his gift but he figured it was as good a time as any. He took a bite of the coffee cake and mumbled his approval as he stood to get the carefully wrapped box.

"Got ya a little somethin', Santa." He put the box next to Clem's plate.

Clem shot a look up at Eli and then back down at the gift. "Ah hell, ya didn't have to do that, fella." Clem put his work-toughened hand on top of the gift and rubbed the shiny gold foil. "Look at that, would yah?"

Eli thought he was either embarrassed or at the very least uncomfortable. "Hey it isn't much and besides, I'm taking it out of your pay anyway."

Clem let out a belly laugh, 'Pissah!"

He tore the paper away and let it fall to the floor like an excited kid might. He pulled out the hat first and held it up, "Ay-yuh, a good one. Look at that, I can wear it huntin' don't yah know."

Then he fished out the slippers and said, "Yah know, if ya didn't get em at the outlet yah paid too damn much. I think next ye-ah I'll put em on with my new hat and drive around in my long jahns—see how people like that! Yah can do that sorta stuff when ya get ta be my age and people just take pity on yah."

Eli finished his coffee and asked, "So what are your plans for the rest of the day?" He looked at Clem in his Santa suit and tried hard to take the man seriously.

"Well I'ma head ovah ta the cemetery to say hello to my Mammy n Pop. Then I'll head ov-ah to my niece's house fah din-ah 'round one. And then if I get ma Christmas wish, I'll be home and in bed by 7:00!"

"That's great, Clem. Does your niece live close?"

"Oh yah, down in Seal Hah-bah. Take a ride down! There's always room fah an extra mouth, fella. Don't you worry 'bout that."

Eli smiled at the invitation. "Thanks, Clem, but I honestly could use a day to just relax and get some things done here that I should have done when I moved in."

"I he-yah that." Clem finished his coffee and pushed his chair back from the table, his shiny Santa belt catching the light from the ceiling.

"Well, Merry Christmas to you, Clem, and enjoy time with your family."

Clem stopped for a moment and wanted to ask Eli about his family but knew there were things a man just wanted to keep to himself. It seemed to Clem that Eli probably lost his wife in some way or another. There was a way about him that Clem recognized.

Eli closed the door behind Clem and cleaned up the coffee mugs and plates. He looked out at Ink and Smudge making a mess of the once pristine snow.

Eli opened his laptop and put on the music he plays when he needs to be in touch with his emotions. At Stanford he concentrated his research on the neuroscience involved in music, memory, and mood. In sessions, he often tells clients he can diagnose them by their playlist.

"You are what you put into your head and as such, you can change your experience by changing what you allow in there."

He pulled up his playlist then: Ludovico Einaudi. "The

master," Eli said. He wrote most of his thesis listening to him.

In the living room, Eli tossed two pieces of oak into the stove. Straightening up and clearing his throat, he looked behind the stove and said, "Stop moving."

27

Eli sat in the auditorium and listened to the principal talk about values and goals and expectations. He shifted in his seat, looked at his phone, crossed his legs, then uncrossed them. *This is the last place I want to be right now.* He looked over at Grace who was staring at her phone as well. She glanced up at him and they made faces at each other. Eli leaned over, "Hey, how long do we have to stay for you to get credit?" He raised his eyebrows at Gracie and she shook her head. "Dad, stop it. We have to stay."

He rolled his eyes at her, "Why are you *such* a rule follower?"

He winked at her and she rolled her eyes, then sat up straight and paid attention, realizing that without her mother here, she was going to need listen because her father wasn't.

When the presentation was finished and parents were encouraged to mingle and ask questions with the staff, Eli quickly asked, "Hey, do you want to get something to eat?" It was a school night and Eli had work to do but he wasn't going to be in the courtroom the next morning and wanted to spend time with his daughter. He had begun to realize she was close to leaving the nest.

"Yea, sure. What time will Mom be home, do you think?" Gracie was scrolling through her Instagram trying to find the sushi place she went to with Brit on their most recent joyride.

"Umm, I don't know. She had two showings back-to-back so probably not 'til nine or so. We can bring her something."

Gracie looked over at Eli as he drove and asked, "Do you love Mom?"

Eli could not have been more stunned than if someone told him he would one day be a Stanford trained psychotherapist living in a cottage on the coast of Maine, with cats and horses. "Of course I do, Gracie. Why? I mean, what makes you ask that?"

"I dunno. Just wondering, I mean you both work a million hours and like, I dunno. You just seem more like ... more like parents who aren't together but live in the same house. It's weird."

Eli took a breath. "Well, Honey. I mean, when you're with someone a long time ... I mean, life gets busy and well, you focus on your kids and your career. Maybe it shouldn't be like that, but for us, it is. But, yes of course I love your Mom. When I met her I thought she was the most beautiful girl on the planet. I knew I wanted to marry her then."

Gracie relaxed and looked out the window. "Good. It seems like I spend more time with you now and I never see her. But when I was little, it was the other way around."

Eli cleared his throat. "Gracie, I tried. I mean I was working a lot so—"

"No, Dad. It's fine. I just mean now it's the other way around, but it's cool. That's all I meant."

"Oh, that's the place! Dad can we stop there? The place next to the tattoo shop."

"Ha, okay. Maybe we can get inked after, you know for the start of senior year?"

"Omg! Let's do it, Dad! Seriously that would be amazeballs."

Eli shook his head, "Well, to prove my love to your mother, I am going to say no. Definitely not on a school night."

"Hey, Grace!" Eli turned to see who was calling his daughter. She turned to the young man and waved.

"Hey, are you in Trig with Anderson this year?"

Grace looked at the menu and tried hard to ignore Sam. "Yea, I'm one of his victims, are you?"

Eli introduced himself as Grace's father and politely asked Sam a few questions since Grace clearly wasn't interested. When the time was right, Eli used a body language trick he learned in law school to move Sam along.

"So, uh, I'm guessing you won't be going to Homecoming with Sam?"

"He's not my type, Dad."

"Type? I think you're a little young to have a type, Gracie."

"Dad, you just keep thinking I'm a little innocent girl and we will both be happy."

Getting back to the house with takeout, Eli grabbed a beer and asked if Grace wanted to watch Monday night football with him.

"Um, let's see. No." She kissed him on the cheek and trotted upstairs with her sushi and a bottle of water. "'Night, Daddy. Love you."

"Love you too, Gracie." He shouted up the stairs. "And I'm very proud of you."

His phone buzzed a moment later. He looked at it. Gracie: **Thx** and she added a heart emoji.

Eli put the phone on the coffee table and opened his box of food. He looked at his phone but at the same moment realized he didn't have chopsticks. They were in the bag Grace took upstairs. He went out to the kitchen and when he got back, texted Antigone: **Hey Tig—how were the showings?** He waited to see if she would send an instant reply.

The game started and Eli relaxed into his sofa and beer. He looked again at his phone. *She must have gone to the office to write up an offer.*

An hour passed and Eli tried again. **Tig, let me know when you're on your way. Hope the showings were great.**

Finally a response: **He won't care. He never has.**

Eli stared at his phone and tried to make sense of it. He was tired. *At least she's okay.*

Not ten minutes later, Antigone came through the door from the garage. "I'm home, Babe."

Eli walked out to the kitchen where Antigone was reaching for a wine glass. "Hey, Tig, you're home."

She glanced at Eli. "How was Gracie's orientation? I wish

we both could have gone."

"Oh it was okay, just a lot of info we could have gotten in an email, ya know? We got you some dinner. It's in the fridge."

Antigone took a sip of wine. "Thanks but we ate earlier." She stopped for a fraction of a second before taking another sip. "At the office, we ordered out."

Eli watched her expression, "How were they?"

Antigone looked at him almost accusingly. "How were who?"

"The showings, Tig. How were the showings?"

"They were good. Haven't gotten any feedback. Probably tomorrow."

Eli said, "Okay, well I'm going to bed. I'm beat."

He leaned over and kissed her. "And who has never cared, by the way?"

Antigone put her wine glass down. "What?"

"Your text, Tig. It said, "He doesn't care and never has."

She waved at an invisible fly and put her hand on her hip, something she developed as a coping mechanism that, years later Eli would come to understand as such.

"I don't know, Babe. I'm beat, too. 'Night."

She watched Eli walk upstairs, feeling disappointed, something she had varying levels of success dealing with throughout her marriage.

Looking back at the wine bottle, she estimated that there was just about enough wine left to take care of that feeling and any others that might show up.

28

The Jameson bottle he had been friendly with when he moved in was not empty, yet not full enough to get him through this day. Luckily, standing tall behind it in the cupboard was the golden honey-colored Glenfiddich. It seemed to salute him as if to say, "Good Morning, Sir!"

He pulled them both from the cabinet near the sink. He looked out at the wreath he had bought from the Boy Scouts, hanging on the nail on the barn door. It was collecting snow both on the top arch and the red bow on the bottom, giving it a picture-perfect Christmas-card appeal. "At ease, Jameson," Eli put the bottle back in the cupboard. It was his standby, his wingman, his go-to. But today, Eli needed the big guns and fished out the single malt Scotch.

He opened the bottle, reached for the "Virginia is For Lovers" shot glass, but pushed it aside and took out a juice glass. He poured three fingers, took the glass and the bottle into the living room, and set them on the coffee table. He noticed the table could use dusting and for that matter, the carpet needed vacuuming. He thought about his laundry in the bathroom hamper and the grain bag full of trash in the barn. Eli thought of half a dozen things he could do to avoid this looming feat but reminded himself, *The best way out is through.*

He remembered that the first box was the lighter one, but picking it up, he could feel the weight of it. He couldn't recall how many times he had touched this box over the years without ever once having the urge to open it. But at the same time, the thought of not opening it was suffocating him.

He finished the whiskey in the glass and let the fire slowly warm his throat and belly as he took a cleansing breath and then another. He could feel his heart resisting his breath's command to slow down. Pouring another drink, he could feel the first one saying, "I'm heeeere!"

The flaps of the box were bent and ragged, with "This Side Up" staring at him as if to say, "I've taken care of this long enough, Pal. It's your turn."

"*Rip it off fast, Gracie. Faster is better, it'll hurt a lot less. Trust Daddy on this. Ready, one, two, THREE!*" Eli smiled at the memory of Gracie, tortured by the idea of the bandage being removed from her knee, making the hurt start all over again.

He pulled on one box flap and they all came up, like a flower unfurls its petals only when it's ready and not a moment sooner.

The second glass went down easily and already Eli was feeling a little fuzzy, a little protected. He reached in and let his hand fall on the item that was last placed in the box before he had closed it up nine years before.

He pulled out the stuffed bunny. It was battered and dirty and barely resembled a bunny at all in this state. It had one eye and only half an ear, its tail hanging on by four very visible threads. Eli would have recognized it anywhere and yet had not thought of it all this time. "Gracie, Macy and Bunny Boo, too!" He could hear Antigone's sing-song voice calling Grace to calm her, get her into her car seat, crib, high chair: wherever she needed Gracie to go without a fight, Bunny Boo led the charge.

Eli pulled it closer and examined it in the way anyone who has ever had a buzz can relate. He knew what it was, felt what it meant and told himself, "It'll be okay. You'll be okay."

He put the bunny on the coffee table in the shadow of the bottle and reached back into the box like a game of "This is Your Life." *Which memory will slap me next?*

It was Gracie's baby ankle ID tag in a plastic bag.

Cranston 01/12/1992 Mother: Cranston, Antigone L
Baby Girl
Jeffries, Raymond, MD
5692436

And next to it, was the one Antigone wore on her wrist. He moved the bag but didn't dare open it, imagining a movie scene where he would be swept back twenty-seven years to the moment Grace drew her first deep breath and screamed. He placed the bag next to Bunny Boo.

Hearing snow whipping against the bay window, Eli looked out toward the road and wondered if it was snowing again. *I hope so. I hope it buries me in this house.* His head was swimming a little as he reached into the box again.

A school picture. Gracie's hair still lighter than it would become when she turned twelve, her bangs complementing a missing front tooth. On the back, in Antigone's handwriting: Grace A. Cranston, 2nd Grade, Mrs. Peclet's Class September 1999. He turned it back over and looked at her perfect little face and eyes that matched his; her pink dress with the ruffled short sleeves, hair stopping just beneath her square chin, a beauty statement matching her mother's; the dimples she got from neither of them, a recessive trait that said, "I am unique and you cannot claim this part of me nor would I have it if it weren't for both of you."

For a moment Eli thought he saw Grace's eyes glisten in the photo. He reached down and wiped the tear away, and then another. He crumbled then, the anxiety and fear, exhaustion and regret. It all tumbled down onto his head. All the years, all the running and hiding, changing careers—becoming a healer, flushing out the wounds of others rather than rubbing in the salt. "Gracie, my little Gracie. I miss you more than I thought a person could survive."

The sobs took turns with gulps of air, his nose running and mingling with tears that couldn't get out of his eyes fast enough, as if they'd been held captive for too long.

He beat the tops of his thighs with his clenched fists and screamed, not words but primitive sounds, like those he heard from Antigone just before Gracie appeared and again years later when she learned her daughter wouldn't be coming home. He didn't try to stop it and probably couldn't have if he had in fact tried. "It's been so long. How can this still feel so awful?"

He whimpered and covered his head with his arms, just the way that Kate had done when she told him she couldn't keep trying, that it was too hard. He rocked forward and backward, trying to comfort himself. All his training was just that, training. It was meant to help others and it did, for the most part. In that moment, though, Eli realized that all the education in the world cannot negate being human and everything that entails.

"I needed you, Gracie. You changed me, you did. You were perfect and I ruined that. I lost you before I even knew what was happening. Why didn't I see it?"

As if the fire hadn't burned enough, he said, "One more. I can do one more," like a bloodied soldier ignoring all signs that he should stop while he still has breath in his body. He reached back in and came out with Grace's cheerleader jersey. It was so soft in his hands and so small. She was only 5'6" and 110 pounds. The jersey had the pin he remembered Brit giving her at Homecoming their freshman year. Gracie and Brit were like sisters until it became apparent they had become something else entirely.

Eli picked up the Glenfiddich and ignored the glass, pouring liquid comfort directly down his throat between crying jags. He closed the box furiously, as if it had the power to destroy his world again, and hurriedly brought it back to where it had been sitting. He placed it on the other one and backed away as one would when a wild animal shows its teeth.

Racked by a new wave of emotional nausea, he let his weight crash onto the recliner as he brought the blue and white jersey to his face, hoping against hope, it didn't smell like Gracie.

The knock at the door roused Eli enough for him to realize his head was killing him. He hoped he imagined it or that it was actually his head making the sound. But it came again and this time he decided he needed to make it stop. He grunted as he dragged himself off the bed. It was light out but wouldn't be much longer. He was disoriented, not sure if it was Christmas night or early the day after. "Coming," he said, not daring to raise his voice for fear his head might shatter.

He reached the front door and opened it. No one. Then movement in the middle of the driveway caught his eye. He reached for the lamppost light switch. It was Hope. "Hi, Eli. Merry Christmas."

Eli's voice betrayed him at first so when he tried again, he overcompensated, shouting. "Merry Christmas, Hope. Are you heading home?"

She was walking back toward the porch. "Yah, I just wanted to say thanks for the presents. You didn't have to get me any-thin'."

"Oh sure I did, you're my best employee." He tried to keep himself from smiling. He looked at Hope in the snow. The air had a bitter sting to it especially when it reached the lungs.

"Would you like some hot chocolate before you go?" He wasn't in any shape for company but had to try anyway. "I could make you a cup to take for the road."

To Eli's surprise, Hope accepted. "Okay, that would be good."

He held the door open for her and she stepped inside, the smell of cold and hay clinging to her, the gift box under her arm. She wiped her boots on the moose head doormat and looked around. Suddenly Eli wished he'd had a Christmas tree or at the very least an electric candle in the window. There was a whole box of them in the basement. He ushered her into the kitchen. "C'mon and have a seat while I make my super-special hot cocoa. He reached for a mug and heard the slight giggle again, "What makes it special?"

"Well, what makes it special is if I can make it at all." He fished out the blue and white box of Swiss Miss and pulled out a packet. While the water warmed in the microwave he asked Hope how the horse's water was and if the kittens were behaving.

"Yea, I chipped the ice out and only filled the bucket halfway so it'll be easier in the morning, like if you want to bring some hot water up. It's easier that way. The kittens are crazy, they like, throw themselves off the hay and like, do these ninja moves."

Eli smiled at her overuse of "like," a familiar habit he knew well.

"Yea, I know," Eli added. "I tried to corral them all on a bale to get a picture but as soon as I had them all together, one or two would hop like a frog—right off." He showed her with his hand how they hopped and bounced. He could see her tiny hands were bright pink with cold and wondered where her gloves were.

The beep of the microwave interrupted their stories. Eli mixed the brown powder with miniscule dots of marshmallow into the mug. He turned to see Hope had gotten up and gathered under her arm the unwrapped box containing her gifts so that she could take the warm mug from Eli. "Thanks."

"Ride home?" He shrugged his shoulders.

"No, thanks, I'm just down the road apiece. Takes me five minutes to get home."

"Okay, well be careful, please. Oh and I meant to ask if you'd be able to feed everyone Friday morning, too. I'll be away Thursday night.

Hope's eyes rose to look almost directly into Eli's. "Yea, I could do that. I would just hafta check on my Mom first."

Eli almost asked if she meant to say check *with* her Mom, but given that this was the most he had ever gotten out of her, he certainly didn't want to make her uncomfortable.

"Great. I am really happy you left me a second note about helping with the crazies. You're a big help."

She stepped carefully off the porch, laden with gifts and cocoa and silently drifted down the driveway, fading into the growing darkness. Eli had no idea those were the only gifts the girl had received this Christmas or for the last three for that matter.

Eli Cranston survived Christmas *and* opened one of the torture boxes *and* made hot cocoa for Hope. He nodded his head, looking up at the crucifix on the knotty pine wall and pictured what that must have been like, to be nailed to a tree, hanging, the weight of your own body helping to hasten your death—one you'd undoubtedly be pleading for. He reminded himself of something he often told his grieving clients.

"You don't know what's coming next, but I can promise you that one day you will be glad you survived this. You will have opportunities to use your pain to relieve the suffering of others, and that alone will give meaning to what you've endured."

He picked up the blue and white cheerleader jersey and went back to bed.

29

Hi Hope—I have a delivery of hay coming but it shouldn't arrive until I get back. I told Fred about the kittens so he'll be careful if he does come by. I put a spare key in the storage bench on the front porch. If you need to warm up or need water for the animals, it's there. (Saw on the news it's going to be close to 0°). There's more super-special hot cocoa in the cabinet, too. Help yourself. In an emergency, call the number on the business card in the pic—it's Clem, the man who is working on my house. He's had the flu so won't be working while I'm gone, but he can help if need be.

Thanks!

-Eli

Eli left the note on the grain bin and double-checked the faucet and spigot. He climbed the steps to the loft and heard the mewing and hissing and thumping of kittens. He left extra food in the dish for Bumblebee and returned the now emptied, makeshift litter box and filled it with kitty litter. "Okay, you guys all set?" He checked the water bowl, which currently wasn't frozen, and knew that Hope would be sure to check and refill it. "I'm gonna miss you guys." He bent down and scooped up the feisty runt and held it to his cheek, feeling its heartbeat in his hand.

Back in the feed room Eli tried to find the scissors that was normally just inside the cabinet under the sink. He knew they were there last week when he opened the hay bales, which is what he now needed to do. They weren't hanging on the nail but he caught a glimpse of the bright green handle lying next to an unopened bag of Friskies. He reached in and got them and opened the bales so Hope wouldn't need to worry about it. He glanced around, making sure everything was as it should be. "Why am I so nervous? Geez."

After returning the scissors, he bid Ink and Smudge farewell and begged them to behave.

Eli took his usual right at the end of Ogden Point Road and headed through town. The snow banks were grey and iced over and not as festive looking as they were the day after the storm, but he loved the downtown area and savored the sunlight warming him, inside and out. The lobster trap Christmas tree was still as stately as it was pre-holiday and seemed to say, "This is Maine, if you were looking for sandy beaches and more warm than cold, don't let the door hit ya on the way out."

Eli made his way onto Route 3 and wished he'd thought to stop at the Independent and get a coffee cake to bring to Otto and Elise. Coming up on the Bloomfield Road, he slowed and laughed at the memory of his little freak-out over realizing that's where Rebecca's farm was located. He could see a sign on the telephone pole but it didn't appear to be the one he saw weeks ago. Slowing more, with no one behind him, he squinted, remembering that he was still supposed to pick up some glasses at the Rite Aid. He saw:

Christmas Clearance

Full Circle Farm

Store Hours 9-3

He took the left fast, heart pounding. *Store?* "Well, I do owe her money for trimming the ponies' hooves." Eli laughed at himself. *Are you seriously trying to convince yourself that you need a legitimate reason to go to a local business and see what you might be able to purchase on your way to a friend's house?* "Yep."

The truck meandered slowly around a bend as Eli was not in a hurry to feign surprise that he had happened upon Rebecca's farm. On the right, the trees began to thin and through them he could see a large open field, with a white coat of sugar sparkling on the landscape. The sign, Full Circle Farm, with the arrows chasing each other around the letters, was on the same post as the mailbox. He pulled into the fence-lined driveway and was relieved to see seven parking spots ahead were occupied.

The cheerful yellow store was attached to a large old white farmhouse with the date 1862 on the plaque next to the pumpkin-colored front door. To the left of the store stood a large old dairy barn, almost as large as the house and store combined.

Eli hopped out of his truck and walked up to the door on which a sign read in large letters:

Leave Your Troubles at The Door

As he got closer he could see in much smaller print underneath:

But Please Don't Forget to Take
Them When You Leave

A young couple with twin toddlers was exiting, Eli hastened to hold the door wide and smiled at the sight. The parents barely noticed him as they both pushed and pulled the bundled kids out of the warm store.

Inside, Eli was greeted with the scents of vanilla, coffee, and freshly baked brownies. Shopping there were about a dozen people, chatting about Christmas and telling their children not to touch anything breakable. Opposite the door was a rolling kitchen rack, the top two shelves laden with loaves of banana, pumpkin, cranberry walnut, and blueberry breads. Underneath the breads were pies: pumpkin, lemon meringue, apple, and blueberry. He knew immediately what he would purchase, but wanted to poke around a bit. From behind the half-wall separating the store from the kitchen, he could hear a faucet running and Christmas music (still) playing. He turned to view the rest of the store and was happy to see tables set up with rows of mittens, scarves, felted animal figures, socks, and hats. Next to the tables stood more shelves, which tempted with preserves, pickled beets, garlic cloves, and cucumbers, three bean salad, peaches and pie fillings, maple sugar candy, and Treadway's

Tonic and honey. *It's like the farmer's market but here, right where Rebecca lives.* In the corner stood an old Coca-Cola refrigerated case filled with pint and quart containers. Completing his visual tour, he saw directly to his left a countertop behind which stood a young man around sixteen, wearing a dark green Full Circle Farm sweatshirt, busily wiping down the scale that sat next to the cash register. Eli watched as he moved quickly to ask an elderly man if he could help carry his items to the counter. "I could have gotten yah'a basket, Sir." The man shuffled slowly and said, "My rule is, only buy what yah can carry, a basket would break the bank!"

The young man looked nervous, as if he wasn't sure if the man was making a joke. "Now when my wife comes in, she will definitely need the biggest basket ya got!"

Eli caught a glimpse of Rebecca in the kitchen, ponytail poking through the back of the Full Circle Farm ball cap on her head, apron over her sweatshirt and jeans. She was carrying a large tray and trying to find an open spot on one of the three stainless steel top tables. Eli quickly moved over to the Coca-Cola case and surveyed the offerings: Chicken salad, chicken pot pies, pasta salad, baked beans, Italian wedding soup, hummus, meatballs in red sauce, coleslaw, and family-size platters of cheese and fruit with stickers that read 50% off and adorned with big red foil bows.

Eli was making mental notes of all the "not pizza" options his future held when he heard, "Eli?"

He turned to see Rebecca with that smile that made him want to kiss her. "Hey, Rebecca. Happy New Year a little early."

She stood with her hands on her hips and wished him the same. The young man called, "Rebecca, what's the price for the pasta salad?"

Rebecca held up her finger to Eli and sprinted to the register, standing behind the boy and pointing to the screen on the register. Eli took the opportunity to see if she was sporting a ring yet. *Nope.*

He picked his way back through the shoppers and made his way to the shelves he first perused. He chose a blueberry bread and a cranberry, too, stacking them on top of each other, the plastic wrap still warm, promising freshness. Not wanting to seem obvious that he'd like to talk to Rebecca but wanting to talk to Rebecca, he let a customer go in front of him while he waited, nervously. When it was his turn, to his surprise, Rebecca said to the boy, "Jack, can you cut the pan of brownies, they should be cool now." She smiled at Eli, "How are the Littles? Was Santa good to them?"

Eli stopped for a moment wondering if people actually got gifts for their horses. "Uh, yes. Spoiled rotten. How was, uh, how was your Christmas?"

The brief flinch on Rebecca's face was not lost on Eli but he wasn't sure what to do with it. "It was good, quiet," she said as she pulled out a brown paper bag for the bread. Eli realized in his nervous haste that he had missed an entire display rack next to the register. "Oh wait a minute, here." He pushed the bag back toward Rebecca and sidestepped to get a closer look, squinting to see the labels. Rebecca said, quietly, "You and that coffee..." before greeting the next customer. Eli looked for the Blueberry blend but didn't see it, so went with the Cinnamon Roll. He stepped back in line and listened to Rebecca explain what else she offers in the spring and summer months at the market and on the farm. When it was his turn again, he asked where his favorite blueberry coffee was.

"Oh, that's a seasonal one. You'll have to wait for that." She pulled out another bag, and Eli, his wallet. Rebecca stood back, arms crossed this time. "Well, I mean if you can't wait, I could possibly make you a batch, custom."

He feigned suspicion best he could, "Really? Is there a custom price attached?"

Rebecca, now showing him mostly the lid on her ball cap, said, "Maybe."

Back in his truck, Eli almost forgot he still needed to drive an hour and a half to Dr. Gunther's. He put on some music, and replayed the last sixteen minutes over and over, all the way to Camden.

"That was köstlich, Eli, delicious. Thank you." Eli wiped the cranberry breadcrumbs from his mouth and nodded. "You'll have to share the rest with Elise when she gets back."

Otto turned in the parlor chair and bent forward toward Eli, "I owe that woman more than das brot. Without her, I would not have survived as a young boy." His gaze drifted past Eli as he was again reliving a scene Eli knew was as real to him as the memory of it.

"Tell me, Eli, have you ever thought you would not survive something but you awoke each day to find that you had and ...."

Eli nodded his head, knowing he needed to carry his end of the conversation but wanting to hear more at the same time. "Yes, Doctor. I have felt that. I'm still not sure how I survived it."

Otto seemed to come alive then, pushing himself to the edge of the seat. "Ah, yes. But are you glad you did? And, Eli, what will you do with that gift?"

Looking at his hands and not wanting to offer too much information for fear his Christmas Day wounds would begin to weep, Eli said, "Well I think that the work I am doing now is helping not only the clients who sit with me but all the people they will ever meet. You know, for many years, the mantra has been that trauma is passed down through the generations and I just feel that, well, healing can be, too. I mean for future generations."

"Elias, you have much to give the world. This future life progression is a fascinating realm that you work in. I have to admit that though it is unorthodox, to say the least, it has made quite a stir in the field. But you need to defend it. It's your wahrheit, your truth."

"Well, it has definitely gotten some harsh attention, that's true, but Dr. Gunther, the lives that have changed, the quality of life, I mean, it speaks for itself."

Otto nodded, "Yes, the proof itself is proof." He sat back against the chair and said, "You know, the day the camp was liberated, I will ... I will never forget that day, April 15th, 1945. I was in the barracks and I was very sick. I had no life in me to go out of the barracks to the latrine and the last several times I had tried to get there, I didn't make it before the water came gushing out of me. I think back now and wonder how close I was to death. There is only so much a body can endure. I had no control of my own body, it was just skin and bones, das skellet. I heard the shouting but it seemed to be a dream; it sounded like the noise was coming through cotton around my head. Some of the boys sat up from the bunk and went to look outside. Others came in and smiled, shouting, "Wir werden frei sein! We are going to be free!" I remember thinking that I must be dreaming or that maybe I had died."

Eli listened as Otto recounted the horrors of the camp that had become his every day existence. Three camps, this one, by far the worst. "My mother and Hannah had been gone almost as long as my father but you see, I didn't know that then. I waited for that day that I had dreamed of. So sure I was, that I would be with them again when this was all over. Every time a new train came, new prisoners, I was looking for them, trying to imagine what they would look like starved and dirty, heads shaved. I was certain I would know them anywhere. Only once in those seven years did I think I heard my sister's voice. But when I turned to look, I could not see her anywhere. We were separated from the girls but that didn't mean we did not see them. I called to her over and over through the wires and frozen air but there was no reply." He turned so that he could be sure Eli understood what he was about to say. "I heard my sister on the day she died." He pointed, not at Eli but rather, toward the sky, elbow resting on the arm of his chair. "She said to me, Eli, you are kräftig, so strong. You must believe this, bruder. You have to find, die hoffen. You have to find hope."

Eli felt the chill run through him then, starting in his chest and running simultaneously to his toes and the top of his head and seemingly rushing out through his fingertips. He shuddered involuntarily. Nervous, he sat up straight and gripped the tops of his thighs to center himself.

"Many years after the liberation, and Elise I had begun to build our lives, I was able to see rosters of the registered dead from Ravensbrück. How many more souls lost that were not even registered? I realized Hannah died shortly after arriving there, my mother a week later. I wonder now if I would have survived all those years, all those camps, if I had known." He lifted his gaze toward the fireplace and continued.

"There was gunfire and shouting and I could not even lift my head, never mind go to see what was happening. It was like my body was gone but somehow I was still there, stuck. I don't remember when it happened but there was a time I realized that I no longer felt der juckreiz, the itch from the lice and infection in my eyes—the itch was never satisfied. But at some point, I don't remember exactly, I just stopped itching. So, yes, suddenly the barracks door opened again and two soldiers came in, British soldiers. They said, "Is anyone alive in here?" They asked it in German and I still think of how strange that was. I hadn't heard anyone ask that before. We never asked that. We just knew when someone had died. The sound of their breathing changed or they would speak in a way that we just knew they were going and then, they were gone. But we never asked if anyone was still alive. A young soldier, not much older than me, put what I thought were pills in my mouth. Red, yellow, green, orange, brown. I chewed them and tasted chocolate."

Eli tilted his head for a moment before the realization came to him.

Dr. Gunther turned to point at the class curio in the corner of the parlor. "That picture there on the top shelf is that very soldier."

Eli walked to the case and peered in.

"That was 1975, thirty-three years and a lifetime later." I found him with a lot of help from my children. Henry Ellis was his name. Elise and I flew to London to meet with him."

Eli saw in the picture the men exchanging packages of M&Ms and smiling.

Eli stood, mesmerized as the sun shone through the glass of the parlor windows, to think about what this man had endured.

"Dr. Gunther, when you sit here in this house and look out at the harbor, do you sometimes wonder if it's even the same life?"

Otto sat for a moment and rubbed his hands together. "Yes, sometimes I think it is a memory from another time, that it couldn't have turned out this way but you see ..." his voice faltered and he cleared his throat, "you see, you can never know what is to come and so you can never quit. That's not up to us, it's up to God. But for all the God-given things Elise and I have enjoyed since the day her mother brought her to the DP, we still have endured many struggles."

"What is the DP?" Eli thought that Otto and Elise had met at the camp.

"The DP is the displaced persons camp. We stayed where we were but it was then under control of the British. They brought in nurses, social workers, and others to help us. First they had to get all of the bodies out of the camp. They were not all in the barracks. They were verstreut, scattered all over the camp. I tripped on them when I tried to get to the latrine at night. Then the barracks were burned to stop all the disease. Typhus and dysentery, they killed thousands and even after the liberation, many more thousands died. But Elise, she came and she nursed me back to health with her mother, Martine. She was younger than me but not by much and she was so beautiful.

"I honestly thought that Elise was there in the camp, too," Eli said.

"No, no. She was there, training with her mother who was a nurse. They brought me back from the edge of death, Eli. They cared for so many of us but I felt then that they took extra time and care with me. Soon the camp was segregated and we were allowed to form our own community and the people from other countries had their own places. And when the camp finally closed in 1950, I was eighteen years old. A year later, I married Elise."

The sun was slowly descending and the warm glow promised that the sun would show up again tomorrow. Eli said, "I'm honored that you are willing to share so much with me, as

I'm certain it can't be easy for you."

"Oh, Dr. Cranston, once I am gone, my story is gone, too, unless someone carries it on for me. And we can never let this happen again. Look at Syria, it is happening again, there are many places it is happening again. And even though I believe your forward life progression is quite useful, it's your past that holds all the knowledge of what you can never go back to. So, you see, it is equally important."

Eli felt a chill run through him, but also sweat running down his back at Dr. Gunther's knowing words.

Eli raised his brows and nodded in agreement. "Your children must have a true appreciation of you and Elise."

"We have been blessed with children who are making the most of the freedom and education we have provided for them. Daniel, our oldest, is a professor of Ethics at Dartmouth. Adelaide is a civil rights lawyer in Washington D.C., and Nathan is a cardiologist at Mount Sinai. They have done well and they give back. That is the most important thing, to give back. My grandchildren, too, they do good things." Otto looked at the dwindling fire in the fireplace. "Mostly," he said.

Otto stood slowly and pulled his shoulders back until he was straight. Out of the well patinaed copper bin, he pulled out a piece of alder and added it to the fire. "Nathan's daughter is uh, she's lost. We don't know what happened with her. She was given the best opportunities, best schooling. Ah, schande, such a shame."

Eli wasn't sure what he meant by lost. "I'm sorry to hear that, Dr. Gunther."

Otto turned to him then. "She was such a shy child, so beautiful, and she looked just like Nathan did when he was a boy. But as she grew older, I don't know what happened. I think perhaps it was depression, but ... hard to say. She disappeared for a while. Nathan wouldn't tell us much, you know, trying to handle things his own way. But eventually Nathan got a call from her. She was alive and that was all that should matter but ... she was like the living dead. First it was marijuana and Nathan didn't think it was that bad but she got hooked on other things, pills, and I don't know what else. She stole from them and even hit her own mother. It broke Elise's heart to hear that her own son had to ask his child to leave the house.

"Wow, I'm really sorry to hear this, Dr. Gunther. I can empathize with you."

Otto continued, "Elise came to me and said she wanted Melissa to come stay with us, help get her on a path, maybe get her a job at the hospital with her. Now, I will tell you that my wife is the smartest, most loving woman I have ever met and I owe my very life to her. There was no way I was able to say no to her. I loved Melissa as much as she did, it's true. I just worried about the drug use. But how could I say that to Elise? She just wanted to nurture her. So we brought her here to live with us and our lives turned kopfüber, upside down. She was only sixteen years old and she was a mess. Stealing, running around town with older men, sneaking alcohol into school. Elise took a leave from the hospital to stay home and watch Melissa as if she was a baby."

"Addiction is a very tough thing, Dr. Gunther, as we both know. It changes a person's brain so you aren't dealing with the person you think is standing in front of you. Their brain is controlled by the addiction. But I'm not telling you anything new."

Eli thought he saw tears in Otto's eyes. "Well, she didn't stay long. We don't know where she is exactly but we get a call once or twice a year still when she is desperate for money. She told us many years ago she has a child but I don't know if I should believe her. Elise asked her to bring the baby to us, so we could see it. She wouldn't come. It's heartbreaking to think that the child, if there is one, is growing up like that, but unless Melissa is willing to get help, money isn't going to be the solution."

The phone buzzed in Eli's pocket, which suddenly broke the hardened clay that encased the mood in the room. "Excuse me, I just want to be sure it isn't ...."

It was a text from Rebecca: **Thanks for supporting local farmers.**

Eli felt a rush of warmth through his body and put his phone back.

Otto sat back in his chair. "So Eli, you see, there is a struggle in each family. No family escapes it completely. And sometimes going backward to heal doesn't make sense. Going forward, now that is the thing that makes sense. Just like me as a boy in the camp with dysentery imagining this wonderful life I now live ... I could not have even entertained the idea of dreaming it, never mind believing it. So for Melissa to believe she could have what she needs without those evil chemicals, she would have to be shown that for her to understand. Eli, I do think your therapy could help a person like her. But we don't even know where she is." Otto looked at the floor then and Eli could see the tear appear on his storied face.

"Like my sister and my mother, I don't even know if she is alive."

Eli leaned forward and said in a hushed tone, "Hey, do you remember the first time we met? You told me, the difference between unbearable and bruise. Do you remember what that was?"

Otto took his glasses off and wiped at his eyes. "Hope."

30

The bench seat was covered in ice and it took more than one tug to lift it. Hope reached in and was surprised when she could hear that she had touched something, because she couldn't feel anything in there. She looked inside the bench and saw the keychain in the corner. She put her hand back in and could hear the key move on the wood and hit the corner. If she hadn't tripped and spilled ice water all over herself, she'd be almost home. Her fingers were almost useless but after a few attempts, she was able to slide the keychain up the side of the box and sandwiched it between both hands. The wind picked up and she thought her ears would freeze and fall off her head. She used her teeth to position the key and push it into the lock. With what seemed more like mitts than human hands with opposable thumbs, she was able to turn the key and push open the door. With relief washing over her, she began to cry. "It hurts so much."

She went to the kitchen sink and turned on the water. She knew not to use hot water but wanted to. "Ow, ow, ow. Mom, I wish you could help meeeee. Oowww!"

Hope watched her skin turn purple and pink and then almost orange as her feet stomped the floor to deflect her pain. "You are my sunshine, my ... ow, ow, ow, make it stop!"

Slowly, her hands thawed and the frozen sweatshirt began to crunch and break up, too. Hope began to calm down. She wrapped her hands in the dish towel from the stove handle and rocked herself back and forth in the chair, "Please don't take my sunshine ...."

The sun had all but set and the last thing Hope wanted to do was try to walk home in soaking wet clothes. She looked around, nervous. She peeled off the pink sweatshirt Eli gave her for Christmas and stood in a torn t-shirt and wet jeans. Peeking around the kitchen wall into the hallway, she flipped on the light and made her way toward the bathroom. Inside, she ran warm water in the tub while she took out a towel from the linen closet. She looked at herself in the mirror and shrugged. She struggled to remove her cold, wet jeans off her bright pink legs and wondered how quickly you could die from a stupid mishap like this.

Lowering herself into the lukewarm water, she began to warm up and wonder how she would get home. She waited until she could feel her fingers resting on her legs and all her toes could move on command and then stepped out.

Wrapped in an Old Orchard beach towel, she stepped back into the hallway and walked to the bedroom. Hope turned the light on and saw Eli's bathrobe on his bed. She wrapped herself in it and pulled on his slippers but couldn't manage to walk in them. Next to the door was a laundry basket with folded clothing and to her delight, the top layer contained socks. She slid into a pair that came up to her knees and laughed. *Now what?* Hope took her wet clothing from the bathroom and guessed the laundry was in the basement. She picked her way carefully downstairs wearing the giant socks and threw her clothing into the dryer.

Back upstairs she decided she wasn't going to attempt to get home in the dark. She texted her mother: Mom, I have to stay over at Sydney's house, I didn't leave in time. I'll be home in the morning. I love you.

She hated lying to her mother. But she hated that her mother had no idea who Rebecca, Eli, or her school friends were, even more.

She remembered Eli's note about the super-special hot cocoa and smiled. While she waited for the water to heat up, she looked in the cupboards. Rice, pasta, oatmeal. Nope. Next was canned baked beans and tuna, coffee and filters, mugs. She raised her brows and pouted her lower lip as if to say, "Okay, getting better. One more try." The third cabinet revealed the jackpot: cereal, preserves, popcorn, tortilla chips, Ritz crackers, peanut butter, sliced bread; Treadway's Tonic and cans of Chicken Noodle Soup and Bar Harbor Lobster Bisque. She decided she was very lucky, indeed.

After eating, Hope went straight back to the bedroom and climbed onto the softest mattress she could have imagined. *Way better than the couch at home,* she thought. She rested her head on the memory foam pillow, the light of the full moon illuminating the room. If she had known the story of Goldilocks, she may have made the connection. But she hadn't had many bedtime stories, not happy ones anyway. Without many more thoughts at all and a full tummy, she drifted to sleep, alone and feeling safer than she ever had in all of her eleven years.

31

Eli got to the Grand Harbor Inn, less than a mile from Dr. Gunther's, and checked in at the front desk. The Christmas tree next to the fireplace was beautifully lit and being admired by a little boy about two years old, by Eli's estimation. He squatted, in his little navy corduroy pants and fisherman's sweater, hands on knees and looked at the "gifts" sitting on the tree skirt. "Ooh wee! Santa! Thank you, Santa!" Eli laughed and exchanged a knowing look with the father of the boy.

Eli carried his overnight bag to the elevator and went up to his room. He was exhausted but wasn't sure why. He thought perhaps it was the emotion, the energy in the parlor at Dr. Gunther's house. He noticed even Peppercorn had become agitated and removed himself after an hour or so. The sadness that had filled that room he imagined was just a fraction of what Otto had felt over his lifetime. Eli was grateful for the experience to be privy to such an account of sheer bravery. It occurred to him that someone like Otto lived almost an entire life with the horrific memories that shaped his young life. Acknowledging that some people turn their most difficult wounds into beacons that attract those who need healing, Eli suspected that this visit would help cement his conviction that his therapy will help heal those very healers.

He opened the drapes and looked out onto the setting sun over the harbor and decided he would have dinner delivered. And for the first time in a decade, he thought it would be nice to have someone to share life with again.

After placing an order, he remembered the message from Rebecca and replied: **Looking forward to trying the chicken pot pie next time.**

He added a smiley, then backspaced, added it again.

"Oh my God, I'm fourteen," he laughed and hit send, the smiley making the cut.

After dinner he brushed his teeth and turned on the TV. He selected a movie to watch and picked up his phone and searched Melissa Gunther. He found a few in the US, one listed in New York with relatives named Nathan and Wendy but beyond that, nothing. No Facebook, Instagram, Twitter.

His phone buzzed, this time with a call from the 916 area code. He declined the call, tossed his phone onto the nightstand and fell asleep with Forrest Gump exclaiming that he and Jenny were like peas and carrots.

32

"Tig, are you serious? What do they mean by that? What? Why are you yelling at me?! Look, just calm down. I'll leave now and we will figure it out. Okay, okay. I'm leaving now, Tig."

Eli pushed his chair away from his desk and walked down the hall to the conference room. "Dad, I gotta run out but I'll be back."

Richard looked up from his computer and nodded. Eli hadn't realized he had his phone to his ear. He looked in at Jay's office. Empty, again. Eli shook his head and wondered how he made partner in the first place. Oldest son ... it was expected he supposed. "If you don't love it, leave," he mumbled as he reached the lobby of the suite. "Lori, I'll be back in an hour or so. If you get a call from Christoff, Christoff and Reagan, put them through to my cell, okay?"

He took the elevator to the garage and hopped into the Alfa. When he got to the high school, he saw that Antigone had parked in a handicapped space right in front of the door. He shook his head. Antigone was not entitled but when it came to Grace, the woman would slay lions, and parking where she wasn't allowed didn't faze her. "That poor principal," he muttered as he walked to the door and waited to be buzzed in. He peered through the window and saw Antigone, dressed in her signature work outfit: skirt, silk shell, and heels with tanned skin, hair sun bleached but beautiful. She stood with one hand on her hip, the other holding her cell to her ear. Eli quietly walked into the air-conditioned office and waved at the secretary. The woman smiled and pointed to the sign-in binder. Antigone's voice filled the room and no one else dared make a sound. A young man sitting in the chair stationed outside the dean's office stifled a laugh as Antigone used her best deeply sarcastic comments for the real estate agent on the other end before she hung up. "Eli. You're here. Come out here for a minute." He followed her back into the lobby where students were taking pictures and decorating for an ocean-themed dance.

"What's going on? Where's Grace?" Eli looked back toward the office to be sure he hadn't missed something.

"She's in with the principal and the police. I didn't want to go in without you and I texted Grace not to say a word until we got in there. Eli, I am so pissed right now."

"Okay, it'll be okay. Her dad's a lawyer, remember? C'mon, let's see what's going on."

Eli put on his stone-cold professional demeanor complete with a poker face to beat the band. Antigone often resented his undying work obsession but when it came down to it, she was proud of him.

The secretary picked up the phone and let the principal know the Cranstons were there and then walked them back to his office.

Inside sat Grace, face dripping with mascara and guilt. The principal and resource officer each stood to greet the parents. Antigone took out a tissue from her purse, handed it to Grace and tried to comfort her.

"Hi Gracie, I am sure you haven't said anything yet, is that correct? Being a minor, I am certain Dr. Clifton and certainly a law enforcement officer would want you to wait until your parent or lawyer could be present before asking too much."

Gracie shook her head and sat a little straighter. The police officer sighed and introduced himself. Eli shook his hand a little more vigorously than was necessary. He stood back, with all his body language shouting about who was in charge and who knew more about the law.

Dr Clifton said, "Mr. and Mrs. Cranston, I am sure this is upsetting and we, too, are concerned but you have to understand that the safety of all our students is paramount and—"

Eli cut him off. "Save the speech, please. Is she being detained here and if so on what charge?"

The principal looked at the cop who was clearly there because he was called, not because he was looking to arrest a girl for bringing her mother's pills to school.

"Uh, no. She isn't being detained but we wanted—"

Eli motioned for his daughter to stand up which she did. He pointed to the door and she looked at him and at her mother with confusion. Antigone guided her out the door but remained in the room with Eli who pulled out a business card and handed it to the principal. "Call me if you have anything more to say about the matter. Do NOT speak to Grace directly without me present. Ever." He waited for a response and got the one he was looking for. Eli thanked them both and ushered Antigone out of the office in front of him.

In the parking lot he opened the door for Grace to get into Antigone's Escalade.

"We'll talk when I get home. Gracie, I don't know what to say about the pills but if you're selling them—"

"Dad! I am not selling anything! What the *fuck*!? Why would you *say* that!?"

Antigone rubbed her temples. "Grace Antigone! Do not speak to your father like that!"

Eli stood back as Grace dissolved into tears. "Go home and stay there. I'll see you guys at dinner tonight." He walked around the truck and gave Antigone a kiss before heading to his car. Sitting behind the wheel, he watched Antigone pull out of her illegal parking space and tear out of the lot. He shook his head, knowing there would be hell to pay at home and for a split second, felt sorry for Grace. He started his car and retreated to Wilshire Boulevard where he found himself in the mood to confront his father about his older son.

33

Hope woke up to the sound of the horses calling to anyone who could hear that they were, in fact, starving. She startled at her unfamiliar surroundings, then took a breath as she remembered her mishap with the water in the cold barn. She hopped out of bed and smoothed the sheets and down comforter, stepped back and decided the pillow needed turning over to reveal the side that didn't hold the shape of her head. She hurried down to the basement and got her now chilly clothing out of the dryer and trotted back up to the bathroom. She dressed quickly and pulled her hair back into a ponytail with the elastic she'd left on the lip of the sink.

After returning the bathrobe and hoping it was in the spot she took it from the night before, she stuffed the socks into her pockets because her gloves were somewhere in the barn, likely as frozen as they were last night. She grabbed the five-gallon bucket Eli kept on the porch for water if the barn water was frozen. Filling it half way with cool water in the bathtub, she went up to the barn, trudging through some fresh snow, taking care with the frozen path underneath.

She assured the ponies they wouldn't starve and trotted up to check the kittens, suddenly afraid it might have been too cold last night. Her heart beat quickly in her chest as she called out, "Bumblebee!" She was terrified at the silence but suddenly Bumblebee popped up from behind one of the bales, meowing loudly. Behind her were two kittens trying to climb the bale. Hope peered over and could see Bumblebee had made a nest with the loose hay between the bales, ensuring her body heat would keep her babies warm. All five rascals peered back at Hope with bright blue eyes. She wished she could call one her own, the tiniest one. He was feisty and attacked her ankles now every day without fail. She fed the momma cat and wondered if the babies were ready to wean. "I'll ask Rebecca," she told Bumblebee who happily purred while she ate.

Hope scooped the grain into the ponies' bucket and laughed at the squeal that came out of Ink as he pushed Smudge to the side. "You two are crazy." Hope loved the barn and the ponies and wished she had a barn of her own. She peered into the empty stall next to Ink and Smudge's. "A Morgan, that's what I'll get. And his name will be Pirate unless he had a really cool name already. Nah, it'd be Pirate either way."

She shivered, which reminded her to keep moving. She finished carefully pouring the water into the bucket that hung inside the occupied stall.

Back to the feed room with the scoop, she tossed it into the bin. On her way out, she opened the cabinet underneath the sink and peered in. She tugged the unopened cat food bag a little to the left and closed the door.

Walking back from the barn, her stomach rumbled. She ignored it the best she could and walked back around to the front of the house. After locking the door and checking to be sure it was secure, Hope opened the bench and placed the key back where it had been. She wondered why Eli had a box of pinecones in there. *Only thing those are good for is fire starters,* she thought.

On her way toward the road she saw her father's Corolla fly by the driveway. She was glad it was not heading in the direction of home.

34

Eli left Camden after a full breakfast at the inn. The sky was darkening with snow in the forecast for the afternoon. On his drive he listened to NPR, more for white noise than anything else. He had a lot to think about. It was nice to have a few days off but he'd feel better once he got back to work and he wondered why he hadn't heard from Kate. He needed to prepare for Kylie's session and he had two intakes this week. But the thoughts that were circling on a carousel in his head were those of Rebecca. He wished he had the guts to ask if she was still with that guy and if so, why she was flirting with him. Or *was* she flirting with him? He shook his head at the angst of it all. "Huh, Eli. You're smitten."

Arriving back in Bar Harbor he decided he ought to stop at the market since it was on the way. He wanted the rest of the day to get things done, but reminded himself that he still had the day off. He turned onto Cottage from Eden and realized he'd been getting around successfully without his GPS for a couple of weeks now. He grabbed a basket and picked out a few items to get him through the week: cold cuts, rolls, and just one frozen pizza. He found himself in the candy aisle and saw, to his surprise, a variety of marshmallows. He got the familiar large white ones he remembered from camping trips but also grabbed a bag of colorful miniature ones. And since marshmallows were boring in comparison to all the other offerings, he picked up two large Lindt chocolate bars.

"Scuse, me sir." Eli looked up and saw the woman in the

black parka in front of him. Until now hadn't gotten a clear view of her face. His heart sank to see the sunken eyes, grey skin and unwashed hair. He realized she wasn't very old. The drug use made it difficult to gauge but he thought she wasn't yet thirty. "Would you happen to have a couple of dollars, Sir? I left my wallet at home. I feel so stupid. I have to get some food—my daughter's at home for vacation and—"

Eli recognized the slight sway as she tried to maintain her posture and the slow speech, too. He reached into his pocket and stopped. *What are you doing?* he thought to himself. You know what she'll do with that. "So uh, I don't actually have any cash on me but if you want to grab a few items, I'll be happy to pay with my card."

"Oh, that's wicked awesome of you but I, ah, actually I really just need a few dollars more to get a ride back home. I think I have enough for mac and cheese and some milk, yah know. Kid would live on that stuff if she had to." Eli said, "Sorry, I just don't have any cash on me. Wish I could help. Do you, uh, do you need any sort of help with anything else? Like maybe finding some assistance with food stamps or, uh, you know just assistance?

The woman stepped away, realizing she wasn't going to get anything from this man. "No, no. I'm all set, Sir, thank you though. You have yourself a nice New Yeah's now."

"Same to you, Ma'am." Eli walked past her, feeling helpless but glad he hadn't given her money.

Back in his truck, Eli started the engine and saw a car pull into the row in front of him. The green Toyota sat running, a man behind the wheel. He waited. The woman in the parka seemed to be arguing with an employee. He was pointing off toward the street and she was emphatically shaking her head. Eli put his window down and discerned that it was in fact an argument. The employee said he was going to call the police again if she didn't leave. She argued that she had a right to be in the store. He countered with, "You're harassing customers and if you were here to shop, Ma'am, you'd have money. People don't want to shop here if this is what they have to deal with!"

The woman told him her father was a doctor and that she was very well connected as was her husband and that the employee's sorry ass ought to be careful how he treated her. She wound herself up and ended with telling him where she hoped he would spend eternity as he pulled out his cell phone. Eli shook his head, knowing it was a tough situation. The woman needed help, but the help she was asking for is something people don't want to take part in.

She slowly made her way over to the Corolla and opened the door. She looked around, saw Eli and flipped him off, doubled down and mouthed "fuck off."

Eli searched on his phone for a treatment center. They were on every corner back home but he wasn't yet familiar with anything local. He called the first one and it rang and rang, no answer, no voicemail. The second one he tried had a recording stating that there were currently no beds available but if it was an emergency, to hang up and dial 9-1-1. He pulled out of the lot and headed home with the intention to make some calls this week just to see what was available in the community.

Turning left onto Ogden Point Road, he was excited to see his little family. The house looked like a fairytale cottage, painted in snow.

He brought his groceries and overnight bag in and placed them in the kitchen, changed into his barn chore clothes and made a mental note of it. "Eli Cranston has, not only barn chores, but clothes dedicated to them." He laughed. "And he still does not have a dog."

He jogged next to the path, knowing the ice on the hill was out to get him and had been almost successful a couple of days before. "I will get a snowblower. I'll ask Clem about it."

He greeted his ponies and could see they had been fed, the last of their hay spread thin on the clean pine shavings, which stuck to the whiskers on their muzzles, making them look like they had spilled popcorn on themselves during a scary movie.

He went upstairs to find the kittens dangerously close to the loft stairs. He'd been worried about it since they became mobile and curious and wondered if he should close off the stairs.

"Maybe they should come inside." His eyes widened then, not sure how many times he had thought it but was now surprised to hear it come out of his mouth, "Bumblebee, what do you think? C'mon inside 'til I can find these rascals homes?" He didn't want to scare her and wasn't sure how to proceed. He went back to the feed room and looked around. Empty grain bags ... eh, that didn't feel right; the grain bucket wasn't quite large enough. There had been a copy paper box he brought out when devising the litter box, finding the lid was sufficient. He saw it recently but wasn't sure where. He looked in the cabinet above the sink but it was too small to fit a box that size. "Ah, underneath," he said. He crouched down and opened the doors. The bag of cat food was there and behind it he could see the box. He removed the Friskies bag and pulled out the box and as he did, he could see there was an envelope behind it. He tossed the box aside and reached into the back of the cabinet. The envelope was not empty, he could tell. He opened it to see several 10s and 20s. He counted the money and shook his head. This is almost the exact amount of money he had paid Hope since she started working there. "What is this about?" He put the bills back in and replaced the envelope.

He took the box upstairs and loaded up the crew, Bumblebee curious but not overly concerned. "C'mon Bumble. I'm not babysitting all night. It's okay, let's go." She didn't immediately follow but he knew she probably would and if not, he'd come back for her. He brought the box over to the stall door and Smudge came to sniff, ears at attention, blowing through his nostrils, his breath visible in the cold air. Ink pushed him aside, Smudge's forelock comically bouncing upward to reveal cartoon eyes, the whites screaming, "I'm gonna tell Mom!!" Ink nudged the tops of the kitten heads and one reached up and swatted at his muzzle. Ink squealed and backed into Smudge, setting him into squeal mode, too. "Oh my God, you two. Go back to eating."

He walked out of the barn, pulling the door most of the way closed to block the wind and he saw Bumblebee on the bottom step, watching. "C'mon, you, I promise, it's warm inside." He was almost to the gate when she bolted through the snow, hopping and leaping in great bounds to catch up and Eli breathed a sigh of relief.

He almost tripped on her as he walked in with the box of babies. She was meowing very loudly and he wasn't sure if she was upset or overjoyed. Eventually he could tell it was the latter.

He put the box in the kitchen with the noisy bunch inside, tiny faces just reaching the top of the box. Bumblebee sat on the edge of the carpet in the living room, tail wrapped around herself. Eli took some of the kindling and newspaper from the bin to start a fire. He looked but didn't see the lighter he kept balanced on the edge of the bin. He looked closer and saw that it had fallen off and came to rest next to the boxes he needed to get back to soon.

He started the kindling and left the stove door open to give the fire a chance before putting any stove lengths in. He glanced over at the bustling box in the kitchen and looked forward to springing the gang out of their W.B. Mason confinement. Bumblebee stretched out then, clearly happy with her good fortune.

Eli put his groceries away and as he did he saw the hot cocoa box on the lower shelf. He remembered it being on the middle shelf. A smile came across his face then, wondering if Hope had taken him up on making herself some cocoa. He looked into the box to see there were six packets left. He smiled, knowing that she now felt comfortable enough to come into the house.

He turned to the kittens to see one had almost made his way out by climbing onto its siblings' heads. He scooped them out one by one and watched as they took over the kitchen floor. Shaking his head at the sight, he busied himself making a litter box and putting out a water bowl and a can of tuna. "Just like the old days, Bumblebee."

Eli put his overnight bag away and finished building his fire, then sat in the recliner, waiting to see if the blaze was taking off or if it needed more help. He pulled out his phone and tried the rehab number again. No answer. He saw that he had missed a text from Hope: Hi Eli—ponies and cats are all set. I'll be back tonight.

He responded: Great! If it's too cold to come out, don't worry. I'm home now.

Feeling restless, he wondered if he should just get to work, the commute was just a few steps away. "You're avoiding." His chest heaved on the inhale.

He looked over at the romper room and watched Bumblebee lick one her babies as it played with its own tail and fell over. *A few months and they go off on their own. Humans keep theirs for so many years. No wonder kids end up with issues.*

Hearing the fire roaring, he peeked in and decided it was a go and closed the door, checking the handle twice. And then as if he was trying to dive off a diving board backwards or get himself to swallow bitter medication, he took a deep breath with eyes closed and pictured the outcome being the best possible thing he could imagine. Then he bent down and dragged the first box back out again and walked over to the recliner.

"No music and no booze. Just straight-up truth."

He pulled out the quasi-bunny and the sweet photo of Grace and put them on the coffee table, noticing it really did need to be dusted. He reached back in and this time pulled out her Kindergarten graduation diploma.

> Grace Antigone Cranston
> Kindergarten Class of 1997
> Mrs. Hawley and Miss Garcia

The only thing he remembered about that day was Antigone telling him how disappointed she was that he would miss such a milestone in his daughter's life because of work. He put it aside and looked in the box. Two Beanie Babies, a tarnished silver rattle with GC engraved on one end and her birthdate on the other, a small piggy bank, an Eiffel Tower jewelry box and a folded, yellowed paper. He lifted it gently and opened it with the care one might handle a venomous snake.

> Happy Birthday Daddy
> You are the best Daddy
> I love you

Let's have ice cream!
By Grace Cranston

He ran his fingers over the blue and pink crayon and little kid writing. At the bottom was a stick figure man in what might have been a dark suit and a tiny stick figure girl with a blue dress and red lips. "I love you, too." He placed it with the other artifacts, the blips of a few selected days from a short life with an innocent child he was supposed to protect. "No, I don't care to reframe that statement."

He pulled the box closer to his feet and moved some of the items aside. On the bottom was a wind-up musical ballerina. He gave it to Grace at her first recital. He put it on the table and sat back. "Yah, nice try, Bud. Pick it up."

He reached for the little figurine in the relevé position. He was surprised that he remembered the name. Eli turned the ballerina a half turn on her base, then a quarter turn more and set her on the table. She began to dance and Eli closed his watery eyes humming along to just a few notes of "Amazing Grace." A vivid flash of little Gracie's four-year-old smile comprising her bright white baby teeth made his heart race. The ballerina was losing steam, the notes coming with gaps between. He opened his eyes as she came to a halt, her back to him.

Peering again into the box, Eli moved the piggy bank over. He saw a thin gold chain and wondered if it was her First Holy Communion necklace. He drew it slowly out of the depth of the box and dangled it in front of his face. The locket that Antigone's mom gave Grace on her 8th birthday slowly completed a pirouette and hung, trembling from the energy in Eli's hands. He carefully opened it and looked at the familiar photo, a tiny version of the one that stood guard over their living room mantle for years. He thought then about all the arguments and joys it had witnessed, the Christmas parties, the stunned silence and absolute devastation. And yet immortalized on canvas stood Eli, Antigone, and Grace, dressed for a photoshoot at the beach, each wearing white, smiling, the sun creating a slight halo around them. He touched Gracie's tiny face, a front tooth missing, remembering that day clearly. Eli had argued with Antigone on the front lawn about such a frivolous waste of a day when they could snap their own photos just as easily in front of their newly landscaped pool. He looked at Antigone's image then. She looked so happy in this picture, despite his nastiness. "I'm sorry, Tig. You have no idea just how sorry."

He gently piled the items back in, one by one, wondering how the tiny ballerina hadn't broken. She looked so fragile and vulnerable and yet after her exile in storage all these years, she dances with innocence and beauty the way she always had, her song just as painful. *Tougher than she looks.* Eli took some of the newspaper from the firewood bin and wrapped her up gently in three sheets. He put her in the box and as he nestled her in place, he saw, staring up at him from the newspaper:

Are You Struggling With Addiction?

Call Now. Counselors Available

24 Hours/ 365 Days.

He dialed the number and on the fourth ring someone answered and asked if he could hold for just a moment.

Eli closed his eyes, "Amazing Grace, indeed."

While he waited on hold, he texted Hope: **BTW, I moved BB and her kittens into the house. Didn't want you to get scared.** He hit send, then sent the scream emoji and laughed at himself.

She texted right back: **I would of freaked LOL I bet they love it.**

Eli got the information one would need if they were seeking help, and also the information a mental health professional might have use for in the future.

The dispersing kitten squad got his attention and Eli decided he needed to find them a safe spot to roam and his kitchen was not going to be that spot. His phone buzzed and he looked, assuming it was a response from Hope. It wasn't.

Eli—I need to talk to you. Please call me.

He looked at the number and thought, "Now that takes balls."

35

"Kylie. How are you? C'mon in." Kylie stepped into the familiar office from the hallway this time since the walkway was a sheet of ice, and took off her knit hat and matching gloves. "Hi. Happy New Year," She smelled like roses, Eli noticed.

"So, today is the day. Tell me how you feel about that." He sat back and mirrored Kylie, who had immediately crossed her legs in the chair opposite Eli. She wore faded jeans, a white button-down shirt she tied in the front, and tall black boots.

"Well, I'm partly excited thinking this could possibly be the thing that does it for me. And then there's the part of me that is laughing at the idea. You know, like, my path is no match for this therapy either."

Eli nodded and sighed, "Well, Kylie, let's work from the positive side of things and assume that there will be changes that occur that will shift you into a different space, allow you to follow a different trajectory. Okay?"

She nodded and folded her arms. Eli asked, "So let's go over some of the questions you answered online for me. I've spent a lot of time reading and though I have a couple of questions for you, I feel like I have a pretty good idea of the events that created the trauma which led to your ..." Eli gestured to her arms and torso, "self injury."

She self-consciously and gently rubbed one of her forearms. "Okay so, before we begin, do you need to use the restroom, get some water?"

Kylie shook her head, this time sending her ponytail dancing from side to side. "Okay, so let's get ready. My phone is off and let's make sure yours is, too. I'm going to clarify a few things, like I mentioned and then we will begin. So, you mentioned in the self-assessment that you were in the foster care system from age four until you were emancipated at age eighteen, and that during that fourteen-year span, you were physically, emotionally, and sexually abused. And you stated that you can recall some memories of your mother, but you'd never met or known who your father is, is that correct?"

Kylie was nodding while one of her hands left the comfort of her lap to begin rubbing her neck, comforting or protective, Eli wasn't sure. What was undeniable was that she was leaving a bold red map of where her anxiety lay.

"So, Kylie, we are going to do some breathing together to prepare for the session and if you'd like to take off your boots, feel free." Kylie shook her head no and seemed to just be in the moment, knowing right where she was, waiting for Eli to catch up to her.

"Take a moment to silently or out loud if you'd like, set an intention. Something you'd like to be, have, or do. And then take a slow, deep breath. It should take a count of four. Ready and one, two, three, four, now hold for one, two, good now exhale for six, two, three, four ..." Eli walked her through four repetitions and he could see her visibly relax. Her shoulders dropped several inches, one of her hands slid from her lap and sat quietly by her side on the chair. "Okay, now if you feel comfortable, close your eyes and I'm going to dim the lights a little bit, too."

Kylie cleared her throat, drew another deep breath and allowed her eyes to close. "Good, now I'd like you to continue breathing at just a regular pace, whatever is comfortable for you. That's good, just keep listening to the sound of my voice and know that at any time you can stop this session because you are in complete control of it. You have more control than you realize and that is part of why FLP is so important. It gives you the power to choose your future. You couldn't control the things that happened in the past, but we aren't going there. We are going forward. Now, there are times when a client might go much further forward and visit a lifetime that's yet to come and that's okay. Don't worry if you don't recognize who or what is around you. Just trust that you are visiting a time you need to visit. Okay, so on the next breath I want you to relax twice as much as you are now. Good." Eli could see she was resisting a bit, her breaths becoming shallow, her eyelids fluttering, almost opening. He continued with the suggestions to get her to a deeper state of meditation knowing it can take up to thirty minutes with some clients.

When he suggested she could open her eyes if she wanted to, but she chose not to, and watching her lashes as he did, seeing there was not so much as a twitch, he knew she was ready.

"Kylie, I want you to see yourself in this room, safe and protected, warm and comfortable. And I want you to imagine that you have a piece of dark green velvet in your right hand."

He watched as the fingers of her right hand moved as though she was caressing something. And each time you feel uncertain or concerned, you will feel this beautiful, soft velvet and you will instantly feel better. In fact, you will feel powerful. And each time you feel this velvet, you will feel twice as powerful as you did before. So now, let's have you watch yourself as you prepare to leave this room. We are going to start our journey. Remember that I am recording this session and you don't need to worry about remembering it although you will, because you are not sleeping. You are far from sleeping, Kylie. In fact, you are wide awake, more so than at any other time in your life. So don't worry about having to speak out loud, but feel free to if you want. You have all the power, all the control.

He watched her chest rise and fall more slowly now. "Okay, let's begin. I want you to imagine that I have handed you a folded piece of paper and you are so curious what is on this paper. It's yours to look at when you are ready. Notice what's on the paper, Kylie. Whatever it is, it's what you need to read about where you are going. This was written by your future self. The best version of your wisest self, the self that has survived awful things at the hands of awful people; this is the self that is guiding you here. This is the self that you are so proud of. That self wrote what is on the paper. And I want you to head out of the room and begin this journey toward this best self in the time that is ideal for you. And I'll give you a moment to process what is written there." He watched as Kylie's other hand slid off her lap and sit, palm up, on the chair. "And now, Kylie, I want you to find yourself walking over a beautiful bridge that arches up and over a calm river and as you walk over that bridge, I want you to look around at where you are, when you are, and how you are. Look down at your feet and hands and see what you are wearing. Take a deep breath through your nose and notice any scents around you. Let them settle into your nose even if you don't recognize them now. And as you step off the bridge, I'd like you to take a walk. Just quietly walk to the place you reside here. And notice any people you see and what they are wearing. If you have any interactions with them, remember what they are and who these people are in relation to you. Remember that any time you feel concerned or scared, you just feel that velvet in your hand. Just drift now, nothing difficult to do at all. Just drift and relax."

Kylie's head leaned back slightly then, and Eli could see there was no resistance now. "Good, Kylie. Now, I want you to see yourself: whoever, whenever, and however you are. And I want you to sit with that self, whether she has the same name or another, it doesn't matter. And for the next several minutes you will sit with her and communicate, share experiences, feelings, goals, anything you want except for fear. There is no fear where you are now, only the best possible outcomes."

Eli watched as her right hand gently rubbed the invisible green velvet. Kylie sat completely still apart from that small movement. He watched the clock on the bookshelf behind her and waited. The house was so quiet, in large part to moving the kittens to the basement just before Kylie arrived. It was still much warmer than being in the hayloft, he reminded himself.

After ten minutes passed, Eli moved Kylie further. "Take a moment now to acknowledge the wisdom your future self has gained. And she gained a lot of it by being this current version of you. Nothing is wasted as you drift and float, just drift and float. Now, Kylie I wonder what would happen if you forgave each and every person who has harmed you in any way at all. I wonder if you could imagine the feeling of that weight being lifted right off your shoulders. It's gone, just like that." Eli watched as she clutched the velvet now.

"And I wonder if you could imagine what it would be like to forgive yourself, too. You know how there were times when you punished yourself for what those people did to you. The people who were supposed to protect you, well, they just didn't do their job. But your future self now completely understands why this had to happen to you. And I want you to see this future time period as one of great joy, accomplishment, and sheer wonder. And now, Kylie, I want you to look at the house you live in and notice if there is anyone there with you. What does it feel like to be there? What do you notice about how you move around there? Are there any scents or colors that you notice in particular?"

Eli watched as s smile slowly appeared on Kylie's face. It widened as a single tear rolled down her cheek. "I wonder what that feels like, to forgive the past and to just let it go and let it be a distant memory that doesn't interfere with your future thoughts or your future happiness and success. Just take all those memories and put them in a bag and tie it shut. Can you imagine now, tossing that bag off a cliff? Just let it go so you never have to see it again."

Kylie drew a deep breath but otherwise was motionless. Eli looked at the clock behind her. "And now as you prepare to leave this house and continue your journey, know that you can visit it any time. It's nice to know it's waiting for you in the future. Just let it be what it is, when and where it is. You can walk now for a bit and think about all the accomplishments that you've had between now and this future time period. Think about all the steps you took, the people who have joined you, and the feelings that got better and better as you moved away from the feelings of being tethered to your past and the people who didn't appreciate who and what you are. They are no longer a part of your existence. You are whole, happy, healthy, and incredibly grateful for your experiences—all of them."

Eli saw her hand move and thought she was going to feel the green velvet fabric, but she didn't. Eli nodded and smiled his own knowing smile. "Now Kylie, I wonder if you can imagine that when we are done with this life-changing journey today, that you feel refreshed and excited about not only your future but also your life as it is today. You will magnetize yourself toward this ideal self and trust every single step of the process even on the days it doesn't feel so good. You have a deep, deep knowing that life is a series of ups and downs, but that it is a very beautiful thing. You have a deep appreciation for this ability to survive and turn something dark into light. Knowing that you are heading in a direction that your own future self has already walked, you rest assured that you will get there in your own time." Eli looked out the window and saw that Hope was arriving to feed the ponies in her new sweatshirt and wondered if he should have bought her a coat.

"Kylie, we are going to finish our work for today by walking back toward the bridge over the river. It's just as safe as it was before. And just as you get to the arch on top of the bridge, look down at your hands and feet. I wonder if there is anything different there. As you walk back toward this room, you do not need to say good-bye to your future self. She is you and she has wisdom that will speak to you if you allow it. And as I count the last ten steps of today's journey you are going to start to come back up toward your awareness of being here in this office with me. With each step, you will feel more and more awake, refreshed, and excited about your current life and your future one. Ten, feeling excited and happy, nine, feeling grateful and enthusiastic, eight, seven, six, feeling like you've just had a great night's sleep. Five, four, three, feeling full of wisdom, two, feeling powerful and courageous, and one, fully aware, awake, and refreshed." Eli watched as she began to shift in the chair. "No hurry, but when you are ready to, you can open your eyes, wiggle your fingers and toes and feel fully grounded here in the office."

Kylie took a deep breath as she opened her eyes, blinked, and looked around. She rubbed the tops of her thighs and smiled. Eli smiled back and said, "Welcome back."

She giggled nervously. "Uh, that was pretty wild," as she stretched her arms and legs out in front of her. "I can't even believe what I saw."

Eli moved the recorder closer to her, "So now we will go through what you experienced. I'll be taking notes but it's all being recorded so you can repeat this session at home. Okay, so I'll let you start when you're ready and just tell me everything. It's important to give me as many details as you can."

She raised her eyebrows and exhaled, nodding. "Okay. Well, I don't even know what to say except I hope I wasn't just making this up. But I mean, it didn't feel made up because seriously, this wasn't anything I would just think up randomly. So, as soon as I walked over the bridge, I could feel something happening. It was like the layers of bullshit just started to fall off and I could feel it. It was weird. And once I was over the bridge, I could tell I wasn't around here anymore. It was more like desert, like the red cliffs. Is that New Mexico, Arizona? I don't know but somewhere out there, And I lived in a cool house with huge windows that looked out on the desert. I was in my office. I worked from home and I think I was a writer or something. My husband is a real estate developer." She laughed then, not realizing how out of character it was for her to laugh. Eli laughed, too.

"This is great. So your office is at home, way to go. I highly recommend that."

She laughed again. "So when I left my office, there was a little girl there in the hallway. I picked her up and she was so cute, sucking her thumb. She put her head on my shoulder and I could feel her breath on my cheek. I know this was my daughter and honestly I feel like crying right now because I feel like I left her there to come back here."

"That's okay, that's to come. She isn't there yet. There's a saying, Kylie. 'What's meant for you won't pass you by.' And so just trust it all. Trust the process. You're doing great."

Kylie looked up over Eli's shoulder and continued, "There

was a whole wall of glass in my bedroom. It was awesome. There were two yoga mats there and the bedroom was so beautiful, like something on Pinterest. I'm not sure what work I am doing but I think I'm writing about how people can change their own lives without having to go through all the garbage first. I just got that feeling. And this man, my husband, he actually was someone whose life I helped change. I think I'm like, a life coach or something. I'm not sure but my husband is so hot!"

Eli smiled at the very nonchalant way she was describing the man she marries as if she would expect nothing less than hot. "And how did you feel in the house?"

She looked at Eli then. He could see something had clicked or was at least in the clicking process. "For the first time in my life I felt peaceful but also, like, powerful. Is that possible?"

Eli nodded. "I do fully believe that is completely possible. And I do believe you are going to feel exactly that."

"You know something, Dr. Cranston? I didn't think I was even going to be able to get my mind calm enough to do this. But it was so real. And you know how I know?"

He sat still and waited. She sat up and shook her head, sending her bangs scattering back and forth like palm fronds. "There were things I would never imagine for myself, like my current self wouldn't choose the southwest or a man with no tattoos. But I was rocking it!"

Eli's head tilted back then and his laugh made her smile. "Of course, you were. I'd expect nothing less for you. So, do you remember at the beginning of the journey when you picked up the piece of paper?" He wasn't sure she would because some people aren't deep enough at that point. Or if they do remember, they don't see anything on the paper because they are still using their thinking brain, not their subconscious.

Kylie looked down then, her hands finding each other in the center of her lap. "Yea, it was my handwriting, but I've never seen this before, what was written, I mean. It said, 'A person is so much more than the sum of their tragedies, whatever they might be.' I think maybe that's the title of my book or whatever it is I write about. It was weird. The paper turned into a key and ..." She shook her head.

"And what? It's okay. It's all important." He was still taking notes and watching her at the same time.

"The key went—" She shifted nervously. "It went into my heart. It's like it just unlocked it. And all this stuff. It was gross, it just all came out. Like weird words and colors, sounds, feelings. It just all gushed out."

"Wow, that's pretty significant, don't you think?" Eli sat forward, not wanting her to feel that what she was saying was being judged. Inside, Eli was dancing and high-fiving Kylie's higher self.

"Yea, it felt pretty significant. It was like a pressure I didn't even know was there was just gone. Like I could finally take a big breath."

"Awesome, that's just awesome, Kylie." Eli looked at the clock again.

"So umm, when you were coming back over the bridge, and I asked you to look at your hands and feet. Did you notice anything different from when you looked at them on the way over the bridge the first time?"

Kylie looked down then and turned her hands over and back again. "Yea."

He waited, pen in hand.

"The chains were gone."

36

"Hey fella, what's cookin'?" Clem stepped into the house and wiped his boots on the doormat. "It's sure a cold one."

"Hi Clem! How are you feeling? Flu knocked you back a bit, huh?"

"Ayuh—sure did. That stuff can kill ya. Wasn't sure if I was gonna make it or you were gonna need'a find a new cahpentah."

Eli wasn't sure if he was kidding but from the look of Clem, it seemed he'd lost a few pounds. "Coffee?" Eli had just finished his and was getting ready to run errands.

"Nah, not now. Gotta run to the lumbah yahd an' get more two by fahs and some other stuff. Just wanted to go measure that wall again. I swear it grows and shrinks every time I'm up there."

"How much should I leave you for materials?" Eli knew Clem wasn't going to ask for the money, which he didn't understand one bit. But there was a pride a man like Clem had and an eagerness to please. "Oh, I think a buck'n a half oughta do it, fella."

Eli checked on the kittens in the bathroom where he felt they were safest and out of the way when clients or Clem were in the house. One was climbing the shower curtain, one was jumping off the baseboard heater onto another's head. Bumblebee, however, had earned her freedom, her babies fully weaned. She was spread out on Eli's pillow in his room and enjoying her current situation in life.

Eli gently pet the bridge of her nose while she purred. He took the cash out of his nightstand drawer and as he did, he heard the gate under his window creak as it closed. He moved the blue curtain and looked out to see Hope walking up to the barn, hands over her face. Eli's heart picked up speed a little.

"There you are, Clem. There's a few extra for gas money in there. I have to get going, but just leave the door unlocked in case I'm not back when you get here."

Eli slipped into his boots and jacket, started his truck with the remote starter and headed up to the barn. Hope only feeds the ponies at night but occasionally she spent time there during the day. Eli guessed it was out of boredom when she wasn't at school, but he also guessed there wasn't a lot of stimulating company at home on the weekends either. He made note of the nearly impassable path and walked through the snow to avoid the ice. "Got to pick up some salt.

He stepped into the barn and didn't see Hope right away. He turned to look in the stall. Empty. The ponies were out in the pasture kicking up snow and biting each other, their squeals could probably be heard a mile away by Eli's estimation. He took a step toward the feed room but stopped when he heard the sound of a muffled sob. His heart ticked up a level again. The sound of a footfall in the loft reached his ears. He moved the broom and the pitchfork that sat on hooks by the door so that she would know he was there. He didn't want to startle her. "I better toss a couple of bales down while it's light." He said it loudly enough that she'd hear it but tried to sound as though he was talking to himself. He added a workaday whistle for effect as he ascended the stairs to the loft. He didn't need to turn on the light; the loft owed its natural lighting to the giant windows on either side of the loft doors.

There on the new delivery of hay, sat Hope, hands still covering her face; her ponytail and yellow sweatshirt the only cheery things about her. Her shoulders shook as she cried.

"Hey, Hope. I thought I saw you coming through the gate. Are you okay?" He waited. The silence was broken by a sound that Eli could only describe as heartbreaking. He could feel the sadness fill the space between them.

A cold blast of memories hit him in the chest, then. Memories of an inconsolable girl: Gracie losing her first tooth in a hotdog and realizing she had swallowed it, Grace finding her hamster dead in its cage; Grace looking at him and screaming, "Daddy, do something! You can't let them do this to me!"

He took a breath and one step further into the loft. He was about to ask Hope again if she was okay, but her voice came through the cold air then, "Yes." She sniffled and wiped her nose with the back of her hand; Eli reached into his coat to the zippered pocket and pulled out a Dunkin Donut's napkin. He walked closer and held it out to her. Her delicate hand reached out and took it from him. Eli stepped back again, not wanting to frighten her. *A fawn,* he thought. She reminded him of a small fawn.

"Can I help with anything, Hope? I mean, you can tell me if something is wrong. I might be able to help, you know."

She shook her head and sent her ponytail in motion. He could see she had been crying for a while, her eyes and nose bright pink in the cold.

"Well, if I can help in any way, just let me know. Or if you want to talk, I bought better marshmallows for the cocoa." He turned to walk back down the stairs.

"My mother almost died."

Eli stopped and took a breath before responding.

"That's awful, Hope. I'm sorry. What happened to your mom?" He didn't turn back toward her. He knew she was more comfortable talking to his back. He could feel it.

"She just has problems. And, I don't know what happened. But she's in the hospital and my father says we can't afford for her to be there and we might have to move." The sob came again, telling the story of a sadness no child should have to know.

Eli's thoughts were racing and his emotions were trying to dictate how he would respond. He centered himself and drew on his training.

"Well, Hope, there's probably a way for your mom to get

some help if she doesn't have insurance. I'm sure there is, in fact. Would you like me to talk to your dad? I've been wanting to meet him anyway."

Hope shook her head no. "It won't help. He won't listen. He doesn't listen to anyone." Eli recognized the black and white thinking and the desperation.

"Hope, sometimes people are angry and they think no one can help them but it's not always true. Maybe we could talk to him together sometime, if you think that would be okay."

She stood up from the hay and finished wiping her nose. "Okay. Maybe."

Eli smiled then. "Okay, good." He walked slowly down the stairs toward the bright late morning sun and turned to see Hope at the top.

"Hey, you know, I'm going to run some errands and I'm bringing back pizza for lunch. Clem eats like a horse and I think he hasn't finished the upstairs because he likes all the lunches I buy for him." He watched as the shy smile spread across her innocent face.

"What's your favorite pizza?" He knew she wouldn't accept an outright offer.

"Umm, pepperoni." She was still smiling.

"Mine, too! Okay then, 12:30. Pizza party at 9 Ogden Point Road. And maybe you can help me figure out who needs kittens. The crazies are ready to go!"

He walked out into the sunshine and heard Hope coming down the stairs now.

Still facing toward the back of his house, Eli looked over his shoulder and said, "You know, Hope. You're going to be okay. In fact, you're going to be better than okay."

37

"Well, where is she then, Tig?" Eli was still holding his suit jacket and files.

Antigone's arms were up over her head as she lashed out in frustration.

"Eli! I don't know where she is! For God's sake, that's why I'm freaking out!"

"Okay, well I assume you called Brit?" Eli stood, helpless, in front of the woman he married, but it seemed he hadn't really seen that Antigone in a few years.

"Oh my God, Eli. I told you, I've called Brit, her mother, her father's office. No one has seen her. The school said she was there today. She's not answering texts and calls go straight to voicemail. Something is wrong!"

Eli looked around at the house as if he expected there to be a teleprompter somewhere with what he ought to say. When she was like this, there was nothing he could say that would be satisfactory.

"And I'm not so sure Brit is the best influence on our daughter, Eli. There is something about that girl I do not like. And I wouldn't trust her as far as I could throw her."

Eli didn't open his mouth but he'd felt that way about Brit since the girls were in sixth grade together. And though at one point he came to realize who her father was, he never mentioned it to anyone. When he made the connection between Rob's elitist behavior and the aggressive phone call long ago about an obviously distressed doctor who assaulted an unconscious patient, he knew who and what he was dealing with. He was never entirely sure, however, if Rob knew that Eli was the lawyer he had spoken to. "Tig, let me call Rob's office and I'll leave a message."

He turned away as if by doing so he wouldn't hear Antigone angrily telling him she already did exactly that.

"Hi, I need to speak to Dr. Williston. It's Eli Cranston, our daughters are friends, and we are looking for Grace and hoped Rob might be able to get ahold of Brit to ask her where she might be. Okay, great. Thank you. Please let him know it's urgent."

He put the phone down and didn't dare look at Antigone. He sat at the kitchen island, picked up the mail which seemed like a calm thing to do, thumbing through the Horchow catalog while Antigone opened a bottle of wine. Before she could pour a full glass, Eli's phone buzzed. "Hello? Hey Rob, thanks for getting back to me. Yea, I just got home and Antigone told me Gracie hasn't been home. I was wondering if she's with Brit, or—" Antigone's arms were up over her head again. Eli turned away to continue. "Okay, yea I'd appreciate it. I don't know what's up with her, but she isn't home as much as she used to be. I know, yea, they are getting older. I wonder if she's at your house as much as she tells us? Yea, I mean, I just wonder. Okay. Great. Thanks, Rob."

Antigone was pouring her second glass of wine when Eli turned back toward her. And before either could say anything, Grace came through the mudroom door from the garage. She stopped when she saw them, swaying on her feet.

"Grace! Where the hell have you been? Why didn't you answer my calls!" Antigone exploded in a way Eli wasn't sure was completely warranted. He put his hand up to her. "Tig, let me."

"Let *you!*? Let you *what*?"

Eli ignored her and looked closer at Grace, sunglasses still on. "Grace, your mother asked you where you were." He waited and watched as Grace swayed and took a step backward.

"Come here, Grace, and take the glasses off." Eli rolled up his shirtsleeves, waiting. Grace came closer and Eli could smell the less-than-pleasant combination of something burnt mixed with perfume, definitely high end. "Gracie, Honey. What is that smell?"

She rolled her eyes at him, but he couldn't see that with her glasses still in place. "Dad."

Eli shrugged, waiting for more. "Dad. I mean c'mon. Brit was smoking in the car."

"Don't lie, Gracie. You're just going to make it all worse for yourself. Now, tell me where you were and who you were with." He felt like he was cross-examining a witness in a courtroom.

"I don't need this bullshit. *You're* never home and now suddenly because *I'm* a little late, you rush home. We all know you don't want to be here. You don't love Mom and you don't love me. You love work! And Mom is too obsessed with her phone and her stupid commission splits to know what the fuck is going on in anyone's life. And it's *me* you're questioning? You two are friggin' ridiculous. I hate it here and I can't wait to be out!" Her voice was cracking and Eli wasn't the only one who noticed the cadence in her voice wasn't quite right.

Antigone came from behind Eli then, wound tighter than an eight-day clock as her father always said. "What the hell is wrong with you, Grace? How could you say those things? What are you *on*? Did you take my pills again? *Did you*?!"

She grabbed Grace's bare, tanned upper arm and pulled her closer. Grace tried to wrest it back into her control to no avail. All at once, Eli was pulling Antigone backward, as Antigone pulled Grace. Together they were a lunatic carousel, spinning madly out of the Parisian kitchen of their dream home that Antigone, just that morning, assessed at 3.2 as they say in certain circles.

Eli's phone buzzed on the island and if anyone heard it, an onlooker would never have known for the molten disgrace that had erupted, sweeping them into the living room, the spot the Christmas tree would stand in a few weeks; the same spot where Eli broke the news to Antigone that this was their new home thirteen years before.

Antigone reached for Grace's sunglasses and pulled them off her face as Grace fell backward, her purse vomiting its contents onto the marble floor. It was as though someone had reached out and hit the safety switch on the carnival ride, the horses continuing their momentum and throwing their riders to the floor.

Eli stumbled but caught himself, jumping over Antigone so as not to fall on top of her. He stared at the floor, not comprehending it all at first. Dozens of twenty-dollar bills, a few hundreds, two cell phones; the only sound was the dozens of pills, tick, tick, ticking on the cool stone and scurrying like termites to the farthest spot they could reach.

Grace pulled herself up, yelling that she was going to move out if they kept treating her like a child. Antigone, sobbing and holding her quickly swelling wrist looked up, stunned at the daughter she had seen, until this moment, as absolutely perfect. "How? I don't understand. Why? Where did these pills—"

Eli helped her up. He pointed toward the staircase, his face red, teeth clenched. "Go! Now!" he shouted at Grace who laughed, "You two are so messed up."

38

Eli opened the door to Rosalie's Pizza, the bells above the door announcing his arrival. He was greeted with the sweet aroma of garlic, peppers, and onions. There was a table of tween girls giggling and taking selfies, clearly trying to capture the man trying to eat his pizza in peace in the adjacent booth.

He stood behind a woman picking up sandwiches and looked at the menu. He was hungry and knew he should not have gone grocery shopping in that state, never mind walk into a delicious-smelling pizza joint. The gentleman behind the register greeted him with a smile he imagined he greeted all customers with, but Eli chose to feel it was genuinely for him.

"Hi, I think we're going to go with a medium pepperoni, a medium mushroom, pepper, and onion, and a medium Rosie's special."

He heard the bells jingle again as he reached for his cash.

The man handed him his change and receipt. "About 15 minutes."

Eli turned to find a seat and ran right into Rebecca's heart-warming smile and shy eyes. Nervous and off guard, he fumbled with his change. "Hi, Rebecca. How are—" He dropped a quarter and his receipt but Rebecca was already scooping it up. He said, "Oh, thanks, how are you?"

"Good! Busy but good."

Eli moved out of her way so she could get to the register. "Hi. Order for Treadway." She turned back to Eli and smiled.

She took her order and walked to the booth where Eli sat.

He straightened up, "Have a seat, or are you in a hurry?"

"No hurry. It's January. I'm busy but January is a slow time on the farm. Fine by me actually, the holidays are so busy, it's nice to have a break for a little bit."

Eli found himself hearing but not listening. He blurted out, "Would you like to go out for dinner next weekend?"

Rebecca froze, her hands betraying her cool exterior, crinkling the paper her sandwich was sitting in. "Uh, yea. Yes, sure. I'd like that."

"Okay, then. Perfect. I figure by spring you'll be too busy with the farm, you won't have any time for anything but, farm ... stuff?"

Her eyes wrinkled at the outside just slightly as she laughed. "Yea, there's a lot of that in the spring."

"So um, on a serious note, I want to get your advice on something."

Just then her phone buzzed and she was momentarily distracted. "Sure."

"Good. I'll ask you next weekend. When I see you. At dinner. Because you agreed to have dinner. With me."

It felt good to be relaxed, silly, even.

Rebecca let out a laugh. "You are something."

Eli watched Rebecca walk out to her van and drive away. "Sir, your pizzas are ready." Eli jumped, pulled out of his reverie. He smiled at the woman with his boxes. He glanced at her name tag and said, "Thank you, Annie." He stopped for a split second, then shook his head as he walked out to his truck.

He arrived home to see the upstairs window was open. Clem tossed out a few scrap pieces of two by four and old carpet. Eli took the hot pizzas off the passenger seat, which no matter how much time went by, reminded him of Gracie. She used to hold the pizza box on her lap when she was little. "It's too hot," she used to say but then refused to let Eli put it in the back seat. Eli said, "That girl loved her pizza." He walked into the house and placed the pizzas on the kitchen table. "Clem! Lunch!"

Eli heard a shuffle upstairs then, "Two minutes, fella!"

Out the kitchen window, Eli could see a cloud of dust being swept out of the barn as Hope put her time to good use. He texted her: "Pizza is here! Come on in."

For the first time in almost a decade, Eli was having lunch with people who felt like family. It was not a feeling lost on him. He pulled out plates, napkins, and glasses. Clem came lumbering down the steps and sat at the table, "I'm stahvin.'"

Then came Hope, quietly through the back door into the kitchen. Eli opened the boxes on the countertop and said, "Help yourself, everyone." He turned to see Hope and Clem looking at each other. "Uh, Clem, have you met Hope, my horse wrangler?" He looked at Clem, confused. Suddenly Clem seemed to come to life, "Hi-ya, young lady. C'mon in."

Hope hung back by the counter and quietly said, "Hi, Mr. LaFrance." Eli was surprised she knew Clem's last name but reminded himself that he himself was the new guy in town, not them.

Hope sat at the table and seemed nervous, which didn't entirely surprise Eli. He opened his laptop and put on some Top-40 music to ease the tension. "So Hope, what on earth am I going to do with those five kittens of ours?"

Hope's eyes lowered to her pepperoni and her smile spoke volumes.

"Well, I think Rebecca wants one. And I told my science teacher and she said she would definitely take two. Her cat just died."

"Whoa, wait a minute. First, how did the cat die? And second, is she going to use them for a science lab or something?" This set them all laughing, and the tension, if that was what Eli detected, slowly dissipated.

"She's wicked nice. They would have a really good home with her."

"Okay, that leaves us with two. I was thinking if Bumblebee stays, maybe one of her kittens should stay, too. So that leaves us with just one who needs a home."

Eli could see that Hope was swinging her leg nervously as she sat on the kitchen chair. She glanced up at him and quickly back down. "I'll take one if ...."

Clem spoke up, "There ya go, fella. Done."

Eli winked at Clem. "Done."

39

"Daddy! I'm right here! Why won't you look at me!?" Eli was looking right at her but he didn't see Grace. He was still searching for her but no matter what he did, he just couldn't see his little girl. He rubbed at his eyes but it only made his vision worse. He tried to dial 9-1-1 but hit the wrong keys over and over.

"Grace! I'm looking for Grace Cranston. Have you seen her? Please, Grace Cranston, she's my daughter. She's 5'6", brunette. She's a good girl. Gracie! Gracie are you here?" He pushed past the people in his way, while they laughed at him, tripping and falling onto the ground. He heard a voice behind him, "Gracie Macie Puddin'n pie. You are the apple of your Mommy's eye!"

Eli turned to face Antigone but it wasn't her. It wasn't anyone. It was just darkness. He frantically turned back and now it was all dark. "Gracie! I'm so sorry. Daddy is so sorry."

One day, when all is said and done, I hope you'll let me tell you my side of the story. You will never know how much I love you.

Eli had agonized for twenty minutes about what to write and wasn't thrilled with what he came up with but it was something. He signed the birthday card, slid it into the envelope and brought it out to the mailbox while his truck was warming up.

The barn was quiet when Eli went to check that the stall door was secure and also planned to hand Hope her week's pay directly. The ponies were quietly eating their hay as the sun was, as it did that time of year, setting early and fast. Thinking he might have missed Hope, he prepared to leave when he heard the creaking of the cabinet in the feed room. He peered through the glass and saw Grace putting her envelope of money back under the sink and pushing a bucket in front of it. He backed away and waited for her to come back into the barn.

"Oh, hi Eli. Ponies are fed." Hope tucked what Eli assumed was money into her pocket. "Hey there—just wanted to pay you in person this time." Eli waited for her to look up which eventually she did. He handed her two twenties and said, "What does an eleven-year-old girl spend all this money on anyway?"

That sweet, shy smile appeared on Hope's face as she flashed her innocent green eyes briefly at him. "I don't really spend money much. I like saving it mostly." Her wistful way made Eli want to shake her and tell her it was okay to relax and have fun, that she was only eleven for God's sake. But Eli was becoming more aware that Hope's life wasn't what he imagined most eleven year olds experienced.

"I get that. That's the responsible thing to do. Are you saving for anything in particular?" Hope kicked at the dirt in front of the ponies' stall. "Well, um," she giggled. "Someday I want my own horse." She looked up at Eli then to see what he thought.

"What? These crazies aren't good enough for you? Geez." He put his hands on his hips for effect. Hope laughed at his sarcasm and reached over the stall door to play with Smudge's mane.

"No. I love them so much. I just always wanted my own horse and I like to ride."

"Oh, I see. Rebecca said you ride her horse. What's his name, Paprika or something like that?"

"Haha, no it's Cayenne!" Hope was more relaxed around Eli now and her laugh was good for his soul.

"Oh, by the way, if you need a safe place to keep your money, I can put a safe up in the loft. I have one in the house I don't use. You can have both keys." He put his hands in the air as if a cop had shouted to do so.

Hope took a deep breath. "It's okay. I've kinda been keeping it here. Most of it. I leave it under the sink." She pointed to the feed room, still drawing designs in the dirt.

"Yea, I saw it when I needed the box that was in there. Was

wondering if you were running a business—selling my hay or something."

Hope didn't know what to say and Eli thought his ribbing might have been too much.

"Hey, I'm just teasing. But I was wondering why you didn't take it home with you."

"Well, sometimes—" Hope's quiet voice trailed off. "Sometimes my mother asks me for money and if it isn't at home then I don't have to lie to her."

Eli noticed her bottom lip quivering. If it was a therapy session, he'd push a little but it wasn't, so he pulled back. "Oh, I totally get it. And anyway, you earned it. It's all yours. Your mom probably understands that."

Hope looked at him, wanting him to understand. "It's not that I won't share, it's just ...."

Hope's little shoulders fell then and Eli could feel the angst but wasn't sure what, if anything, he could do about it. *I gave Grace everything and looked what happened.*

Feeling he had her trust, at least a little bit, he was satisfied.

"Well, I'm meeting Rebecca for dinner but maybe tomorrow we can get your kitten ready to go home. What do you think?"

"I think that would be awesome." She lifted her face, her eyes just one wrong word or gesture away from spilling the tears that balanced on her waterline like tiny ballerinas.

40

Winter and spring had a strange courtship in New England. Through the lens of Eli's therapist mindset, if hard-pressed to describe it, he'd say it was passive aggressive at best and at worst, downright abusive.

"Now I understand what everyone was complaining about," he told the woman at the RiteAid counter.

"Ay-uh, wintah's a bitch around he-ah. And just wait, mud season's comin' and we know what that brings."

Eli felt out of place because he had no idea what she meant. The woman in line behind him spoke up. "Blackfly season."

Both women laughed and Eli decided he didn't want to hear anymore. He was just happy there was more sunlight and less snow.

He paid for two Easter cards and some TicTacs and walked out into the sun. There was something about spring that suddenly made everything okay.

Eli's phone buzzed with an email notification. He contemplated turning off notifications for email but sometimes even in crisis, a client will email rather than call. He couldn't have been more surprised albeit happy to see it was from Kate.

Dr. Cranston—Let me first say I am so sorry to not be in touch. I was in a very bad place and I know I shouldn't blow off everything but I did. I wish it was different. Anyways, if you have an opening, I really need to talk to you. Any time and day or night works for me.

-Kate

Eli inhaled deeply and on the exhale said, "Kate. What am I going to do with you?"

He started his truck and pulled onto the street toward home thinking about the upcoming gathering at Rebecca's farm. She invited him, Hope, Clem and her three employees for Easter dinner. He had no idea what to contribute besides a card but thought he'd bring some flowers at least. He had over a week to think about it. And if he was honest with himself, Rebecca was all he thought about when not working.

He pulled into the gas station to fill up and as he waited for the attendant his phone buzzed again, this time with a text: **Eli— Ink cut his leg on something. It's not that bad but do you have any bandages and betadine? I don't see any in the cabinet.**

Not knowing what betadine is or what sort of bandage one might use on a horse, he skipped the text and called Hope.

"Hey there—is it a deep cut? Oh good. Umm, honestly, I don't even have Band-Aids in the house. Where do you get horse bandages? Oh okay, umm, I have peroxide. Oh, you can't? Huh ... I'm useless, I guess. Okay, Salsbury? Yea, that's where I get their grain. Yes. Want to take a drive with me? Okay I'll be back there in a little bit. Bye."

Eli pulled in and saw Hope sitting on the bench on the front porch. He thought someday she would make a very responsible, punctual, and dedicated employee. Then he reminded himself she already was.

He waved to her as she trotted to the passenger side and pulled herself up into the truck. "Hi."

Eli smiled and said, "You know, those ponies are more trouble than they're worth."

Hope shot him a concerned glance but saw Eli's expression, the one she had grown to appreciate as lighthearted, something she didn't have much experience with.

The ride to the feed store was only fifteen minutes but the pair covered everything from growing kitten antics to weather, the business of blackflies—"the state bird, my history teacher calls them"—and Easter dinner in addition to why you don't ever want to use hydrogen peroxide on horse flesh.

They pulled in at the hardware/feed store. Eli followed Hope in, as she told him she knew exactly where the first aid items would be. True to her word, she led him straight to the vet wrap, betadine, gauze, and many other items Eli never knew existed.

"Okay, do I dare ask if we should get anything else while we're here?" Eli squinted at her as if he were in pain. Hope nodded and walked to the next aisle. She picked up an Ivermectin tube and also a Zimecterin Gold. Eli tilted his head while looking at the latter. Hope looked at him as a teacher does with a student who simply doesn't retain info he's been taught time and again. "Regular dewormer and tapeworms."

"Say no more." He followed her to the counter. He spied, sitting next to the register, a small display of gourmet, locally made chocolate bars. He placed two of them next to the ponies' medical regimen. Hope looked up at him and said, "Those are $3 *each*.

Eli said, "Overtime pay. "

Hope was chatting, between bites of chocolate, about her science class and explaining how her teacher shared picture updates with her on the kittens and how some of the other students have been talking to her more now, which she said is, "okay but is annoying sometimes." Eli tried hard to not pretend it was Grace in the seat next to him.

He sometimes questioned if he was trying hard to heal from his wounds or if in fact he was still on the run from them. *You can't get much farther away unless you leave the country,* he had often thought on the tougher days.

Hope was talking about school lunch when they rounded the corner from Mount Desert Street to Main when Eli spotted a cruiser and a fire department ambulance. He slowed as he approached the line of cars in front of them that were being directed to wait as another cruiser came through. Eli was trying to see what had happened since there were no vehicles, no bicycles in view, just emergency personnel. They inched forward and Eli could feel the worry in Hope's voice, "What happened?"

"Not sure." Eli moved forward then, slowly. He saw the medic who had been crouched down begin to stand and step over the person on the ground. Before he could ascertain what might have happened, Hope opened the truck door and screamed, "No no no!"

Eli hit his breaks, heart thumping hard in his chest, "Oh my God, Hope—wait!"

She was out of the truck and running before he could finish.

He heard the officer tell her not to come closer and one of the medics shouted to him to keep her back.

Eli pulled his truck over, threw the transmission into park and jumped out. Hope had made it to the woman's prostrate body on the sand-covered pavement while the medic administered the second dose of Narcan into her nose. Eli's thoughts and heart were competing for attention. His approach got as far as the police officer's outstretched hand. He watched as the arriving officer pulled Hope back and tried to comfort her. Eli looked down at the woman. His mind slipped and stammered and like a greased pole, couldn't grasp how this woman and Hope could possibly be connected. And though she wasn't wearing the parka, he recognized her Uggs. The realization slammed into him like a car on an ice-covered highway, no chance of stopping. He looked at Hope as she sobbed and pleaded, "Mom, please be okay, Mommy, please wake up. Mom, *please!*"

41

"Hey, Kate. How are you?" Eli could see she wasn't in the same spot as she had been when they had their last session. Where are you now?"

"Hi Dr. Cranston, I'm at New Horizons, been here for a few months. Got three to go."

"Good, Kate. That's a good place and one where you can really get a handle on this. You've never done a full nine-month program with follow-up care."

"Yea, I feel good about it. I actually talked to my mom, no word of a lie."

"Wow, that's a step and a half. Do you want to start there today?"

Kate shifted in her seat, which appeared to be in an office at the rehab. "No, not really. It was good though."

"Okay, well where shall we begin?" Eli was looking at the date of their last session—just before Christmas. Kate was telling someone she needed the room for an hour and why.

Eli flipped through her paperwork. Her first FLP session with Eli was 2016, following months of talk therapy and EMDR. She was one of his first clients after all his post-doctoral work, internships, and licensing. His eye fell on a sentence, partially covered by an insurance document. ... *your daughters and grandson are there* ... Eli's arms tingled as the hairs stood on end. He pulled that page and several others out of her folder and set them aside next to his desktop.

He focused his attention when he heard Kate say something about a squirrel.

"What? Hold on Kate, I didn't hear you, what did you say?"

"I said, I'm like a freaking squirrel. I'm all over the place, can't sleep, can't concentrate or finish a sentence and it's really hard to like, function. Oh and do you remember when I told you about Rory? Yeah, he's here, too, small freakin' world. We used to turn up together all the time and now, we're rehabbin' together. And there's a therapist here who just completely sucks. She's such a—"

"Hold up, Kate. One thought at a time. Do you remember a long time ago when I mentioned ADD to you? Attention Deficit?" Kate stopped for a long moment and then she was animated again, shifting in her chair, tapping her vape on the desk, pulling her hair up into a ponytail and down again. "Yea, I remember, why?"

Eli bit the inside corner of his mouth, which he could see, in the small split screen of himself, was barely noticeable. He had learned to do this to keep from laughing when in fact a client said something unknowingly outrageous.

After the session ended and Kate promised to keep their appointment the following week, Eli rubbed his eyes. He focused on the screen but the words were still blurry.

He went out to the kitchen and pulled out the remaining chicken parm that Rebecca had brought over the night before and put it into the microwave. He checked his phone and was relieved there was nothing but the time staring at him.

When the microwave had turned his dinner into a molten volcano, he decided to let it cool off for a bit. He poured food into Bumblebee and Honey's bowl and turned to find they were already there waiting. He watched as Honey face-planted right into her dinner, Bumblebee pushing her ridiculous daughter to the side so she could get closer. Mother and daughter happy as can be.

Eli remembered the paperwork he'd set aside and went to retrieve it from his office. He sat at his desk and picked up the pages from over three years ago. It was an FLP session with Kate. He remembered wondering if it was working with her or if he'd have to try again another time. She said some things that seemed odd or that couldn't be true. Later, he changed the wording of his induction and added a few more cues to get her to a deeper state of hypnotic suggestion. He did a second session with her a month later with the same results. Tabling the FLP, he continued working with her but decided that talk therapy would probably be the best course for her. And having success later, with other clients using FLP going forward, he thought it was simply the improved succession of steps.

Sitting back with the notes now, he saw: August 2015—Possible FLP? Kate indicated she might be open to trying it but is showing signs of mania. Will need to manage that first.

He flipped through two pages of notes on her outpatient methadone treatment and continuing therapy sessions until he got to January 2016.

FLP session #1 Kate Cromwell DOB 3/27/1997 age 21.

He skimmed through the specifics of the suggestions he included in his notes. He always kept a copy of the recordings but he preferred notes. Sometimes a client spoke throughout the session, which he could go back and review in the recording if he needed to supplement his notes; but if he learned one thing in law school, it was to take very clear notes all day, every day.

On the fourth page, he found in his notes what had caught his attention earlier:

Kate indicates her future life includes working as a registered nurse and also teaching at a local college. She indicates that she continued to improve her life once her father passed away. She feels that the best revenge is to live a good life.

She describes her wedding in the following manner:

I'm marrying the best guy in the world—Ryan. He looks at me like I'm made of gold and caffeine and Netflix. We met at an airport when I was going home for my father's funeral. He was meeting friends from college after finishing a residency. We lived on opposite coasts but we knew were supposed to be together. Eventually we moved to Colorado but for a little while I moved to the East Coast to be with him. And we got married on a farm out there. It's the beginning of the fall and so beautiful. And believe it or not, Dr. Cranston, you're there??

Eli had added two question marks and continued his notes:

You look mostly the same but your hair is a little more grey but not much and you have glasses.

Kate is humming and trying to describe a nursery rhyme. Little house, back house, barn.

Your wife and your daughters are there and your little grandson. It's a perfect day and it's like coming full circle in a way. I started on a farm out in Colorado before moving to L.A. when I was sixteen. And I know that I continued to struggle after we worked together, Dr. Cranston. But I wasn't ready to take responsibility until I got scared and stayed in a program.

Eli's notes included: Client seems to be dreaming/fantasizing.

Look at script and suggestions. Implement deeper state of hypnosis in next session.

Eli's stomach grumbled, reminding him of his dinner and that he'd ruin it if he reheated it a second time.

He put the notes back into the folder marked Kate Cromwell and went back to the kitchen.

The cats had finished their dinner and had made their way to Eli's bed for the night.

Eli ate as he scrolled through his phone, looking, but not sure for what.

42

The end of the summer saw Eli taking more time away from his office and spending it with Rebecca. He enjoyed helping her prepare items for the farmer's market, which was still in full swing and would be through October. He also caught up with finding a doctor, dentist, and a barber he liked.

Hope was at the barn every day, working on training Ink and Smudge to pull a small cart she found on Craig's List. She purchased bridles and bits of harnesses and pieced together one that worked. The ponies were feisty but peppermint-motivated and if Eli hadn't seen it with his own eyes, he wouldn't have believed what she had gotten them to do.

With her mother living in a recovery home, Hope was more relaxed, the burden of worry lifted from her little, yet strong, shoulders, and riding Cayenne while Eli worked alongside Rebecca on weekends was one of her greatest joys.

"So Becca, I was thinking. For Thanksgiving this year, maybe we can ask Otto and Elise to join us here at the farm? This will be the first year none of their kids can make it. What do you say?"

"I love it! The more the merrier. I've been wanting to meet them. Hey, any word on Clem?" She smiled now with what Eli would consider women's intuition: a knowing without proof until the proof reveals itself.

"No, the old guy's been pretty tight-lipped. I wish he'd spill, it. The suspense is killing me."

"Well, maybe we will get to meet her at Thanksgiving."

Eli still couldn't believe he'd been here a year, often marveling at all the things that had changed since that day he arrived, three days before the closing on the cottage. There was too much time for him at the hotel, waiting. He wasn't a patient waiter. He knew he wanted a dog, for company if nothing else. Finding several animal rescue organizations, he chose the closest one and checked out their pets for adoption.

When he arrived at the Second Chance Rescue, he realized there weren't just dogs and cats but chickens, ducks, sheep, goats and yes, two lively little ponies the woman at the rescue seemed quite eager to place. "They're great for farrier, vet, trailering, will stand for a bath, easy keepers, too. Would make a great addition to a lesson program, great with kids, bombproof." Eli had no idea until much later that people described horses in the same inflated way real estate ads were worded. Antigone had learned the art and often came up with new and inventive ways to describe a home that needed updating, was on the smaller side, or had little in the way of parking space.

He explained to the foster woman that he had a barn with two stalls but he was really looking for a dog.

"Oh yes, we have dogs but unfortunately, they've all been spoken for."

He thought back at how enamored he was with the ponies and how they searched his hands and pockets for a treat. *I had no idea they were going to be therapy horses.*

He turned and stepped into the doorway of the farm kitchen, remembering the first nervous time he spontaneously popped in to buy something on the way to Otto's.

Out beyond the parking lot, to the left of the barn, Hope was cantering over a low cross rail in the arena on Cayenne, who was flicking his tail and shaking his head. Eli watched as she reached and patted his neck for a job well done.

"You're on the clock, Buddy," Rebecca pointed out, reminding Eli that work was never really finished on a farm.

Eli turned back to the worktable and wrapped the apple

pies while Rebecca poured the warm spiced brine into jars stuffed with sliced cucumbers from the field.

"Who knew how much I needed a place just like this." He said it under his breath on purpose.

"What's that?" Rebecca looked over, waiting for a response.

Eli said loudly, "Who knew what a harsh boss you'd be."

Eli didn't see the dishrag coming until it landed perfectly on his face, hung on for a moment, before falling onto his hands that were already struggling with plastic wrap.

Without looking up he said, "I just can't work like this."

Rebecca's laugh had now tied Hope's as his favorite sound.

After Hope cooled down Cayenne with a cold hose and plenty of walking, she turned him out to the pasture he shared with the new donkey that Rebecca was asked to "watch for a month" while the owner "got her life together."

Rebecca had explained to Eli on their first date that it was how she had gotten almost all the animals that were on her farm. "I wouldn't have it any other way," she explained. "This place was a new beginning for me, too, and I found myself still returning to all the issues I'd left home with. New places, new faces, but same me."

"Ah, the famous geographic cure," Eli smiled at the thought of it. "What were you running from?"

Rebecca sat up straighter then and took the last sip of her wine. "I wasn't running away. I was running back. I grew up on a small farm but thought I needed a fancy education and big job in Boston if I was going to be successful. And by the definition I held for success, I was exactly that. I lived in a suburb, commuted an hour and a half into town, paid insane amounts of money to park, worked nine or ten hours, drove home sometimes two hours to a big house I now had to keep the job in order to afford, was miserable toward my fiancé. I was sick a lot and realized I needed the job for the insurance but was only sick because of the job ... I tried to cram as much fun into Friday night and Saturday because on Sundays, I cried, knowing I had to do it all over again the next five days. I did that for *years*."

Eli nodded. He'd heard the exact same scenario from many of his clients. The rat race that people can't wait to start begins to wear them out but they continue. They tell him, "I can't just quit my job." When Eli challenges their rigid thinking, they defend it, teeth bared, foam rising on their mouth. "That's just your ego, your conditioning trying to keep you where you are. It's fine, you can stay there. It's your choice. Just know you *do* have a choice." He caught himself. The last thing he wanted to do was sound like he was conducting a therapy session.

"So, tell me more about your plans for the expansion of the farm."

He watched as her eyes lit up like fireflies and he couldn't help but wink.

"Well, I want to offer event space for weddings, parties, reunions. I only use half the barn as it is, so I want to make the other half a cool venue."

"That's amazing and of course you'll cater?"

She smiled and nodded, "I already have menus planned."

Eli asked Rebecca over the shared turtle cheesecake and coffee that arrived, "So what was your turning point?"

She went to sip her coffee but it was still too hot, so she took a breath instead.

"When I realized I was too old to start a family, was suddenly single and—" Her eyes went to her coffee cup again. He watched her eyelashes dance as she thought. "All I had to show for all the hours I sat in airports and all the cities I traveled to but didn't actually get to see, and the sleepless nights I spent working to make other people wealthy ... all I had to show for it was a big empty house and a car I was paying way too much for. I wasn't really living."

And all these months later, he was starting to realize he knew much more about her life than she did his. She was careful not to pry but he knew the time was coming when he'd have to tell her about his need to run far, far away.

Hope came into the farm kitchen then, something green highlighting the dirt smeared on the side of her neck. Eli laughed, "What happened to *you*?"

He pointed to the small mirror that hung next to the coat rack where clean aprons hung. Hope stood on her tiptoes and peered in. She giggled and wiped at the mess on her neck. "Cayenne sneezed on me with a mouthful of grass."

Eli shook his head at how it just seemed so perfect. All of it.

Hope and Eli got back to the house as the clouds began to roll in fast and unforgiving. If you lived here more than a season, you learned to listen to the forecast. Soon after that you didn't need a forecast; you learned to observe and feel. "Storm's coming, better feed quick!"

Eli went into the house while Hope trotted up to the barn. He grabbed his laundry from the hamper and on his way to the basement he heard the rain start. By the time he started the washing machine, the rumbling began. "Moving fast," he told his dirty socks.

Back upstairs, he peered through the kitchen window to see that the barn door was closed already. "Geez, she's fast."

He crossed over to the living room window then and saw her leaving the driveway. "Oh no, you don't," he said, and grabbed his keys. Eli flinched at the overhead lightning as it illuminated his property. But the thunder that came a split second after was more frightening. He ran to his truck and backed out onto the road. Hope had on only a t-shirt and jeans but was holding one of the grain bag totes she and Rebecca started making to sell at the store. He pulled up next to her, rolled down the window and yelled, "Get in!"

He thought she was going to keep going but the lightning and thunder arrived at the same time now. She screamed and clawed her way up into the truck, drenched.

"Oh my God!" Eli could barely hear her; his ears were ringing from the near miss. "Jesus!" He looked at her, "Are you okay?"

She was shaken, he could see and though she normally would never allow him to drive her home, this evening, she didn't protest.

Clem had shown Eli where her driveway was on the way to

pick out hardwood floor for the upstairs. He really thought Clem was mistaken until one day he was heading down to Southwest Harbor and saw the green Corolla pull out of the woods at the same spot.

The rain was so heavy; his wiper blades were no match. He put his lights on which did nothing to help him see. Eli leaned forward and put on the defrost, but still the visibility was slim to none. Hope said, "There! That's my driveway." She reached for the handle but Eli hit the lock from his door so she couldn't bail like she did the day her mother OD'd on the corner of Main Street.

As he pulled off the road into the woods, his view was now dark forest ahead but at least he could see. The pine needle-covered tire ruts were well worn but the ferns in between and on the sides were also well established. He wondered what it must be like in the winter. The rain sent down leaves and a small branch onto his windshield, making him unsure this was any safer than being on the road.

The driveway slowly took him around a bend to the right and there ahead was Hope's house. He looked over at her as if she was going to be as surprised and exasperated as he was. The cabin, up on cinder blocks, was "nestled in the pines", as Antigone might have written. The blue tarp on the roof was covered in needles and moss, denoting that it wasn't newly placed. The green tarp covering one window looked a bit more recent. Eli's mind had a hard time formulating A) what he was seeing, and B) what he was thinking and, C) what he should say to the nearly twelve-year-old who called this place home.

"Hey, think I could meet your dad? Is he home?"

Hope looked at Eli, the trepidation clearly brimming.

"I don't see his car." She looked around.

Eli looked, too, and realized he had no choice but to unlock the door. She hopped out, "Bye, thanks for the ride."

She ran to the steps and turned as Eli saw headlights in his rearview mirror.

He rolled his window down and felt the humid pine air rush into the cab. He could hear the thunder rumbling further away now. Stan Barlow hit the accelerator and pulled up next to Eli's truck, narrowly missing the sapling on the edge of the driveway. He slammed the door of his car and stood looking at Hope, frozen on the steps of the cabin.

"The *fuck* you want?" His voice was cool and calm as he turned to Eli now, who felt he ought to get out of the truck and at least try to introduce himself but the Corolla was too close.

Eli nodded, "Hey, I'm Eli Cranston, nice to meet ya. Hope's been taking care of my animals for—"

Stan Barlow, wearing green chino work pants, a worn leather motorcycle jacket and a "Don't Tread on Me" ball cap, staggered back a step and pointed at Eli. "You don't need a give my kid a ride anywhere—he-ah me? She needs a ride, I'll give 'er one."

He turned and pointed now at Hope. "Get in the house!"

Hope disappeared behind the door then and Eli's heart raced and sank at the same time. To him, Stan looked like he could be Hope's grandfather.

"Hey, the storm came up and I didn't want her to get struck by lightning, Sir."

"Sir? Are you fuckin' kiddin' me? I ain't a cop. Don't sir me. Get the fuck outta he-ah."

Eli's mind raced, adrenaline hitting his veins. Fight, flight, or freeze.

He looked back at the house and could see Hope in the glass of the door, holding Buttercup, the now almost full-grown runt of the litter. She shooed her hand at Eli as if to say, *Get while the gettin's good.*

Eli put his truck in reverse and slowly backed out onto the road, hearing the forest whisper, *You too were once judged by appearances.*

43

"Hi, can I speak to my mother please, Missy Barlow. She's in B Wing. Okay, thanks."

"Hi Mom! I miss you. When are you coming home? Why? What do you mean? So when? I have to go back to school soon. I wish you could come home before—oh, okay. Yup. I just miss you. Yea, he's good. Can you tell Linda to bring me to visit? Dad said he can't because he's not supposed to drive and if he gets— yea, I know. It's okay. I just miss you. Yea, it's been good. Really? I've never heard you talk about them. I wish—oh okay. It's okay. Okay. I love you, Mom."

Eli didn't mean to eavesdrop but he could hear the conversation from where he stood and decided to hear it out, his stomach lurching with each sad syllable. Eli poked his head out the office window, "Hey Hope, when you're finished out there, can you stop in for a minute?"

She agreed to and went back to picking rocks out of the pasture and putting them into the wheelbarrow.

Clem was finishing the baseboards in the upstairs rooms and Eli was getting ready to finish his paperwork. He dropped a stack of folders he'd set aside while purging old files from his horizontal cabinet and swore louder than he realized, causing Bumblebee to jump and scurry from the spot she always claimed, roughly a half inch from wherever Eli's feet were.

Eli bent to pick up the folders and managed to keep them from spilling their contents. A lone purple folder remained at his feet:

John A Corcoran Jr, PhD C.Ht
Making Peace With Your Past ©
Integrated PLR and How it Changes Realities
Feeding Hills, Massachusetts
info@piperonceandagain.com

Eli had attended a weekend conference in San Diego while working toward his Ph.D, because he was fascinated by past life work and had read lecture notes on Dr. Corcoran's website at the suggestion of another candidate he sometimes joined on Skype. But it was Dr. Gunther he had hoped to hear this particular weekend. His seminar on Healing Historical Trauma was full to Eli's chagrin, but as it turned out, he was thrilled with Dr. Corcoran's workshop. Eli remembered it as one of the pivotal weekends he credits with helping him focus on what his thesis would eventually be. The other, he has yet to come to grips with.

He sat with the folder, having not seen it in many years. Inside was the usual: a copy of the slides from the presentation, an announcement about lunch, restrooms, Wi-Fi password, CEU certificates and the agenda for both days, on the back of which Eli had taken copious notes. Behind that was a Courtyard by Marriott notepad also filled with Eli's shorthand.

>> Clients need to go back to acknowledge what their initial trauma was before they can work with the current time period. (is that really true in all cases?)

>> Clients will ultimately choose the lifetime(s) that need visiting for healing, etc.

>> Never underestimate the power of the client's mind to open or close to any suggestion not in alignment with their purpose. (but what if their purpose is to not relive the trauma? What if their purpose is to move forward further and faster in spite of it? What if the past is what holds most people from reaching their potential?)

Eli has always believed timing is essential to just about everything in life and this was no exception. He flipped the pages back and forth and read the quick bio about John and his wife Piper, and their incredible life and particularly her past.

Underneath the bio was a final line: *Free consult with John via phone/Skype for any Lic. Mental Health Professional.

Eli quickly sent Dr. Corcoran an email asking if he could set up a time to speak with him. He put the folder on his desk and heard Hope come into the kitchen. Eli collected his thoughts and walked out to meet her.

"Hey, Hope. How's the rock farm out there? Pretty good crop, huh?"

"Yea, you could say that." Her face was flushed, and her hair drenched with sweat.

Eli took a bottle of water from the fridge and handed it to Hope. "Have a seat for a minute."

Hope sat at the table opposite Eli. He picked up a tax bill from the table so as to divert his gaze. "Listen, I happened to hear you on the phone with your mom and if you think your father might be okay with it, I would be happy to give you a ride. Or if not, then maybe he'd let Rebecca."

He looked at Hope out of the corner of his eye. She sat up a little taller.

"You would!?" I don't think my father will care. I just won't tell him. Please."

Eli hadn't expected that. "Listen, you know I'd love to not ask your father, but I gotta play by the rules. If he found out, and he probably would, I could get into some sort of trouble, you know?"

Hope didn't know but she was no stranger to disappointment. She simply nodded.

"So um, Hope, is there anything you need, I mean with your mom not home? I mean with school coming up. You're heading into middle school and that can be a big change. Rebecca and I were wondering if there's anything you can think of that you want to ask or anything? I mean, if you have any questions about anything at all, fire away."

She sat for a moment, expressionless, shrugged her shoulders and very matter of factly asked, "Why do you have pinecones in your bench on the porch?"

44

Hope clung to her mother and inhaled deeply. She smelled like coconut shampoo and Bounce dryer sheets. To Hope, that meant more than a pleasant scent; it meant her mother was clean and being cared for.

"I wish you could home now, Mom." She looked up at her mother's deep blue eyes and dark hair. If Hope had her mother's eye color, she'd look like a throwback picture of Missy at that age. Physical hallmarks aside, no one would ever pin them as, in any way, related. "Well, you seem a lot better, Mom! I know you'll stay this way now. Right?"

Missy pulled back and looked at her daughter, wondering when she last really did so. "You're getting so grown up, Hope. I just—" Missy's voice wavered and she caught herself, pulling away from her daughter and moving over to the edge of the bed to put some distance between them. "So uh, I have something for you, Hope. It's something that I got a long time ago before you were bahn. She reached up and unclasped the chain around her neck. The hamsa pendant was familiar to Hope, as her mother wore it often. "My grandmother gave this to me when I went to live with her. Her mother gave it to her so it's an heirloom. See, she put their initials on the back. Got to add mine and yours. It's supposed to be good luck." She let out a laugh then that startled Hope. "Maybe it'll give you bettah luck." She put it around Hope's thin neck and turned her around by the shoulders to get a look at it. Hope touched it, incredulously. She'd never worn a necklace. "I want you to take care of it and give to your daughter someday, okay?"

Hope nodded with anticipation and for the first time in many years, a feeling that things would somehow get better.

"Listen, Sweet-haht. I can't come home. Ya know what I mean? It's not a healthy place and it just ... it just isn't good for me if I'm gonna stay clean and everything." She looked at her feet then and for the first time in her life, recognized that she was in an unhealthy relationship with her husband, herself, and anyone connected to her.

Hope stood up and looked at the other side of the room, the one her mother shared with a woman named Sheila. As if Sheila was going to break it all down for her and explain what her mother meant by this, Hope searched the eyes of the older lady with the yellow sundress and bare feet. Sheila looked up, realizing what was coming next and excused herself, cell phone and sunglasses in hand. "Nice meeting you, Sweetie. Enjoy your weekend."

Looking back at her mother, Hope's heart began to beat faster, the butterflies in her stomach suddenly feeling more like angry bats, a metamorphosis gone wrong.

"So *when* are you coming home then?" Hope could hear her heartbeat in her words, a pulsing that wanted to scream and bleed and be noticed.

Missy stood then and walked to the small window that looked out over the small courtyard where people visited with their families, exchanging hugs and words of encouragement. She watched a father scoop up his toddler son and whirl him around before saying good-bye for another week, his wife wiping at tears with the promise of a new start when he's well enough to come home.

Missy Barlow didn't turn back around to see her daughter's face again. She put her hand up to the glass of the window and looked at the scars on her skin, indelible reminders of the life she led as a heroin user. The older ones she recognized as needle tracks, the newer ones, blood draws and IV port footprints. What shook her the most, though, were the scars she couldn't remember getting.

"I'm not coming home, Hope. I can't. And I am so friggin'

sorry—more than you could evah know. I love you more than I have evah loved anyone but ... but I was a *kid* when I had you for Christ sake and ... I know some people might think it's self-ish but I need to find a life for myself and get outta he-ah." She rubbed at the fingerprints on the window.

"I need to get better and going back home would friggin' kill me. It almost did a million times. And it's not you, baby. It's not you. But I can't take you with me 'cause yah fath-ah would *never* let me take you. The day you were bahn was the happiest day of my life. All ya need is hope, as they say. You're a smaht girl and you need to finish school." She laughed then, "Hell, one day, maybe I can come live with you—you'll probably be a doc-tah or somethin'—it's in yah blood yah know. You're so freakin' smaht. I don't even know where you came from, to be honest."

By the time Missy finished her long good-bye, Hope was al-ready back in the lobby, safely in Rebecca's embrace. Her tears told a story words would only serve to cheapen. How does one describe an act so brutal as the voluntary severing of a sacred bond God entrusted only to women?

45

"Oh my God I am going to need a new kitchen. Good thing Clem is already planning for it." Eli backed away from the stove with his hands in the air.

Hope quietly giggled, "I know. I can't believe we are actually doing this."

The pot of softly bubbling wax beckoned the first pinecone to dare take a dip as the smell of honey filled the kitchen. Hope looked over her shoulder and said, "Remember, this was your idea."

"Wait a minute here. I'm not sure it was a hundred percent my idea, young lady."

Eli had been trying hard not to react to the devastating blow, one of many, in Hope's short life. He wanted to be a confidant and safe haven but he also knew it wasn't his place to try to be her father. Rebecca suggested he strive for "funcle "You know, fun uncle," she told him. As with most ideas she had, Eli thought it rather brilliant.

"Oh, yes it was a hundred percent your idea." Hope carefully wrapped a piece of wick around the top third of the pinecone, picked it up with salad tongs and gently dipped it into the bubbling beeswax fondue. She let it sit for a few moments, turning it side to side as if she were toasting s'mores. "Oh shoot, get the waxed paper! We forgot the waxed paper!" Her voice held the energy of a rollercoaster virgin—nervous anticipation with a smidge of fear.

Eli jumped into action and grabbed the roll of Cut-Rite on

the counter and tore off a piece. He smoothed it out on the cookie sheet next to the stove. "Okay, careful now, that is very hot stuff." He watched as she gingerly guided the dripping pinecone to its destination. The waxy sheen quickly cooled to an opaque pale yellow and made the pinecone look like a chubby snowman. "So cool!" Hope was ecstatic. "We are going to sell so many of these!"

"Um, how many coats of wax do they need?" Eli held the Pinterest image on his laptop close to the experimental fire starter for comparison.

Hope said, with conviction, "Two to three. But I think two will do it."

"Okay, well we have a ton of beeswax and Becca has a lot more if we need it. Might need to go pinecone hunting later."

"How much should we sell them for? I've never sold anything before."

"Well, we will have to see what the market calls for—supply and demand. But I was thinking $.60 each, two for a dollar. The ones I saw at L.L. Bean were way more, so I think it'll be all about the presentation. Maybe we'll get little boxes or something."

Hope placed the second fire starter on the paper, little drops of wax falling onto the floor and stepstool on which she was perched. "Oh, I know, maybe like, some ribbon or something, make it fancy."

Eli looked at his email.

Dr. Corcoran following up regarding their Skype session last month. *This will be interesting!*

Kate with good news about a job and possible apartment. *That-a girl!*

Home Depot reminding him of items in his cart he hasn't yet purchased. *I know, I know, waiting on Clem.*

Rebecca forwarding a link to the Office of Child and Family Services. *She didn't waste any time.*

Clem walked down the stairs, one at a time, Eli could hear. "Hey fella. That plumbing is brand new and if yah know what kinda commode yah want I can swing ovah to Home Cheapo and pick it up fah ya." He looked over at Hope. "Hey kid, whatcha got cookin?"

Hope held up the first and coolest wax concoction and said, "Fire starters. We're going to sell them on the last two farmer's market days."

Clem stepped closer. "Oh, would ya look at that? I could use those up ta camp. We get that fire goin' every night. I'll take a handful of 'em when they're ready. Jack likes to use cowboy juice but yah eveh get caught, yah get yerself in a jam fah sure."

Eli shook his head, "What on earth is cowboy juice?"

Hope giggled. Clem said, "Oh it's nothin'. Just a little gasoline, kerosene, or chah-coal lightah. Hee heee! It sure does get it goin, no fah-tin' around waitin'. But that's why Jack has no eyebrows, either."

Hope looked over her shoulder and exchanged an "Oh my God" with Eli.

"So ah, Clem, you still on the fence about bringing a guest to Thanksgiving this year?"

"Just give me the kinda terlet seat yah want, fella, before I just install a five-gallon bucket. They got nice ah-range ones at the sto-ah."

Eli wrote down the stock number for the toilet, pedestal sink, and faucet he wanted and sent Clem on his way.

Hope carefully added more beeswax and wiped her brow, "He cracks me up."

Eli laughed, "He cracks me up, too. But he's a really good guy. You know, not everyone you meet in life can go through tough things and still be a good person. He's one that can. People like that are worth more than gold."

He waited to see if Hope wanted to add to the sentiment but she didn't. She just quietly added to the pot little bits of wax, like a worker bee herself, contributing something seemingly insignificant, not realizing that without her, the honeycomb wouldn't be complete. Little did she know that there were those who believed she ought to be treated like the queen.

46

"Dr. Corcoran, it's Eli Cranston. I'm great, how are you? Yes, we're getting ready. It's been great weather, hard to believe it's Thanksgiving tomorrow. Yes, so I've been thinking nonstop about our last email exchange. I'm fascinated. And yes, I'd love to join you in Boston next month. Thank you, I'm honored, to say the least. Yes, yes, she's great, we are down to once-a-month sessions and I couldn't be happier. I just wasn't sure if that initial session with her was accurate, the things she was seeing. Yes, it's mostly because she saw me and I mean, it would be highly unlikely that I'd be at her wedding, and well she mentioned daughters and, well—Yes, yes. Future stuff. I know, Dr. Gunther says it, too. "You just can't imagine it so you have to trust God and let life take you there. I do, I really do. Sure, send me your thoughts and I'll start to get a working description together. Fantastic, enjoy your holidays."

He reached into his desk drawer for a pen and stopped when he felt the RiteAid bag. "Shoot. This'll arrive late."

He pulled it out and placed it on the desktop. He took out a pen and gathered his thoughts.

Of all the things I have been given in my life, I'm most thankful for you. Even if you can't understand it now, I hope one day you will.
You will never know how much I love you.

He signed the card and with the tom turkey, his plumage, soft velvet against the matte cardstock and guided it into the envelope. He checked the address twice and walked out to the mailbox. The cool air woke him up and reminded him to have firewood delivered. *A whole year,* he thought. *Another year gone by and another year closer.* He closed the squeaky mailbox door and thought how, a year ago, he was quick to hit anything vaguely squeaky with WD-40. But this year changed something in him. Imperfection became not only okay, but valuable. Not knowing was not anxious but exciting, and opening his heart became not painful but enlightening.

He looked at his watch. "Oh geez, I'm late." He jogged up to the house, checked on the cats' food and water and told them to hold down the fort. He grabbed his overnight bag and pillow and texted Hope: **I'm heading to Rebecca's now. I'll come get you in the morning after you feed the ponies, around 7:00 okay? And please invite your father—if you want to.**

She texted right back: **Okay. I'll see you tomorrow.**

Hope watched from the barn window as Eli backed out of the driveway. She waited twenty minutes to be sure he was gone and hadn't forgotten anything before trotting down to the front door and unlocking it with the key Eli had made for her.

47

"Daddy, you have to come get me right now! No, Daddy, now. It's an emergency. Oh my God, Dad please just come get me now!"

Eli sat up in bed, Gracie's voice startling him. His phone read 1:12 a.m. He shook Antigone's shoulder but she didn't rouse. Eli got out of bed and used the light of his phone to illuminate the walk-in closet. He pulled on a pair of jeans and a sweatshirt, and trotted down the stairs to the kitchen where his keys sat on the island. His cross trainers were the only shoes he had left in the mudroom leading to the garage, so he slipped them on.

He looked at his GPS screen and shook his head. He knew exactly where he was going. Brit Williston lived not far geographically but in Eli's mind, in a completely different universe. Brit was as spoiled and angry as they come, the youngest daughter of the high profile plastic surgeon, the one Eli knew was guilty as sin the moment he heard the man's voice years ago, before the girls were born. He and his socialite wife were as fake as they come—physically and in every other way. Brit flaunted her pedigree and her lack of morals to anyone who would look. He tried over the years to like the parents for Grace's sake but he just couldn't get there. And even if he could have, Antigone blew up any sort of civility that had been maintained when the girls were little. She blamed Brit for Grace's poor grades, her drug use, her poor choice of loser boyfriends. Eli tried to balance her view by asserting that, influence aside, Grace was making all of those choices on her own.

He pulled onto the Williston's street but was five houses away when he had to stop. The cruisers and ambulance were double-parked on the street, which was lined with cars.

He threw his car into park and ran to the door. There were kids on the front lawn, some in tears, one was vomiting. The front door was open and the commotion inside was a scene from a movie Eli once saw. He had said to Antigone at the time, "That's so ridiculous. I don't care how wasted you are. If the cops show up, you beat feet."

Surveying the room, he was certain Grace wasn't there. He called her cell but it went straight to voicemail. As he approached the gathered teens at the foot of the staircase he shouted, "Hey I'm looking for Grace Cranston. Have you seen her? Please, Grace Cranston, she's my daughter. She's 5'6", brunette. Gracie! Gracie are you here?" He pushed past the kids who were too stoned to move out of his way.

He got to the fourth step when he heard a man's voice, "Hit her again." Eli took the rest of the steps by two at a time, hauling himself up with the help of the walnut bannister.

On the white carpet in the long curved hallway, a medic was checking for a pulse on the motionless body. Again, he said, "Nothing. Hit her again."

Kids, many Eli recognized as classmates of Grace, were pushed back by officers. Eli tried to focus on the scene in front of him. The medic continued chest compressions while another prepared a syringe, but Eli could see blue lips and grey skin. His stomach lurched as an officer approached. He asked him his name and if he was the homeowner. Eli shook his head and looked at Grace, shaking his head. He wasn't sure if she spilled a drink or wet herself but under the circumstances he guessed it was the latter.

He slowly descended the steps on autopilot, his full weight landing on each one. He paused, his mind trying to catch up as he attempted to dial his father.

48

Rebecca was chopping celery when Eli arrived. Her hair was pulled up in a ponytail and her apron was already showing signs of Thanksgiving preparation kicking into high gear.

"Hey! I was beginning to wonder if you were going to bail on me!" She wiped her hands on her apron and before she could finish he pulled her away from the table and kissed her. "I would never bail on you, Miss Treadway."

She blushed then, and tucked her hair back behind her ears. She never thought she'd be with someone like Eli.

"Okay then, are you ready for this?" She pointed to her to-do list and then around the farm kitchen to all the prep tables on which were gathered ingredients, pots, pans, utensils, and recipe cards. Eli let out a low whistle. 'Oooh boy. It's ah, it's gonna be a long night, huh?"

Rebecca tossed an apron over his shoulder and said, "I'll make it worth your while."

Eli sprung into action then, and washed his hands in the industrial sink. "Where do I start?"

Rebecca pointed to the spot next to her cutting board. "Right where you'll finish, next to me."

Side by side they, chopped butternut squash, and sweet and white potatoes; onions and stale bread for the stuffing. They brined the twenty-one pound turkey and set it in the walk-in refrigerator; baked pies, and made cranberry sauce, all the while listening to 80s music and telling stories of their respective Thanksgivings past.

"What are you doing?" Rebecca watched Eli squinting at the recipe card in front of the bowl he was using to mix his pumpkin pie mixture.

"I'm making pies." He threw her a feigned sarcastic scowl.

"I see you're trying to but can you even see which spices you're using?"

"Yes. Yes I can. You just worry about yourself."

Rebecca gently took the spice jar out of his hand, looked at it and stood back, hand on her hip. "Really. So garlic in the pumpkin pie is umm, a Cranston tradition?"

Eli's eyebrows climbed toward his hairline. "What?!"

Rebecca turned the jar around dramatically and held it up in front of Eli's nose.

"Well, I think it will be a new Cranston tradition, thank you very much."

Rebecca was stunned. "Did you really put some in there?" She looked closely at the pumpkin mixture and back at him.

"You'll have to wait until tomorrow to find out." And with that, he started the mixer and happily combined ingredients until smooth.

By 11:45 that night they'd finished cleaning and took their well-used aprons off. Rebecca shut out the farm kitchen lights and led Eli by the hand through the breezeway between the store and the house. "Big house, little house, back house, barn." Rebecca said.

Eli's heart skipped, "What was that?"

Rebecca turned and smiled. "What?" She opened the door to the side entrance of the farmhouse, leading to the pantry off the kitchen.

"What did you say just now?"

The look on Eli's face took Rebecca by surprise. "Oh, it's just an old saying here. Big house, little house, back house, barn. It's a New England thing, adding on to the homestead, everything connected so you don't get lost in a blizzard trying to feed your animals. Literally, that happens."

He loved how she filled with light when she explained things. "Oh, gotcha. I feel like I should know where that comes from, but I don't know why I think I should."

"It's late. Maybe it'll come to you in a dream or first thing in the morning."

"Yea, maybe. Big day tomorrow." He changed the subject but couldn't shake the feeling that what she said was oddly familiar. "I told Hope I'd pick her up when she feeds the Littles in the morning."

Rebecca took off her sweatshirt and sat at the kitchen table. "I heard her telling Stan she's staying over at Sydney's house tonight so he won't ask where she's going tomorrow. I can't imagine having to live like that. It's the saddest thing to watch. She hasn't said much to me about her mother but I know she must be heartbroken."

"Denial, it helps soften the blow for a little while. She'll have to face it at some point."

He pulled Rebecca to him then. "You would make a good mom."

She pulled away from him. "Yea, I would have, but that ship has sailed. I'm forty-one now."

Eli backed away, "Oh my God, so freakin' old."

"Hey, you've got twelve years on me, Buddy," she said. "Which is why your eyes are failing you." She laughed. "Go see Dr. Randall. He's great. Get a pair of glasses, they aren't that bad. You just need them for reading recipes."

Later as he lay next to Rebecca, he wondered how different his life would have been if he hadn't joined the family business. If he had become a firefighter or an accountant, would he have had a quieter existence in the long run, a quieter mind?

49

Hope pulled herself up into the truck wearing the new jeans and sweater Rebecca took her to the mall to pick out. It was the first time Eli had seen her in anything beside her sweatshirts. The dark sweater set off her hazel eyes, making them look bluer.

"Happy Thanksgiving!" Eli said and shifted into reverse.

"Happy Thanksgiving." Hope peered out the window as they swung onto the road.

"So are you ready to meet Clem's mystery date and my good friends Otto and Elise?"

Hope was preoccupied with something she was seeing in the side view mirror, her hands tucked under her legs.

Eli glanced into his rear view mirror and saw the familiar green Corolla. He watched Hope out of the corner of his eye, her eyes never moving. Instead of taking a left on Park Street and meandering through the side streets like he does on days he knows downtown will be jam-packed with tourist traffic, he turned at Mt. Desert. He watched with anticipation as did Hope, as Stan kept straight on Main.

"What kind of pie is there going to be?" Hope asked, now looking at Eli.

"Let's see, we made apple, pumpkin, and mincemeat."

"What? Meat pie? For dessert?" Hope's surprise changed to disgust and Eli tried to keep a straight face.

"Yea, it's tradition, I guess. I don't know. I'm not from around here."

Hope stared at Eli's profile for a moment. When she looked away, Eli looked over at her. She noticed and turned toward him again. "Are you joking?"

"Yes. I'm joking. There's apple and pumpkin. I think. We were up pretty late getting everything ready. It's going to be a big meal for sure!"

Eli pulled the truck up next to Rebecca's van and cut the engine. He turned to Hope. "So at Thanksgiving a lot of times people go around the table and say what they are thankful for. Just a heads up. I remember always getting nervous and saying something dumb when I was a kid. So as I got older, I'd think about it for like, three months before, so I'd have something to say."

"Oh, okay. I um, I don't think I'll have a problem coming up with something. We do things like that at school."

"Oh, cool. Good to know." Eli took a breath.

"My teachers sometimes send me on an errand so I don't have to answer."

Eli sucked in air as quietly as he could for someone who felt like he'd been kicked in the gut. "Oh, who?"

"Mrs. Haverfeld, she's my guidance counselor." Hope opened the door and hopped out, just like she did most things: heartrendingly matter-of-factly.

Inside, Rebecca's house smelled like spices and coffee. "Hope! Happy Thanksgiving to my favorite twelve year old." She hugged Hope and Eli could see it was something that Hope was getting used to more and more.

"Happy Thanksgiving. Hey, can I bring Cayenne some carrots for Thanksgiving?"

"Of course. Just not the ones in the roasting pan." She laughed as Hope went straight for the refrigerator, grabbed a handful of carrots, and went out the door.

"That girl is horse crazy." She turned to Eli, who was watching Hope through the dining room window as she ran to the barn.

"I would have to agree there." He looked at Rebecca then. "So, what still needs to be done? And by that I mean, anything that I can't mess up."

"Well, I locked up the garlic powder, so we won't have to worry there. And basically, now it's just getting the dining room ready and then timing everything. Turkey should be done at noon so if the Gunther's arrive by 11:30 it'll give them time to unwind and we can all visit for a bit before dinner. And you said Clem was going to come right at noon?"

Eli heard Rebecca, but mostly he was just captivated by her heart and her genuine love for life.

"Yes, that is the plan, Ma'am! I am so hungry but I don't want to ruin my appetite."

"Good, because there's enough food for a small army here."

Hope came back in looking happy and like she belonged here. Eli glanced at her, "Okay, you—time to work."

She looked at him as if to say, "That's all I do!"

He pointed to the dining room table. "We are going to set that table and make it look like something out of Better Homes and Gardens."

She raised her eyebrows. "Okay, let's do it."

Rebecca opened the whitewashed hutch that stood by the window and took out her grandmother's linen tablecloth to hand to Hope. They unfolded it and smoothed it onto the long dark table; Eli began removing the beautiful Homer Laughlin china dinnerware and gently placing it on the table. Together, they set out seven place settings. Hope marveled at the silverware serving set that was wrapped in burgundy velvet and stored in the bottom of the hutch. "This looks amazing. It looks like it belongs in a castle or something."

Rebecca said, "This all belonged to my grandmother, my mother's mother. I was lucky to get it because I know my sister has had her eye on it for years!"

"Well, did your sister get anything?"

"Oh yes, she got plenty. She wanted things that were worth money, but I preferred the sentimental things."

"Do you remember your grandmother?" Hope looked up

at Rebecca quizzically.

"Of course! She was like a second mother to me. She stayed with me when my parents were working and I spent all summer with her watching soap operas and *The Price is Right*."

Hope was learning more and more that her experience was far different from those of people she knew. "Oh, I wonder what that's like. I never met my grandparents. I wish I could. That would be cool to see—" She stopped and nervously moved a serving fork to point in one direction, then another, a compass gone crazy.

Eli, watching from the other side of the table said, "Um, are we just letting people sit wherever they want or should we have those things. What are they called?" Eli knew full well what they were called but wanted to *keep moving.*

"Place cards," Rebecca said softly from the doorway. "I have some things we could use to make some cool ones. Wanna help, Hope?"

"Sure." Hope stood back and looked sheepishly from Eli to Rebecca, the two people she trusted most in the world. But if there was one thing she needed and wanted more than anything, it was her mom.

Rebecca followed Hope into the back office which had a drafting table and a regular table with chairs around it that Hope used as a crafting room, designing and creating items for her store. She pulled out several boxes, one with cardstock, another with markers, and one with the fire starters that hadn't sold at the market. She turned back to see what else she had as Eli watched from the hall, standing still so as not to make the floorboards creak.

At close to 11:30, Eli watched the driveway a bit nervously. He was relieved the weather was cooperating but knew it was a long drive up from Camden. He inhaled deeply, the aroma of the turkey and roasting vegetables filling his nose and making his stomach growl. He turned to watch Hope play with Butterscotch, the kitten Rebecca brought home from Eli's. When he turned back to the window, he saw Drs. Gunther's car rolling down the long winding drive toward the house.

"They're here, Bec!" He couldn't hide his excitement as he put his shoes and coat on and rushed out the door to greet them.

Hope, a bit shy with those she's never met, picked up the kitten and comforted him, though he needed no such thing. "It's okay, they'll be nice. They're Eli's friends."

The front door opened and in with it came a gush of cold air. Hope backed up and turned to head to the kitchen.

"Rebecca, the Gunther's are here, Honey."

"Coming!" Rebecca had gone upstairs to change her outfit and put on some makeup. She trotted back down to see Eli positively beaming as she came into view.

"Hello! Welcome!" She stood next to Eli who put his arm around her waist.

"Rebecca, this is Dr. Otto Gunther and his beautiful wife, Dr. Elise Gunther." He turned to them and said, "My girlfriend, Rebecca Treadway."

Hope watched from the kitchen, the adults shaking hands and complimenting one another. She felt out of place and wanted to go out to the barn. Suddenly she wished she had stayed home. Her father would be lying on the couch, next to the woodstove, watching TV and yelling for her to get him a beer. Hope would be trying to stay warm upstairs because even though heat rises, it doesn't always go around corners. And even if it wasn't ideal, it was home. It was her comfort zone. The kitten wriggled out of her arms and zoomed down the hall toward the office, leaving Hope alone to fend for herself.

"Hope! Come out here. I've been wanting you to meet my friends. Come!"

Eli waved her toward him. Her body language was clear, she was nervous.

She reached Eli's outstretched arm and as she did, she felt the weight and warmth of Eli's hand on her shoulder. This man, who seemed to care more about her than both of her parents combined made her feel safe, said, "Hope, these are my friends I've been telling you about. Remember that picture of Peppercorn I showed you? He belongs to them. This is Otto and Elise Gunther."

Hope felt all the eyes in the room on her and though her hands insisted on hiding in her jean pockets and her feet wanted to turn and leave, she stood and raised her green eyes. "Hi."

Elise clutched at her scarf and stammered, "Oh, uh, he, hello, Hope. It's a pleasure to meet you." She reached out her hand to shake Hope's and waited for the little hand to reach up.

"Happy Thanksgiving, young lady," said Otto. "We have heard so much about you. I hope to learn more today." Elise watched Otto as he shook Hope's hand. She looked back at Hope. When she caught a glimpse of the hamsha sitting at her clavicle, she touched Otto's arm. But Otto was beginning to take off his scarf and Eli invited them to come sit in the dining room. Rebecca excused herself to check on the turkey.

Eli asked if Hope wouldn't mind hanging their coats in the hall closet.

Rebecca returned with a tray of glasses filled with a bright pink punch and announced that dinner would be served in twenty minutes, as soon as Clem arrived.

Elise watched as Hope scooped up the returning kitten and kissed his nose. She smiled at the sweet gesture. Otto watched Elise as she watched Hope at play.

"I know what you're thinking, Elise. But it isn't. It isn't."

Elise didn't seem to hear and perhaps she didn't.

A loud knock at the door sent the kitten scampering a second time and Hope giggled at the screech he made to announce his departure.

Eli answered the door, "Clem, Happy Thanksgiving! C'mon in!"

Clem stood back and allowed his guest to step in ahead of him.

"Eli, this is Annie. Annie, Eli Cranston I been tellin' ya about."

His mind whirling, trying to piece all of the bits of information together and still be coherent, Eli said, "Annie, hi. Happy Thanksgiving! Pleased to meet you. I, uh, feel like I know you from somewhere."

Annie laughed, "well, if ya like pizza, ya prob'ly know me from Rosalie's."

"That's it, yes. C'mon in, please. Come meet everyone."

Eli winked at Clem, understanding why he had been so private about the "sweet girl" he was seeing. She was the same sweet girl he had been pulling wrappers off straws for since 1975.

After introductions were made, Rebecca brought more punch in for refills and said, "Hope, did you tell everyone about the place cards?" All eyes moved again to Hope, the little girl with the dark ponytail and striking eyes.

Hope reached for the fire starter with the pretty orange and yellow ribbons around it, holding her nametag in place. She explained the messy process and how Eli tells everyone he needs a kitchen remodel so Hope could sell fire starters at the farmer's market. Everyone laughed at her recollection of Eli's one-liners and facial expressions.

"But we did make a lot of money, so it was totally worth it." She looked up, relaxed now in the company of people who were glad to have her there.

Otto laughed, "And what did you do with your windfall?"

Hope looked nervously at him, "Windfall?"

"All that money of yours," he said and smiled at her, looking down over his glasses.

"Oh, I'm saving it. I like to save my money."

Otto nodded, "Smart girl, smart girl."

Elise leaned forward to look around Otto and watched Hope. Her heart quickened and she opened her mouth to speak but heard Rebecca in the hallway say, "Turkey is done!"

Like an intermission in a play, the announcement set everyone in motion. Hope jumped up, glad for the interruption. Eli followed her out to the kitchen, Butterscotch spinning his wheels on the wide pine floor like a cartoon cat to keep up.

Clem turned to Otto and Elise, "That girl, she's somethin', taking care ah them hosses like they were hers. She handles 'em like nobody's business and they listen!" Annie rubbed Clem's arm, "Girl like that shouldn't be worryin' bout nothing at her age. I think those hosses are a way to get outta that house. I don't know how anyone has let that go on fah so long."

Clem sat back in his chair, "Well, everybody's got a diff'rent way ah livin', Annie. Can't say one is bettah than anothah."

Annie said, "Well, I think if the office ah families knew "bout them, they'd have somthin' ta say."

Elise said, "Do you know ..." she hesitated, "the family?"

Otto turned to look at Annie then.

Annie said, "Everybody knows of the family but I wouldn't say anybody really knows 'em, would you, Clem?"

Clem shook his head, "Nah, Stan's a piece ah work, that one. Not right in the head. What happened to him, prob'ly drive anyone ta drink, you know? He drinks wicked."

Annie added, "And his wife, for a long time I thought she was his daught-ah, she was so young."

Elise fidgeted now, wanting to blurt out all the questions she knew Annie probably had all the answers to.

"Where are her parents right now, do you know?" She reached for Otto's hand then, for comfort.

"I dunno. My guess is at home, drinkin' and yellin' at each otha. That's what they do all round town."

Eli reappeared first with the platter of turkey dressed with roasted vegetables all around. Then came Rebecca with a rolling kitchen cart from the store on which were bowls of steaming hot mashed potatoes, roasted root vegetables, stuffing, light and airy popovers, and a gravy boat with beautiful pink and blue flowers that matched the china place settings.

They began covering the table with all their offerings, Eli preparing to slice the bird. Clem took a deep breath and turned to Annie. "Happy Thanksgiving, Annie Fannie."

Otto stood to help Rebecca with the serving utensils. Amid the exclamations and compliments in the bustling dining room, Hope bought more time in the kitchen. She picked out a chunk of hot potato from the pan on the stovetop. Touching it to her tongue, she decided it was too hot. She blew on it and popped into her mouth. She turned to take another and when she turned back around, Elise was standing there in the middle of the kitchen, one hand on her chest, feeling it race like a spooked horse.

"Sweetheart, is there anything else that needs to go out to the dining room?"

Hope wiped her mouth with the back of her hand, abashed. She looked at her feet and shook her head no.

"Where is that kitty friend of yours? I bet we could find him a spot under the table where he might catch a few bits of turkey." She smiled at Hope and tried to restrain herself.

Hope started to walk toward the hall that led to the dining room when Elise reached out and lightly touched her shoulder. Hope stopped and looked up into eyes that matched hers. "Sweetheart, I noticed your necklace. You know, I had one just like that and—"

"There you are!" Eli came up behind Hope and Elise, dishtowel thrown over his shoulder. "C'mon, the turkey is carved and candles are lit! We can't let Clem get his hands on those drumsticks."

They made their way back to the dining room, Eli pulling out Hope's chair to seat her.

Rebecca looked around the table, happier than she could remember being in over a decade. "Thank you, everyone, for coming here to celebrate and give thanks with us today. You've made this a very special day for me."

She turned to look at Eli then. "Eli would you like to say grace?"

Eli fell asleep next to Rebecca, having not slept the night before. Words spoken during the day echoed in his heart as he drifted. "Family, health, friends, love, life."

"Daddy! Thank God you're here. Help me, Dad! I don't belong here. You know this. What happened? Why am I here?"

Eli walked around the giant oak in the forest, hand trailing behind him, the bark rough and filled with stories no one alive was there to witness.

"Gracie, you were a good girl, a princess. You were so beautiful and loving. I just wish I could watch you dancing on the stage again. My little ballerina ... just one more time."

"Daddy! I can't hear what you're saying! Why can't I hear your voice?"

Eli stepped out of the forest and onto the freeway underpass. "Do you know Grace Cranston? Yea, 5'6", brunette. When was the last time you saw her? Huh, interesting. Oh, yah, I've seen her since then, sure. Yea, I'll tell her."

"Daddy. Where's Mom? Why won't she talk to me? I've been calling and calling and she won't answer! Daddy!"

Eli drowned in a thousand dreams and in each one he tried to find answers to questions he wasn't allowed to ask. And in each and every one Gracie looked exactly like the little girl he needed to save. She looked exactly like Hope.

50

"Elise. Hi, how are you? Yes, it's good to hear from you and thank you for making the trip a couple of weeks back. Yes, we had a great time, too. Sure. Uh-huh. Yea, she's a great kid. Tough home life but I'm hoping there might be something social services can do. Yeah, her mom is in a program. I'm not sure but it sounds like she won't be moving back and Hope is, as you can imagine, devastated. Yea, she's been wonderful, I really do love Rebecca. Oh, sure. Hi, Otto. Yes, I can hear you both. Okay, yes of course. Go ahead. Her last name is Barlow. Yes as far as I know. Um, let's see, her father is probably forty-five, forty-six. Hard to say, he doesn't take care of himself. Yes, from what I know he's from Bar Harbor, moved away, and got married. Then lost his wife and newborn many years ago. Yea, tragic and he's been hell-bent on making others suffer for it."

Eli shut off the television and walked out to the mailbox. He reached in and took out the sales circulars he wished he knew how to keep from coming to the house. They were folded around two bills and a card envelope with RETURN TO SENDER stamped in red. Sometimes the ink was blue or even purple. They used to say POSTCARDS ONLY but that changed last year.

"Her mom, yea. Um, Missy Barlow. Yea, I only met her once, sort of. It was before I knew she was Hope's mother. In the grocery store, she was asking for money. Yea, really sad. Addiction is an awful thing. That's all I know, really. Uh, not positive but I think Hope said she would turn twenty-nine soon. Yea, young. Hope is just an amazing, resilient kid. Sure, go ahead."

Back in the house, Eli walked into his office and sat at his desk. He opened the drawer on the right and placed the returned Thanksgiving card on top of all the others: Birthday, Christmas, Easter, Thanksgiving, and the odd Thinking of You. As if something might escape, he shut it quickly and went back to the living room.

Eli waited as Elise and Otto covered their phone to speak in private.

"Yes, I'm here. What do you mean? What? Hope? Melissa? Who is—? Oh, wait. Melissa, your granddaughter?! Oh my God. I—I don't know. How can that—"

51

Hope sat at the booth at Rosalie's with Eli and waited nervously. Eli noticed how long her hair was when not in a ponytail. She was wearing jeans and a Hollister top Rebecca had given to her. She sipped her Coke and swayed back and forth on the seat, her hands tucked under her lanky, still growing legs.

"You look like a penguin," Eli said and winked at her. "Are you nervous?"

She nodded, "Yes, a lot."

"I'm sure, but you've been waiting awhile now and that's probably part of it."

Eli could see she was intent on something over his shoulder. He watched her eyes dart back and forth, pupils widening, pulse visible in her narrow neck.

The bell over the door jingled and Eli turned. "Otto, Elise! You're here!"

He greeted them with hugs and asked if they'd like a drink or if he should order lunch. They accepted the drinks but were clearly in a hurry to sit with Hope.

"Sweetheart, it's so good to see you again." They sat next to each other on the bench across the table from Hope.

Eli came back to the booth and scooted in next to Hope who visibly relaxed then.

"Hope, the last time we spoke on the phone, I mentioned to you something about that special necklace of yours." Elise's eyes dropped to Hope's hamsa sitting on the chain around her neck.

Reaching up and touching it, Hope thought of her mother and how long it had been since she'd seen her. Four months was a long time to not see your mother when you're twelve, even if most of the time she was with you she was too sick to be much of a mom.

She nodded to Elise, lifting her eyes for a flickering moment.

Annie came to the table and said, "Here we are, two ginger ales. I'll be back in a bit to take ya or-dah."

Eli looked up at her and smiled. She winked at him, then turned to look further back into the dining room where Clem sat enjoying his Italian grinder, watching the group. From the distance, no one could see his watery eyes; eyes that were no stranger to reunions.

"That is, if I'm not mistaken, the very necklace we gave to our granddaughter, Melissa when she was living with us. It has initials on the back."

Otto spoke up, "Does yours have initials, young lady?" He was uncomfortable with how nervous she looked. If they were correct, this was their great-granddaughter and the last thing she should be feeling is nervous.

Hope raised her eyes, not letting them completely make contact with Otto's and nodded while she bit at her upper lip. If she could have seen herself, she'd realize she looked like Ink when he had the bit in his mouth, tossing his head in protest to work.

She reached up with trembling hands and unclasped the necklace, knowing all eyes were on her. She handed it to Otto and withdrew her hand back to the safety of her lap.

He turned it over and leaned closer to Elise so she could see as well.

Elise reached up and caught a tear as it fell from her cheek. She looked at Hope and then Otto and finally Eli.

"Hope, Sweetheart. I know that Eli has explained some things to you, hasn't he? Our granddaughter Melissa came to live with us when she was in high school. She was, well, she was a little lost and we thought we could help her start over and—"

Otto finished for her, "And she didn't really want our help. She left us and we never knew where she went. Her mother and father were herz gebrochhen, uh, heartbroken. She called us sometimes but we knew we could not help her."

Eli could see how painful this was for them, not knowing how to word the situation that they had learned to cope with. And here they were, with the realization that when Melissa told them she had a baby, they hadn't believed her.

Otto gently turned the hamsa over and ran his finger over the engraved initials of his wife and her mother.

To everyone's surprise, Hope looked up then, meeting Otto's eyes and said, "My mom loves me. And when I see her again, I'm going to give that back to her."

She reached out and took the necklace back from Otto.

52

Eli arrived in Boston and found the Marriott Copley Place on his third try. "Who made these roads? Makes no sense whatsoever."

He parked in the garage and made his way up to the lobby. He checked in and left his bag at the desk. On his way to find breakfast his phone buzzed. "Hi John. Yes, I just got in. Sure, I'm heading there now."

Eli spotted John at the buffet; three women and a man were also moving down the line. Eli got in line and filled his plate with eggs, bacon, and homefries, a piece of toast and a wedge of watermelon. *Always the same,* he thought. He scanned the muffin offerings and passed them by. He looked back at the baskets they were in, scanning for information. On his way back to the table he spoke to the girl at the hostess station.

"Hey, ah, not to be a pest but I used to be a lawyer. Where's your allergy warning sign?" He pointed over to the muffins. "I see walnuts." The girl scowled at him, "Um, Sir, the sign says cranberry walnut?"

Eli said, "Just mention it to your manager. Trust me, he'll be happy. You might even get a raise."

He made his way back to the table where John was seated. John stood up, holding his tie so it wouldn't fall into his coffee. "Dr. Cranston! Good to see you!"

"Dr. Corcoran, how are you?"

"Great, going to be a great weekend. The workshop is full, got a few more participants last couple of days."

"Can't wait. I had a tough time sleeping last night, although not as tough as navigating the streets here."

"Ha! First time in Boston?"

"Yup."

"So, I have some questions for you later, after we knock this out of the park. I have some ideas about how to approach the integration of past life and future life therapies but—"

John looked at Eli as he waited for him to continue.

"But what, Eli?"

"I'm just wondering if—" He straightened up and took a sip of ice water. "If the past is supposed to just stay in the past. I mean, it makes you and your experience with it essential to your authenticity."

John nodded, "Yes, that's exactly true. One train of thought is that your past is a fingerprint of sorts, it dictates your future. But a past life, well, it can be seen that way as well and as a new baby coming into the world, is that really fair? Why not go back and deal with it head on, clear up that karma and start fresh."

"Ah yes, I do agree with that. And I think, too, that one's future can be affected in such a way that the karma is tied up in the time between the FLP sessions and the life the client sees many years down the road. I believe it sort of hastens the clearing of the trauma or family legacy, sort of accelerating it so you can get on with life and enjoy your future sooner. Does that make sense?"

"A hundred percent. Now, let's go tell the others."

After breakfast, John went to the front desk to inquire about a delivery he was expecting.

Eli sat in the lobby answering emails. A text from Rebecca popped onto his screen.

Hey Eli—the plumbers had to tear out the wall to get to the leak. Ugh, no water which means no heat either!

He texted back: **Oh no! That's not good. Stay at my house. I'll call at lunch break.**

She texted back: **I might need to. Love you.**

In the ballroom, clinicians began to file in, chatting and introducing each other as they sat at round tables in the beautiful ballroom. Close to two hundred people from all over the country were waking up to the possibilities that John and Eli were bringing into the mainstream.

John began with a story of a woman who lived an unfulfilled life that prevented her from fully loving herself or anyone else. He told this incredible story of how she, after very difficult lessons and the sudden loss of her husband, sought out past life regression.

The attendees were taking pictures, tweeting them out, taking notes, nodding heads.

John spoke for about twenty minutes about this incredible transformative leap of faith, finishing by explaining this woman is now his wife, Piper. "Now I know what you're all thinking about patient/client boundaries. As it turns out, Piper wanted nothing to do with me! It wasn't until many years after my wife Kayla passed, that Piper reached out to me and the rest, as they say, is history." He turned as he clicked the remote toward the monitor, to look at the screen with the picture of Piper, standing in a field of lavender in Sault, France. "We have gone several times to visit this serene place she once called home. It's a place like no other. The wine is phenomenal, too."

People clapped and turned to talk with one another, excited at the outset of the conference.

John sat in the back, observing, taking his own notes. He was thinking of Otto and his horrific young life and Hope with her own trauma, born into such dysfunction. And then he thought of Grace. He felt his heart quicken and took a deep breath to center himself. *Keep moving.*

That afternoon after the question and answer session, Eli stood at the exit handing out feedback forms and wishing everyone a great evening.

Over dinner that evening, John and Eli discussed the story John had shared about he and Piper.

"So that story is incredible, just fascinating. I mean, almost hard to believe."

John nodded, "Yes, I know. It took me a long time to share it. I was afraid of judgment or being accused of embellishing. Truth be told, I've left some pretty amazing details out because I know how it sounds. But yes, it's an amazing experience, this life thing."

Eli was stunned that he started to feel a rush of emotion, then. All the angst and sadness he had kept hidden for so many years began to rise to the surface like steam in a pot about to boil. He took a deep breath and a sip of his vodka tonic.

"Hey, you okay, Eli?" John asked, concerned.

"Yea, I'm fine. Just thinking about some of the stuff my family has gone through."

John asked, "Rebecca?"

Eli flinched then. "No. Rebecca is uh, she's not my wife. I, um. I meant my family back in California."

"Oh, okay. So when I saw you out there years ago, you were living out that way?"

"Yes, that was my old life as I refer to it. Actually, I was in transition at that time. I was a lawyer and my life just—" He cleared his throat and felt he might be losing control.

"My life just blew up."

The waitress came to the table and asked if they'd like dessert. John looked at Eli with a questioning expression. Eli said, "No. Thank you, I think we're all Grace. I mean, I think we're all set. Excuse me."

He got up from the table, wiped his forehead with the napkin and walked to the restroom. He closed himself in a stall and vomited his five-star filet and lobster tail, still looking very much like filet and lobster tail. Feeling relieved and once again in control, he washed up at the sink and headed back to the table.

"Hey, Eli, you okay?"

Eli sat for a moment, straightened his tie and said, "I don't know, John."

"Anything you want to talk about? I mean, I'm more than

happy to listen, help if I can."

Eli looked out at the street, stores lit up with Christmas lights. He suddenly wished he was back in Bar Harbor with Rebecca and Hope, the ponies and the crazy cats.

"Hey, wanna check out the Christmas lights, take a walk?"

"Yea, sounds good to me."

They walked out into the cold air, Eli taking in a deep gulp. "That's what I needed."

John buttoned up his coat, "Fresh air is medicine itself."

Eli looked at his phone. A text from Hope: **Hi Eli—A lady came here looking for you. She asked when you would be back.**

Eli quickly responded: **Ok thx. Probably a client. Did she tell you her name?**

"So John, I wonder if there's any sense in me telling you this but ..."

John looked at him as they walked toward the giant lit Christmas tree, "I have something I carry on my shoulders every day and try to pretend it isn't there. I haven't told Rebecca or Clem or anyone. I thought I would, I mean, I intended to but—" He looked up at the tree, so full and bright, drawing exclamations and excitement from kids and parents alike.

"I just don't know what to do with it. It is what it is. I don't know if it's my fault or if it's no one's fault. I have a hard time thinking it's karma or predestined. I just don't know that I ever dealt with it. I mean, I did, in therapy but ... but I think I just went through the motions. I don't think I came to terms with it."

John quietly waited for Eli to get it all out. He sat on a bench and Eli followed suit.

"You know, we could have a session if you'd like, when we get back to the hotel."

Eli stared straight ahead, nodding, slightly.

John continued talking to him with words of encouragement but he could see Eli was elsewhere. When he glanced in the direction Eli was looking, he saw the usual sights. Cars hitting brakes, swerving around confused drivers; people hurrying through the crosswalks; packages in big bags, filled with Christmas gifts.

Eli continued nodding as he focused on the billboard for the Nutcracker Ballet.

"Yea, I think it's time, John. I think it's definitely time."

Back in the hotel, John went to his room to shower and relax and told Eli to do the same and meet him at his room at 8:00.

Eli called Rebecca but she didn't answer. He looked at his watch and realized she was probably at the farm feeding all the animals and probably lugging jugs of water from her truck into the barn. He wished he was there to help.

He texted her: **Hey Becca, wish I was able to help. Hope it's going ok. Can you do me a favor when you get to the house?**

Then he sent another text: **In my office desk—top drawer, there's a copy of** *The Alchemist*. **I need you to find a certain page and take a picture of it for me. Call me when you can and I'll tell you about where to look for it. Thx**

He saw a reply from the last text he sent Hope: **No, she didn't say her name but she was pregnant and asked if I was your daughter.** Eli laughed at the emoji rolling its eyes.

Rebecca looked at her phone, gloves on. "Oh, it's gonna be a while, Eli."

She was indeed, carrying jugs of water, eight in all, to the animals. She loved her farm but winters were tough and doing it mostly alone was a lot. Still, she cherished it over the rat race she had left behind years ago.

Eli got back to his hotel room just before midnight, exhausted and drained but knowing he would be okay. He changed out of his clothes and slept nude in the bed, asleep within minutes of his head hitting the pillow.

"Daddy, don't hide! You're going to be so proud! I'm going to be the prima ballerina, you'll see!"

Eli watched as little Gracie stumbled, arms out in front of her, crashing to the stage. She got up, the audience laughing, recording the funny performance.

She got up and she continued the routine, the other tiny dancers never knowing she had missed a step.

"Daddy, I'm going to try until I get it right. I'm going to be perfect."

Eli left the auditorium and stepped into the courtroom. He watched the chess game unfolding and held his head in his hands. They were doing it all wrong. All wrong. Those bastards! Those liars! The one time he needed to be in control, he wasn't allowed to touch even one pawn.

53

Eli awoke feeling a sense of peace and also purpose. He showered, dressed, and met John for breakfast at the hotel. The agenda for the day included a three-hour practice and wrap-up session and then he'd head home. He was eager to see Rebecca and tell her he was ready to take their relationship to the next level. He knew what he needed to do to forgive himself for the past and to truly move on. Moving to the opposite side of the country was but a band-aid until he was ready to let go of the guilt he had tortured himself with for so long. And that was lifted during his session with John. Never would he doubt the power of healing the past again. He had a very clear vision of how to integrate the past life regression with the future life progression. He couldn't wait to get started.

Rebecca sat in the kitchen of Eli's house, waiting for the coffee to finish brewing. She watched Hope slide down the hill as she tried to fetch the water bucket she placed on an icy patch. It slid down the hill like a Plinko Chip on *The Price is Right*. Rebecca giggled.

She looked at her phone. Eli: "Becca, hope you're ok? Did you get my text last night? Call me, I'll be leaving soon."

She pushed the phone away and put on her boots to head back to her farm.

Eli pulled into his driveway just before 5:30 p.m., ecstatic to be home. He knew this was where his future had begun but it was only going to get better from here. He glanced over at his sign and wondered how easy it would be to have Clem add PLR to the sign. Out of the warm truck, the refreshing cold air reminded him he was alive. Carrying his bags into the house, he was delighted to see Bumblebee and Honey scurry around the corner from the hallway to greet him. "Hi Girls! I missed you. Did you miss me, too?"

They meowed and rubbed up against his leg with their answer. He scooped them both up, feeling the warmth of their bellies and the vibration of their purring. He squinted as they rubbed their faces on his, Honey playfully biting his nose. "Oh, geez, I need that, you crazy cat."

He brought his bags into the bedroom but remembered he needed to start bringing things he didn't use every day upstairs. He trotted up the Berber covered steps noticing the smell of fresh paint and new carpet. Clem did an exceptional job with all the work. Two bedrooms and a lavish bath, no orange Homer bucket toilet.

He dropped the bags in the middle of one of the closets and peered out the window that still had stickers on it. The barn door was closed, which meant Hope had fed and put the ponies to bed.

Back downstairs, he took another bag, acquired on the trip, into his office and put it into the drawer. There he saw the copy of *The Alchemist* sticking out under a postcard from Clem from back in the spring. He'd gone to Vermont with his "new" girlfriend and Eli was happy to see the mood it had put him in. Never in a million years would Eli have pegged Clem to be a postcard-sending sort of guy.

The book was right where he'd left it, seemingly untouched. He wondered if Rebecca had come to the house at all and suddenly felt an urgency to speak with her.

His phone buzzed just as he was about to call her. He let out a sigh of relief. It was a text from her: **Hi, I imagine you're home now. I didn't want to send this while you were driving. I think we need to talk about something, but not tonight. I am pretty floored and I am not so sure that me giving you time and space about your past was the way to go. For you, maybe, but not for me. I went to look for the book you wanted a passage from and I found something else entirely.**

Eli could feel his heart chomping at the bit. *What is she talking about?*

He looked around his office as if he would gain some meaning.

Then another text from Rebecca: it was a picture of the stack of cards addressed to Cowchilla, CA.

Eli let out of his lungs the rattling, stale air that was hiding in there, then took a deep breath and held it.

It was go time; it was time for the truth at all costs. The good, the bad, and the really ugly.

He called Rebecca's phone but by the third ring he knew she wouldn't answer.

He checked on the cat's food and water, then walked into the living room on a mission. He took the top box and placed it on the coffee table as he'd done twice before, once aided by alcohol, then full on feels with no buffer. He turned back toward the other one; the one he couldn't bring himself to look in—the one that had collected dust for a year and four months in his new home and many years in his heart.

He picked it up, feeling the weight of it. It suddenly felt like the twelve pounds in reality it always had been.

The sound of an engine reached his ears and he said, "Rebecca!"

He glanced out the window but without his porch lights on, he couldn't see the vehicle. He turned with the box and then decided he'd put it back so they could talk first. He was glad she was here. He had so much to tell her now. Everything he was holding back now wanted to come gushing out. Mostly, he wanted to calm any fear she was feeling from finding those envelopes. His mind raced with all the things she could be thinking. The doorbell rang. "Becca, come in!"

He took the box from the coffee table and replaced it on top of the other. He turned toward the door. Still closed.

The doorbell rang again. Confused, he went to the door and flipped on the porch light.

Eli opened the door and there in the cold night air of Bar Harbor in December, two weeks before Christmas, thirty-two hundred fifty-four miles from where he last saw her, stood Grace Cranston.

Beautiful.

Grown.

Pregnant.

54

Rebecca was painting the new wall in the kitchen when her phone rang. She looked at the phone on the kitchen table and saw it was Eli. "Not great timing," she said and let it go to voicemail. "I don't even know what to say to you anyway." She dipped her paintbrush back into the can and wiped most of it off before climbing the step stool to reach the trim. Buttercup walked across the countertop and headed for the paint can. "Oh no you don't, kit cat. Get off there, shoo!"

She stepped back off the stepstool and as she did, her phone rang again. She shook her head, picked up the cat and put her in the office with her catnip toy.

Back in the kitchen she saw that Eli left a voicemail. She put her hand on her hip and decided she would listen to it later. She climbed back up, paintbrush in hand and said, "I suppose you have a perfect explanation of why your ex-wife, oh who knows maybe you're still married to her, is in jail. I really do know how to pick them. My mother was right about that."

Clem had left his plastering tools so he could finish the drywall taping and mudding in the bathroom upstairs where the leak started. She moved them to the front hall so that she could bring them upstairs when she next went up. The snow falling on the fields caught her eye and she stopped to enjoy the scene. She looked at the lamppost with the wreath adorned for Christmas under which Eli first kissed her at the end of their first date. It stood as it had for many decades, not judging, just shining light when needed. She wanted to stand there again on the anniversary of their first date and have him kiss her that way again. She shook her head and headed back to the kitchen. She had felt high hopes about Eli and it crushed her to think she fell for a liar. She picked up the paintbrush for the third time and stopped again, sighing heavily.

Eli's voicemail: "Rebecca, I need to talk to you. Something has happened and I—I need you to call me. Clem said he was at your place so I know you're there. Please, I'm really worried and I can explain everything. I'm heading ..." She stopped the message when she heard a woman's voice in the background telling Bumblebee how adorable she and her daughter are.

She sat hard on the kitchen chair and stared at the picture hanging there: Eli and Hope at Thanksgiving dinner in the dining room. Hope's face beaming at the place card holders she was so proud of, obscuring Eli's mouth in the photo, but Rebecca recognized the smile in his eyes. She wondered if people could really fake emotion or if in fact he was as happy as he seemed that day. "Who knows." She heard Buttercup meowing from the office and went to let her out. When she got back to the kitchen she jumped at the sound of her doorbell. It didn't ring often and when it did, she was usually expecting it. A delivery, a plumber, the UPS man would all warrant a ring, but she wasn't expecting anyone today.

Heart pounding at the thought of who or what the answered door might bring, she peered out and saw Eli's truck. "Fuck."

She composed herself, smoothed her hair at the top of her forehead as she always did when wearing it in a ponytail and filled her lungs with pine-scented air.

"Becca! Oh my God, I was so worried." Eli stood with his hand over his heart, wearing his black overcoat and gloves, snow sticking to his hair. She could smell the faint scent of his cologne and wished the last 48 hours hadn't happened. She just wanted to welcome him into the house and tell him that she wanted him there forever and Hope, too, somehow; that they should be a family. Instead she crossed her arms defensively and waited to see what fantastical story Eli had for her, at no time stepping back or in any way indicating that he should come into the house.

"Rebecca, I need to talk with you. So much has happened and my head is spinning. Can I?" He gestured toward the spot next to where she remained still and just stared blankly at him, waiting.

Eli's heart beat faster as if to say, "I think I can, I think I can."

"Becca, I need you to hear everything. I brought something to show you." He stepped aside and looked down behind where he had been standing. There sat the dreaded box containing remnants of the most horrible months of Eli's existence.

Rebecca looked up from the box, which meant nothing to her. She inhaled deeply and looked up past the porch to the lamppost and felt Eli's kiss.

She stepped back from the doorstep and turned toward the dining room, her pinecone place card along with Hope's and Eli's, nestled in the middle of a bittersweet wreath at the center of the table.

Saying nothing and not planning to, she led him back toward the kitchen. She looked at the paintbrush and thought, *Wasn't meant to be today.*

Eli placed the box on the table and opened it. He picked out a handful of unopened, returned greeting cards and letters he had added that morning from his desk drawer. Putting them on the white wooden surface, he began lining them up squarely. They looked like evidence of sorts and he thought, *Once a lawyer, always a lawyer.* He placed the rest of the forty-three cards in a pile and stepped back. He took a step toward Rebecca whose body language told him not to get too close.

He stopped and took off his gloves. "Becca, I have a lot to tell you. But I need you to trust me and hear me out. I know this is confusing and I am still in shock myself, I mean, just last night—"

All of Rebecca's hurt and disappointment boiled up to the surface then. All the old feelings of abandonment and fear, outrage and heartache, both self-inflicted and otherwise, fair and

unfair came bursting forth. Eli absorbed every bit of the con-
cussion.

"How dare you come to my home! Why would you even
start something with me? We talked about a future together—
with Hope! How can you just lie like that? What is wrong with
you? What the fuck is *wrong* with you!?"

Her tears betrayed her angry tone and Eli stood, speechless,
but waited, knowing there was more and he also knew she
wouldn't hear anything he had to say in this state of confusion.

"I love you, Eli. That's the kicker. I actually fell in love with
you despite my reservations. And *you* were the one who con-
vinced *me* you had your act together! That's what makes me
more upset—not the ex-wife you're still in love with—the fact
that I *believed* everything you told me. What I should have worried about was what you *didn't* tell me!"

Eli's mind raced. He realized Rebecca had put pieces of a
puzzle together while he was gone but they weren't pieces from
the puzzle they had started together.

"Wait, Rebecca, no. No." He held his hands up as if to say,
"Don't shoot!"

Rebecca's face was red now; anger and hurt, but definitely
not confusion, shone brightly in her complexion.

"Rebecca, please, calm down." He had learned long ago not
to say those words to anyone: client, wife, child, parent, when
they were anything but calm. He slipped.

"Calm down? Did you say *calm down*? How about you get
the hell out of my house?" Her tears were streaming now, eyes
sad and hurt like a puppy's.

Eli thought how different his life would have been right
then if he had just gotten the dog he set out to get. No barn, no
ponies, no cats, no Rebecca, and no Hope. He was overcome
with gratitude for the woman who forced the crazy ponies on
him.

Everything happens for a reason.

"She's my daughter! Grace is my *daughter*, Rebecca!" He
pointed to the pile of long-ignored, cross- country well wishes
on the table.

The silence that blanketed the kitchen of the farmhouse was not unfamiliar to its original walls, the new wall being baptized right out of the gate. It wasn't entirely different from the frozen hush when the Saint Pierre Family received news their son wasn't returning from the battlefield in Virginia in 1864. Nor was it dissimilar to the vacuum when the Wheaton Family lost not one, but two children to the flu of 1918.

Rebecca's face changed as she tried to unravel all the information that had been tangled quite differently since she found the envelopes in Eli's desk while looking for a book he needed her to find.

"What? Grace is—" She looked down, to the side and up again, above Eli's head as if the answer might be there above the door frame.

Eli took a breath and let his shoulders sink a little. "Can I take my coat off?"

Rebecca shook her head, not to say, "No, you can't," but because the tangled information still had some knots to be picked apart.

"Yes, take your coat off."

Eli opened the box then for the third time in over a decade. He reached in and pulled out a stack of legal-sized folders and placed them on the table, covering up several callous RETURN TO SENDER stamped messages.

Rebecca looked at the folders emblazoned with Berkowski, Berkowski and DeWitt. "What are these?"

She looked at Eli and braced herself against his sad expression, the tears forming in his eyes.

"These are all the disgusting details of how my life blew up one night and all the misery that came after it. This is why I left the courtroom forever. It's why I had to change my life completely or—" His voice cracked. "Or I wasn't going to survive."

He opened the first folder and saw words that brought back the bolts of lightning that struck he and Antigone day after day of the highly publicized trial: *Without regard for her childhood friend Brittany Williston's young life, Reckless abandon that resulted in the death of a beautiful young woman who trusted her with her life,*

Deranged and wonton behavior that drove her to kill Dr. Williston's only daughter out of jealousy over a lover, several witnesses who swore under oath that Miss Cranston was the one who provided the fatal dose."

Rebecca was reading over Eli's shoulder and the picture became much clearer. Eli took his new glasses out of his coat pocket and reached back into the box. He sniffled as he looked for a particular sheet of paper, Rebecca holding her heart back the way she held Cayenne back before a jump, knowing you can control the pace and the timing but not the outcome. You just had to trust he knew where all of his hooves belonged.

Eli found the paper he was looking for, the one signed by the judge who regularly golfed with Dr. Williston and his legal team. The paper may well have been signed nineteen years before, when Eli had refused to represent Williston who was clearly guilty of sexual assault on an unconscious patient in his recovery room. And there had been many allegations since.

Remanded to the Central California State Women's Facility for fifteen (15) years with the possibility of parole in ten (10) years.

It all came together then in Rebecca's mind, but she had to hear it with her ears to cement it. "So, these are cards you sent to Grace in prison? Your daughter?"

Eli nodded, still looking at the papers, now strewn about the table. He looked at all the paperwork, the cards, and the box that had contained his painful secrets for so long. He often told his clients that we sometimes, on those darkest of nights, create monsters out of things that, freed in the light of day, are easily slayed.

Rebecca's arms around his neck and the feeling of her body pressed against his opened the floodgates in ways that other things never could. Not the therapy he sought, not the therapy he facilitated, not even the years of lonely nights he spent wondering how it would all turn out. Eli cried for all the years he struggled with anger and resentment, the misery he put Antigone through in the wake of the sentencing, the sadness that lost out to rage when she left him for Jay and moved to Sacramento to be closer to Grace. He cried for all the years he spent back in school to try to heal others, ignoring the obvious healing he so badly needed.

It dawned on Rebecca that she wasn't sure whose voice she heard on the voicemail but was more than sure this was not the time to inquire. But before she could form a sentence that would, by some miracle, sound normal, she saw Eli's phone light up with a text. It was Hope: **Grace is so nice! We are going to cook dinner. Bring Rebecca back with you. Does she even know you have a daughter?** She added the crazy-eyed emoji.

And then another text: **This family is getting bigger!**

Eli's phone lit up. It was from the 916 area code again. He sat up straight as Rebecca's arms slowly released him. He knew he had to answer. He was done running, hiding and ignoring what needed attention. He rubbed his face hard, picked up the phone and closed his eyes, bracing himself. "Hi. Yes, she just arrived, Tig. She's safe with me."

55

The gentle breeze in the warm, early October air swirled the stray leaves of gold and crimson around the rose-covered arbor. The barn with its fresh coat of white paint and twinkling lights stood proudly, ready to serve a new purpose, the perfect backdrop for a down-east celebration. In front of it stood a long farm table covered with flower-packed buckets and set with china, a bottle of Treadway's Tonic to be poured as the toast to good health and happiness. Eli had practiced for weeks.

Kate stood in a form-fitting mermaid dress with most of her tattoos covered, hair a natural sable, lips a muted bronze. Eli watched as she held Ryan's nervous hands, listening to his vows.

Eli pushed his glasses back up after wiping at a stray tear, Rebecca squeezing his arm, her diamond glinting in the early afternoon sun. Clem and Annie stood with Elise and Otto under the clear blue sky we all stand under while Pirate, hitched to a white carriage, called to Ink, Smudge, and Cayenne out in the pasture.

Hope held Kate's bouquet with pride and giggled quietly at Grayson who made faces as he pulled at the ring on the pillow he was holding. Grace gently reached down and tugged at the ring and put it in his chubby two and a half-year-old fist so he could hand it to Ryan.

Eli watched as Grace straightened her back and tossed her long hair over her shoulder, looking so much like Antigone a million years before. *My little prima ballerina,* he thought. *My perfect little Gracie. You will never know how much I love you.*